D1532349

RICHARD TRACKLER

THE ROLL - CALL VOTE

Richard Trackler is a retired physician
and an avowed political junkie. He
lives with his wife in San Diego.
The Role-Call Vote is his first novel.

THE ROLL - CALL VOTE

A NOVEL

BY

RICHARD TRACKLER

Pentland Press, Inc.
www.pentlandpressusa.com

PUBLISHED BY PENTLAND PRESS, INC.
5122 Bur Oak Circle, Raleigh, North Carolina 27612
United States of America
919-782-0281

ISBN 1-57197-277-3
Library of Congress Control Number: 2001 131113

Printed in the United States of America

For Family and Friends
in memory

The President . . . "shall nominate, and by and with the Advice and Consent of the Senate, shall appoint . . . Judges of the supreme Court" . . .

—The Constitution of the United States
Article II, Section 2

. . . "There is a tide in the affairs of men
Which taken at the flood leads on to fortune;
Omitted, all the voyage of their life
Is bound in shallows and miseries." . . .

—*The Tragedy of Julius Caesar*
Act IV, Scene 3
William Shakespeare

THE
ROLL - CALL
VOTE

ONE

The nine-passenger corporate jet bounced upward, whipped by fierce wind and rain. Seconds later the plane took a steep plunge and then steadied. The pilot came on the intercom and said calmly, "I know it's choppy, folks, but the tower has just given us an OK to head in for landing. We should be on the ground in about twenty minutes, right around 10:40 PM local time."

In the cabin, the two women and seven men tightened their belts. The younger of the two females looked at the man next to her and whispered, "Charley, I'm so scared. This could be . . . and the kids . . ."

"It's going to be all right, honey. Believe me." He gently wiped a tear from her cheek.

The other woman grasped the arms of her seat, fixed her gaze straight ahead, and said in a barely audible voice, "The Lord is my . . . "

Her younger seatmate patted her hand reassuringly, but his own fingers were frigid. "Aw, don't worry, Your Honor. I fly all the time. You get used to it."

The small jet circled over Lake Michigan once more before heading toward the airport. Rain pounded the windows. A deafening roar of thunder, followed by a close flash of lightning, rocked the plane, jolting the cabin occupants against the windows, then back toward the aisle.

A bushy-haired man in the first row bellowed, "We don't have a prayer. This crate's doomed."

Suddenly, the jet listed sharply to the right, corrected for a moment, and then immediately rolled over on its back. The passengers' belongings scattered and flew around the cabin.

"Goddamn it, we're goin' down," the shaggy guy shrieked, "gonna crash, gonna drown!"

". . . I fear no evil, for thou art with me," the older woman prayed faintly.

The formerly composed pilot grabbed the radio mike. "O'Hare! O'Hare! This is Nancy-One-Two-Four-Yankee-Yankee. We've inverted. Falling fast. I can't hold this thing together!"

SECTION I

THE NOMINATION

TWO

Two and a half hours later

Gloria Hernandez sank into an overstuffed beige armchair in her music room. She tried to realign her thoughts in this, the favorite room of her expansive San Marino home. Strong white moldings and her favorite oil paintings accented the light cream walls in the serene, high-ceilinged salon.

Her Tuesday-night bridge club had just left. Cuffy Singleton, loyal and constant to a fault, had once again made a series of boneheaded responses to every opening bid, causing them to lose all but one of their hands. In a few minutes, Gloria knew, Cuffy would arrive home and call to apologize several more times and beg for a forgiveness she already had. Gloria glanced at her watch: 10:58. Without leaving her chair, she aimed her remote at a Spanish-style armoire. Soundlessly, the center doors opened to reveal a television screen that instantaneously snapped on.

> "... All nine passengers and crew of three are presumed dead. We have an unconfirmed report that U.S. Supreme Court Associate Justice Marianne McBride was on board the corporate jet that plunged into Lake Michigan earlier tonight."

"Oh dear Lord," Gloria's hands flew to her mouth. "Oh, my God. This can't be." Images of huge waves crashing against the Chicago shoreline, spraying up from

rocks and pilings, and pounding against lakefront
windows played across the screen.

"... says they won't be able to begin search
and retrieve operations until morning ..."

Lord, please don't let her have been on board, Gloria prayed
silently. *She's even younger than I. God, Jon'll have a fit, after all
the deals he had to make to get her confirmed! What a horror. I've
got to call her husband. Darn! What is his name? I can't ask Jon.
He'd have a fit about that, too. Of course now, they'll probably
overturn my Drew v. CHP ruling. Oh, Lord, forgive me. What a
dreadful thing to think about at a time like this. I'll call Anne.
She'll know. No, not tonight, it's after two there. Well, maybe
they awakened her.*

"Excuse me, Mrs. Judge."

It took Gloria a few moments to notice the housekeeper
leaning over her with a worried look.

"Judge Hernandez? Ma'am?"

"I'm sorry, Celia. What's the matter?"

"You have a call on line one."

Gloria shook her head, "Tell Mrs. Singleton I'll talk to
her in the morning."

"Oh, no, Mrs. Judge. It's not the lady with the too-small
car. It's the White House, the lady said to me. Calling for
you. On line one."

Gloria blinked at her chubby, earnest housekeeper who
kept track of the people in Gloria's life by the size and
color—but not the names—of their automobiles. She
rubbed her temples apprehensively. "At this hour? Are you
sure?"

"Oh, yes. You want I should bring the phone in here?"

"No, thank you. I'll take it in my office." *That was fast,*
Gloria thought as she headed toward her study.

She settled herself behind a sprawling, mahogany desk
littered with legal briefs and recent law journals. A silver-
framed photograph of a handsome young man steadying a
small, curly-haired boy on a beginner's two-wheeler sat at

the center edge. She had to move a few files to get to the phone.

"This is Judge Hernandez."

The voice on the other end responded immediately, "Please hold for the president."

"Glory! Have you heard the news?"

"I was just watching it when you called. I'm so sorry. Are they sure she was on the plane?"

"Yeah. We reached her secretary, who was completely distraught. She said it was a private jet, and then she went on about what a wonderful person Marianne was and, well, it got pretty garbled with all the sobbing."

"Well, of course, poor woman. Please tell me her husband wasn't with her."

"No, but one of her clerks was. Just graduated last year."

"Oh, what a disaster! Where were they going?"

"Marianne's secretary said she was supposed to give a talk at the kid's law school. That's the last coherent thing I got from her. Anyway, that's all I know. I was awakened at midnight. We're getting bits and pieces here. Stuff they haven't released to the media."

Gloria positioned the phone's shoulder attachment to free up her hands and wipe at her eyes.

"It's too soon to know when the funeral will be, of course," the voice on the other end continued. "I mean, they have to find the bodies first. The Coast Guard says they can't start looking until morning, and maybe not even then, if the weather doesn't let up."

"You'll have to give one of the eulogies," Gloria said thickly, knowing this was probably why he had called. Jonathan Morgan was a shrewd businessman, a wonderful friend, and a better-than-average president, but she knew he'd rather undergo a root canal than have to speak at a funeral. "I promise when I die, you won't have to say a word. Just show up and throw jonquils."

"Kyle does it better, you know."

"What? Give eulogies or toss flowers?"

"No way out of it," he said, ignoring the sarcasm. "I owe her and Greg that respect."

"Greg, that's right. I knew it was something like that."

"Gregory. Like the gray in his hair links to the Greg in his name."

"Did I say that out loud? Forget it. I knew the name all along."

"Of course, you did. By the way, how are you?"

"Since yesterday? Fine. Why do you ask? Is something else wrong? Has your son almost gotten himself arrested again? I heard about last weekend's fiasco with that little blonde *muchacha* in Philadelphia. Thank God she's twenty-one. She looked a *lot* younger on TV."

Across the country, Jon grunted. "His mother's harsh words would soften cotton candy. Her idea of reading him the riot act was: 'Michael, you've got to be more discreet. You know how unforgiving the press is these days.' I almost felt sorry for him, but he makes it tough. Damn fool. We had a big argument right here in the Oval Office. 'Dad, you're giving me two intolerable choices,' he said. 'Marriage or the monastery. I'm only twenty-seven!' And I yelled, 'Yeah, going on sixteen!' He stormed out."

Gloria stifled a laugh. "So what did you do?"

"Signed a wildlife refuge bill I'd been reviewing. It protects the desert tortoise and the cholla cactus out near Palm Springs."

They were silent for a moment, and then both broke out laughing.

"I dunno what to do with that kid. Give me a trip to the Middle East any day. The leaders are unreasonable but, thankfully, they're pros about it. Been practicing for centuries. I think the only thing that restrains the boy from causing a major scandal is fear of hurting his mom."

"Which is as it should be." There was a brief silence. "So, what else is wrong?" Gloria finally asked.

"Well, you know, I'm going to have to replace her."

"Marianne? Isn't it a shame? She was so young." A shiver ran down Gloria's spine as she visualized steel crushing in on Marianne, rushing water engulfing her nose and mouth, her final moment. She shook the feelings away. "You can handle it," she said, forcing Jon's face into her mind to replace the frightening images. "Just call up the next name on the last list. Who was it? Rittenhouse? Go with him. Play it safe. You told me your top advisors wanted him in the first place."

"Everyone except me. Look, I pulled out the old list of names from when we were deciding on Marianne's nomination. Got it before me on my desk right now. I'm not about to put another Kirkland clone like Marky Rittenhouse on the Court. I don't care what it costs me."

Just the opening she needed to focus on. "Speaking of which, and I apologize for being so self-absorbed here, but could you make sure it's someone who won't overturn that case I told you about last week? I know it's going up to the Court. The attorneys for the CHP as much as told me when I handed down my ruling. Kirkland and his pew mates always side with the police."

"Well, that's my point."

Gloria gave a short laugh. "You had a point?"

"I was thinking of you."

"Uh-huh. So?"

"So, just that. I was thinking of you. To replace Marianne. I want to nominate you for Associate Supreme Court Justice."

"*Jesús Soberano!* Have you lost your mind?" Gloria held the phone away from her head and stared at it. Jonathan kept talking, but she didn't want to hear the words echoing through the air.

"Jonathan Andrew Morgan!" she finally exclaimed into the mouthpiece, cutting him off in the middle of whatever he was saying. "This is the most absurd thing I've heard you say in thirty-eight years." She stopped suddenly, "Oh, I get it. It was a joke. Ha, ha, very funny. Why do you do these things to me? You have a real mean streak in you, Jon."

"It's no joke. I mean it," he insisted.

"This is impossible. I'm getting a headache."

"No, it isn't impossible. And you are too the best person for the job, for all the reasons I just gave you and more."

"I wasn't listening. I think you've finally lost your sanity. Bob predicted as much, years ago, remember? When you decided to sell off your multi-billion dollar company and run for governor?"

"It was millions, not billions, and I won, didn't I? So how crazy can I be? Listen," he said, rejecting her protests before she could get them out, "just think about it, OK? Think, don't answer yet. You'll never get this opportunity again, you know. No other president is ever going to nominate a naturalized Argentine immigrant to the Court, no matter how many of your rulings get upheld, or how many of your books get on the mandatory reading lists, or how beautiful your eyes are. Glory, listen to me. This is your big chance, before you get any older."

"Thank you, Jonathan. You certainly know how to bring a girl's feet back to earth," she said, choosing to ignore the remark about her eyes, which Jon had once likened to coffee with just the right touch of cognac and cream. When she'd had to marry Arturo in place of him, he'd used some pretty negative words instead to describe her light olive skin, high cheekbones, and aquiline nose. *Thank God for Annie,* she often thought. Jon's wife had been the one to make sure everyone had remained friends—and only friends. And Arturo had been none the wiser, even after all those years. "If I recall correctly, I am exactly one month and four days younger than you."

"Which just proves my point. It's now or never. Think about it, will you, Glory? Oh, and don't tell anyone for now. Especially . . . you know."

"Who? You mean my son?" She raised her eyebrows at the photo on her desk. "I shouldn't even talk to my own son?"

"Your indulged son," the president scoffed. "I had words with him a couple of weeks ago, or didn't he mention it? He probably referred to it as a 'discussion.' Please, let's leave him out of the loop until you make up your own mind."

"You don't seem to know Eduardo Arturo Hernandez as well as you think you do," Gloria responded lightly. "He isn't interested in my life. He's too wrapped up in his own."

"My very thought. By the way, who is this new *friend* he's got now?"

She groaned. "Please, Jon, between my bridge partner, the crash, and your crazy offer, I've had enough for one evening. Don't start with me about my late husband's son."

"Oh, now he's Arturo's son! I seem to remember the size of your belly right before he was born. I'm pretty sure the kid is yours."

"At the moment, I'm not claiming him. I don't have that much energy at this time."

"Well, leave him out of it and get back to me after you've had a chance to think."

Gloria closed her eyes and leaned her executive swivel chair as far back as it would tilt. "What does Anne have to say about all this?"

"I haven't told her yet. I've told no one. Good grief, I wasn't planning on Marianne's plane going down! Listen, I've got to get off. I still have a government to run. Think about it, will you? And call me when you've decided. Sleep tight."

Gloria couldn't help but smile at the familiar sign off. Too many thoughts ran through her mind for any of them to make sense. She gently laid the receiver in its cradle, then, just as gently, propped her elbows on the desk and buried her face in her hands. A mixture of laughter and tears filled the room.

THREE

Bob Peterson let his subordinates chatter briefly, while he settled himself into one of the high-backed chairs in front of the Oval Office's fireplace. The coals still glowed faintly. Even this late in spring, the welcome fire warded off the chill of rain that had been dripping down the windows and sloshing off the sidewalks and streets for almost two weeks. The navy blue, leather upholstery sighed softly under the chief of staff's husky frame. Presently, he called the shirt-sleeve meeting to order.

"We've narrowed it down to seven candidates," he began wearily. "As you know, I've spent the last couple of days in one closed-door session after another with Ben Carothers and Ron Jordan. Ben, of course, had some kind of objection to every single one of the hundred twenty-three names we started with, but Ron and I joined forces and strong-armed him down to fifty real possibilities."

"*Santa Maria*! How'd you ever get from fifty to seven with Ben in the room?"

Bob cocked an eye at the interruption, rubbed his forehead with the base of his hand, and decided he was going to need a lot more coffee to get through the rest of this day. Perched on wing-backed sofas that faced each other across a too small, too low, coffee table, his staff looked a good sight more rested and energetic than he thought reasonable. Antonio (Tony) Avalos, for example, who could turn that part Mexican part Texan accent on and off like a faucet, had to have partied until the wee hours this morning; yet here he was at 9:10 AM, just as alert, cheerful, and easygoing as always.

Either I'm too old or he's too young, Bob reflected, watching the well-built Latino run his fingers through a crop of thick, black hair which contrasted sharply with his own gray head and bushy eyebrows. The press secretary shifted around in an apparent effort to get comfortable on the couch. Tony's biceps and abs flexed as the president's blue-eyed, cool, blonde, personal aide rolled her eyes and clicked her tongue against her teeth.

Ha! You haven't got a chance, sonny boy, Bob said to himself. *Too slick, too pushy. Hell, I'm not old,* he decided abruptly, *I'm seasoned.*

"I confess, I cheated," he said now, putting an end to the gender match. "Whenever Ron and Ben locked horns on a candidate over some fine point of law, I'd say, 'OK, then, she's in' or, 'he's out.' They were too consumed with their own rhetoric to notice we'd moved on."

"Anybody else know who the seven are?" Dan Mendelson, a thin, tightly-wired man with unruly, dusty-brown hair and sharply angular features took up the whole other sofa, more with his barely restrained energy than his size. He seemed, as usual, about to spring into the air at any moment.

"Just us and the senate majority leader, of course. In fact, I asked Forrest to figure out which of the seven could win confirmation most easily without a senate battle. I don't think anybody here is ready for another upper-chamber fight. He did an off-the-record with three or four judiciary committee members."

"And the decision?" Mendelson nudged.

"The first choice across the board was Marcus Rittenhouse. You've all heard this before, but I'll recap: Seventh Circuit Court, Chicago; married; three school-aged kids; Presbyterian; graduate of elite schools; moderately conservative, but flexible; decorated Vietnam veteran; no known enemies or indiscretions; former counsel to the very committee that has to approve him; and, of course, more important than all the rest," Bob paused to give the troops his famous lopsided grin, "highly regarded on both sides of the aisle. A veritable shoo-in."

The blonde squinted her eyes. "And a white male," she noted. "You forgot that oh-so-important advantage. He's the same nice, clean, white male he was last time, when we decided not to go with him, I believe for that very reason. Aren't there a few females on the list this time?"

"Of course there are, Claire," Bob said, arching his brows. "Circuit Judges Chloe Doubilet of New Orleans and Gloria Hernandez of Los Angeles—both from the previous short list—and Federal District Judge Maria Romero from Miami. All fine candidates."

"And all not standing a ghost of a chance."

A heated discussion erupted at once. Bob allowed the old, familiar debate to drift just beyond his consciousness. Sometimes, in fact, he imagined the president kept Claire Baldwin on staff not so much because she could anticipate his thoughts or make his backbreaking schedule tolerable, or even because she was more than pleasant to look at, but because being stalwartly independent, she was the political compass that kept Jonathan Morgan's office on track. But now, as she once again defended the idea that the Court already had too many conservative white males for the public good, Bob had time to pay attention to the tightness in his stomach that had started when he'd noticed his boss shift ever-so-slightly in his chair at the mention of his old friend, Gloria. *My God, he can't really be considering her! He'd have to be out of his mind. He must know I only kept her on the list for appearances, like Romero and Perez. Later, maybe, if he's reelected. Ben and Ron would have my head on a plate. "I want a hassle-free confirmation, what with the election just seven months away," he'd said. How can he even think about—?*

The argument had made it to the raised-voice stage, cutting into his thoughts and bringing him back to the Oval Office. Dan had leapt to his feet.

". . . cannot pick a candidate simply on the grounds of gender!"

Bob tapped the cap of his pen on his chair's arm. "OK, OK, everybody count to ten and take a deep breath. Dan, please sit down and take it easy. You're too young to stroke out on us."

"And at least half the office staff would think seriously about missing you," Antonio joked.

"Tony, enough."

Dan glared at Antonio before dropping back onto the sofa. Bob waited until everyone quieted down before he went on.

"Look, nothing has been decided yet. All seven candidates are still in the race. Let's move on. The next choice was Glen Hayward."

Now it was Dan's turn to be incredulous. "My God! Did Forrest Garrison swallow his entire bottle of politically correct pills? The Secretary of Commerce? Give me a break!"

Bob flashed Dan an annoyed, I'm-still-talking glower. "Look, he's well qualified. A few adversaries, but no real enemies and no skeletons that have come out so far. He did a great job as a federal judge in Houston before he got into Congress, where, I might point out, he'll be strongly endorsed by the Black Caucus."

"And," he added, turning to Claire, "he's not a nice, clean, white male." Claire looked at him dolefully, but nodded.

"Actually, Glen's kind of a folk hero in Texas," Antonio offered. "Especially back home San Antonio-way. We'd have elected him senator if he'd tried for it."

"So is it Rittenhouse or Hayward?" Leave it to Claire to cut to the chase. "And who've we got for backup, just in case? We can't afford a second, tough conflict if the first nominee fails."

"Howard King." Bob lifted the page in his leather-bound notebook, "Former three-term senator, took the presidency of the University of Iowa after he opted out of his last race. Centrist Democrat, consensus molder.

Originally a law professor and constitutional scholar. We'd get all forty-nine Democratic votes and plenty of support from Republican friends. No judicial experience, but the cleanest background you could imagine. Safe, very safe. Purely political option."

"Which we may need," Dan put in.

"Even if we don't nominate a woman," Claire countered.

"Woman! Woman! There's already a woman on the high court, or have you forgotten Margaret Louise Jackson?"

"I try to forget her, the darling of conservatives. Her with her flaming crimson hair and fiery oratory! Works post-adolescent, redneck males into frenzies on campuses across the nation."

"Sour grapes," Dan taunted.

Once more Bob tapped his pen sharply on the wooden curve that jutted beyond the leather of the armchair. *That's the problem with having a staff full of high-powered experts,* he mused. *Everyone's a prima donna.* Finally, he turned to the man on his left. "Well, Mr. President? Is Markus Rittenhouse acceptable to you, with Howard King as a backup? Or would you rather go with Glen Hayward?"

Jonathan Morgan sat low in his seat, his long legs stretched out before him, his elbows flailed out on the chair's arms. The still taut skin on the back of his hands now formed into a loose pyramid on which his lips rested. His staff had a running bet on whether or not he dyed his hair, or if nature's graying process had just managed to stop at the temples. He often claimed to feel a hundred ten years old, but barely looked past the minimum age requirement for the President of the United States. His eyes, whose blue deepened and widened when he got very angry, were half-closed. He looked almost unconscious, but Bob knew he had heard every word, noticed every expression and every twitch. Now he spoke without moving. "People, I appreciate your ideas and hard work. And Bob," he lifted his head and pushed his six-feet, two-inch frame into an upright position, "I can't tell you how much I appreciate the trials you went through closeting yourself with both Ben and Ron simultaneously."

"All that notwithstanding," he went on, "I have made an independent decision. I'll explain it, but won't debate it. I'm going to nominate Ninth Circuit Judge, Gloria Hernandez, for our next Supreme Court Associate Justice."

For a moment, no one in the room seemed able to breathe easily, much less speak. Then the tension burst forth again and everyone started talking at once.

"Mr. President, think of the ramifications—"

"Sir, the Democrats will drag up every little piece of dirt—"

"Mr. President, as much as I wanted another female voice, Judge Hernandez is hardly—"

Bob subtly felt his bounding pulse, while pretending to adjust his watchband. He looked down and inhaled slowly, then tapped his pen once more, this time more briskly. "All right, people, time to settle down. Less talk, more thought. The president has made his decision. We'll take questions one at a time."

"Mr. President," Dan began tightly, taking the lead. "May I just ask why? Why her? And with the election only seven months away."

"The president doesn't have to explain his motives to you," Bob started, but Jonathan cut him off.

"Good question, Dan. The media and Senate will no doubt ask the same. Let me make my position clear. One, the woman is an excellent jurist, with twenty years' experience on the federal bench. She has the strongest record of major decisions, among the seven final candidates. You all know that. Two, a lot of people out there share Claire's point of view. We need another moderate female voice on the Court to replace Marianne. Replacing a woman with a man would be political suicide at this point. And three, she's Latina. We don't even need to go into that, do we? You all know what would have happened if we hadn't won California, Texas, and Florida with Latino support, four years ago. We'd be nothing more than a footnote in the history books by now. Besides," he added quietly, almost to himself, "it's time."

Antonio spoke with composure. "Should I prepare a statement?"

"No," Bob cut in quickly. "Not yet. For now, if anyone asks, just say we've narrowed it down to a short list of superb candidates." He stood up. "Dan, dig up everything negative you can find so we can get prepared to counter it." His gesture indicated the meeting was over. "Thank you, everybody. We've got our work cut out for us, so let's get to it."

The staff members exchanged looks as they trailed out of the Oval Office. Bob waited until he heard the door close before he spoke to the man still sitting pensively in the massive leather chair.

"OK, Jon, I am surprised. You really got me. This was the last thing I expected. Have you talked to Anne?"

"No, not yet." He paused, "I'm waiting for Glory's decision."

Bob let out a long breath and stared into the fire, "I don't suppose I can talk you out of this." It was a statement.

"No."

The president stood, finally. His chief of staff turned to face him. They held each other's gaze without words, each trying to tap into the other's mind. At length Morgan broke the ice. "Look, Bob, I'm asking you to back my play, one more time. You were against my selling the company, but it made us both rich. You were against my running for office, but we held the governor's chair for eight years. I know there'll be problems with this, but I honestly think we can pull it off. It's the most powerful political move we can make. You can't deny that. Bold and unexpected, like the sell off and the governor's bid. More to the point, it may be my last chance to put up a Hispanic nominee."

"Powerful. Bold. Unexpected. Well, Jon, yes, it's all that. Not to mention dangerous, frightening, and potentially disastrous." Bob held his old friend's eyes for another second or two, then spread his palms upward. "All right, Mr. President. If you call the long pass, I'll be out there fighting to catch the ball. But—"

"You'd rather go with the run."

"You're calling the plays."

Jon's entire body seemed to relax. "Well, hell, Bob," he said, "if it doesn't work, you and I can always open that one-room law firm near the courthouse in Santa Monica."

Bob gave a short laugh. "And handle nothing but high-profile paternity suits with multiple defendants."

"*Rich* multiple defendants."

"Oh, but of course!"

FOUR

Gloria shivered slightly in the late morning sun. She threw a white, terry cloth robe around her shoulders and patted her swimsuit dry while her mind tried to sort through a hodgepodge of thoughts and emotions. Jon had been right about one thing: No one else would ever offer her this chance again. And in the back of her head, she could hear her father's voice lecturing about duty to her people. This would make her the first Hispanic in history to serve on the U.S. Supreme Court. On the other hand, if Arturo were alive, he'd probably point out how she'd gone as far as she could reasonably expect him to tolerate on the Ninth Circuit Court, and how it was now time to retire gracefully, as befitted a woman of the social standing Arturo expected her to maintain as his wife. Yet there was Jon, once again, encouraging her to go after whatever she wanted and not let anything or anyone stand in her way. As for her own desires, well . . .

Gloria looked out toward the azure pool where her son continued to swim laps, his strong, smooth, rapid strokes barely rippling the surface. *He swims like Arturo,* Gloria mused. *I wish he'd get married.*

Eduardo splashed her playfully, before pulling himself out of the twenty-five meter pool. He tossed his head from side to side to get the water out of his ears, and then grabbed a handful of towels to rub himself dry.

"Don't do that," Gloria warned automatically. "You'll hurt yourself."

"Nah. That's how Dad always did it."

True. Arturo had been an accomplished swimmer who took great pride in his dark Latin physique: strong shoulders; well-muscled chest, arms and legs; flat abdomen; lean waist. Slapping the water now from his brief, black racing suit, Eddie's body build mirrored that of his father, however his facial features differed: the well-shaped, slightly upturned nose and startlingly blue eyes. Arturo's hair had been pitch black, as had his father's and his father's before him, but Eddie had thick brown hair and eyebrows.

"Ready for lunch?" Gloria asked. "I told the girls to bring our food out here. I don't want you dripping water across my freshly shampooed carpets."

"Got any wine?"

Gloria stopped herself from frowning. "I have some of that heavenly chardonnay left, that you sent me last month, the new buttery varietal from Sonoma. But, please, only one glassful."

"OK, Mom," he waved with a shrug, "I promise."

Eduardo finished drying himself with a large yellow towel, then sat down across from her at a table shaded by a huge blue and white umbrella. Large white china plates held a variety of crackers and cheeses—Brie, Camembert, Stilton—along with slices of honeydew melon, apples, pears, and clusters of red grapes. He lifted the wine from the sterling silver cooler. "This hasn't been opened yet."

Gloria looked at the bottle, started to speak, stopped, thought about calling Celia to berate her, and stopped again. Finally she said, "I guess I finished that bottle with some friends last week. I found more in a Pasadena wine shop. Actually, I love it."

"Well, I'm glad! You know, Isamu chose it for you. He's got a real sense for what you like. Poor guy, he had such a rough week . . ."

"Oh, are you still with the same boy?"

Eduardo stiffened slightly, "Yes, Mother, I'm still with the same *man*."

He gave her an icy stare and then went on as if he hadn't been interrupted. "His father called the office Wednesday. Just to raise hell again. 'Why aren't you here working with me?' He's in Kyoto, you know. 'I've killed myself to build this company. You dishonor me not carrying on the family name. You disgrace your mother and your ancestors.' Blah, blah, blah."

"Oh, what a shame."

Gloria bit into a piece of Stilton and looked away. Eduardo grimaced as he wiggled the cork out of the bottle. "Yeah, well, and later Issy told me this bizarre story about his mother."

Gloria put up her hand. "Really, Eddie, please. Let's not ruin lunch again. I wanted us to have a nice visit. You're hardly ever here anymore. This big house. Your home. I really miss . . ."

Eduardo gave his mother a dark look, splashed a little wine into her glass and filled his own. He took a large gulp. "His mother has been miserable married to that domineering old fart. You'd think we were still back in the days of the shoguns! She should have left him years ago. They only had the one kid." He leaned forward and spoke in a conspiratorial whisper. "Did I tell you that when she married, her own mother included a dagger in her dowry? If the marriage to Narita failed, her parents didn't want her back home. They'd rather she committed suicide."

Gloria tried a lighter tone. "But that was the grandmother, Eddie. Years ago. Things have changed in Japan by now. Try some Brie . . ."

"No." He balled his hands into fists. "Don't you get it, Mom? This is a true story. This is his mother. Issy sobbed when he told me."

"Well, look, didn't you once say he's depressed a lot? You know, this really is very good wine. I don't think a little bit will hurt you. At least he got *this* right."

Eduardo polished off the rest of his glass. Gloria started to bring her hand up in protest, then let it drop. "Anyway, there was something I wanted to talk to you . . ."

He brought his fist down on the table. "Mother, please. I'm not finished."

Gloria forced a halfhearted smile and steadied the teetering wine glasses. "All right then, go on."

"Until we met, his best friend was one of his cousins. About five years older and had also defied his father. Instead of going into the family's import-export business in Osaka, he studied film production in Tokyo and became an *avant-garde* director." He paused to refill his glass and take another gulp of wine. "Yeah," he continued, waving his arms expansively, "one hit film and he moved right into the fast lane. Died of a heroin overdose. He was only twenty-eight. Issy was at Berkeley going for his architecture degree."

He thrust his right hand at her, but Gloria didn't react. "Anyway," he went on, "you can imagine how hard it hit him. He was really bummed out. That's when the Berkeley docs got to him. Shipped him right off to Langley-Porter in San Francisco and he ended up getting electroshocked." Eddie widened his eyes and vibrated his head and torso. "And, God, he wound up staying with the shrink who was treating him. A woman. Unbelievable." He slumped back in his chair, his arms dangling at his sides.

"How awful." Gloria tried. *Why would I care?* her mind said. *He won't give me grandchildren . . .*

"He adores her," Eddie pushed on, desperation creeping into his voice. "And now he's trying to show that he likes you, too, but I know he can't figure out why he isn't here with us this weekend."

Oh, good Lord. Gloria resisted the urge to roll her eyes. Instead, she reached across the table and rested her hands on his.

"Sweetheart, this is all very fascinating, but can't we talk about Isamu later? I need to discuss something with you privately. That's why I asked you to have him stay home. It's a little secret between us for now, OK?"

He pulled back, concern sweeping across his face. "What's the matter?" he asked anxiously. "Have you heard something I should know about? Something about my business? About the grant I want the foundation to fund . . ."

"No, nothing like that," she cut him off. "It's about me."

"Oh my God! Are you sick? You don't have cancer, do you?"

Great, I've done it again, she thought. *What in the world was I thinking about, giving him wine?* "Eddie, darling, I'm fine. There's nothing to fret about. You're getting upset over nothing. I only wanted to talk to you, that's all. Have you taken your meds today?"

He pushed her hands away. "I'm fine, Mother. Don't start with me about my medication. I can take care of myself without your help, thank you very much."

She started to answer but thought better of it. They munched absently on fruit and sat quietly for a few minutes. Presently he settled back, inhaled and exhaled deeply. "OK, sorry. I'm OK. What was it you wanted to tell me?"

"Well, I think it's good news," she said, trying to sound casual. "The president has asked me to be his nominee to replace Marianne McBride on the Supreme Court."

"*Jesús Soberano!*" Eduardo's face turned pale. His lips and chin trembled.

"You know what? I had the same reaction. I couldn't believe it when he called me that night."

"He called the night she died?" he almost screamed.

"Uh huh. My bridge club had just left."

For some reason, that seemed to mollify him. "Oohhh," he squealed. "The girls of San Marino. Cuffy duh. Sugah sweet Virginnea. Tight-assed Mildred."

Gloria narrowed her eyes and fired back. "That's enough, Eduardo Arturo. Don't start with me, child. I don't make cracks about the boys of San Francisco."

"Uh huh. Well, Mother, but what do you think about Uncle Jon's offer? Won't you have to make our finances public?"

She blinked, "Of course."

"And the foundation?"

"Yes, sure."

He leaned forward accusingly. "Wouldn't you have to tell everything about us . . . you, me, Dad?"

"They ask a lot of questions, Eddie. Yes, they could ask about our lives."

"On TV?"

"Yes, the hearings are televised."

Drops of sweat formed on Eduardo's forehead and perspiration streaked down from his armpits.

Uh oh. Don't panic, mijo.

Eduardo abruptly slammed his fist down on the table. His wine glass toppled off and shattered on the ground.

"Why the hell is he doing this? He's fucking our privacy. I've never been happier in my whole life, for Christ's sake, and now he's ruining everything. How can you even consider doing this? Don't you ever think about me at all?"

"Now wait just a minute, Eduardo Hernandez, this isn't about you. This is my life. What are you so worried about, anyway?"

"What do you think?" he whined. "Weren't you listening?" He pushed back from the table and stood up, his hands clenched on his hips. "How can you even think about putting Isamu through this?"

"Isamu!" She rose to meet his gaze directly. "Eduardo," she said, purposely lowering her voice to keep her anger in check, "you're not thinking clearly now. This doesn't have anything remotely to do with your friend. You're not being rational." She took several deep breaths. She spoke again, in a softened tone. "*Mijo,* you're having an anxiety attack. We can discuss this later. Why don't you go inside and rest for awhile."

He glared at her, his nostrils flaring with his rapid breathing, his eyes moist with rage. "So what are you going to tell him?" he snapped.

She snapped back without thinking. "I'm probably going to say yes!"

"You are so goddamn selfish!"

"*I'm* selfish?" She closed her mouth and held her lips together. *What am I doing?* she berated herself. *I should never have let him have anything to drink. His medication and alcohol always react like this. What is the matter with me?*

"You're really going to do it?" Eddie was saying on the edge of her hearing.

"Yes," she replied, all at once calm about her decision, "I am. This is the greatest opportunity I've ever been given. I've worked for it all my life, and it will never come around again. Why should I give it up?" she went on, her voice rising again. "Just so I don't upset your little life in San Francisco with your special friends?"

He glared at her without speaking. Tears ran down his cheeks. His forehead, chest, and abdomen glistened with nervous sweat. *I'll pay for this later,* she thought, surprised at her impetuous determination. *But I'm not backing down. The boy has to grow up sometime. I'm entitled to a life, too.*

"I'm outta here," Eddie roared suddenly and turned to stomp away. Abruptly, he spun around. "Just what is it between you and Uncle Jon anyway?"

FIVE

One week, and dozens of conversations after he first offered his friend a place on the U.S. Supreme Court, Jonathan Morgan sat in the Oval Office with his old Stanford roommate and current chief of staff. Winter's prolonged bleakness had given way to signs of spring, and the sunlight streaming in through the windows had prompted Bob to sit to the president's right, rather than across from him. In the world beyond the White House grounds, Washingtonians and tourists flocked to see the countless, pink blossoms adorning the Japanese cherry trees that line the Tidal Basin. They were mindful that capricious, seasonal breezes could send the fragile blooms cascading to earth.

"It's remarkable," Jon was saying. "Plain, downstate Illinois language. I mean he was direct!" He mimicked a midwestern twang. "'Mr. President, there are rumors all over the capital that you're gonna nominate your old Stand-ford friend to the Court and frankly, I don't care for her. Not even born here. Rich Mexican, inn't she? And all mixed up with those Catholic bigwigs out in Los Angeles.'"

Bob arched his eyebrows. "No one ever accused the Chairman of the Senate Appropriations' Committee of being subtle. Straight shooter from Decatur, our Quentin Ravenswood is. That's ethanol country, pardner." He fleered. "What does the man want and what's he gonna give for what he's after?"

Jon shrugged. "Simple. He wants Rittenhouse nominated so he can be the senate sponsor."

"Yeah, no way Stanley Popowski would champion another republican to the Court, even if he does come from Illinois."

Jon tilted his leather chair back and rubbed his forehead. "Strange as it may seem," he mused aloud, "I feel less comfortable around Quentin than Stanley, even though he's a democrat. Remember Abe Dankowski?"

"No."

"Sure you do. California Senate? Same kind of guy as Popowski? Bucked us on everything but big, spending bills. Predictable, always predictable." He cocked his head at Bob. "Stanley talks like a street urchin, but you always know what he's going to do. Quentin speaks plainly enough, but his actions are bewildering. The only thing I'm sure about is that he doesn't like me."

"Well, hell, I don't always like you either. But then, I've got good reason."

Jon laughed. "Sure, 'cause I've made you into the miserable success you are today. But Quentin's another matter. He doesn't like me because I did in twelve years what he hasn't been able to accomplish in thirty-six. After eighteen years in state positions and the U.S. House, he finally made it into the Senate and progressed stolidly up the hierarchy for three terms and now, he's reached the top rung of his personal ladder. And he knows it."

Bob shook his head. "Nice theory, but I don't think that's it."

"Oh? You've got some kind of magical insight into the heartland mindset?"

Bob flashed his lopsided grin. "I think he hates you simply because you come from California. A lot of them do, you know. 'Golden Boy from the Golden State.' The party, desperate for a presidential victory, practically hands you the nomination after only eight years in politics. Why wouldn't he think you don't know what you're doing?"

Jon frowned. "Isn't that what I just said?"

"Yeah. But I said it better. So what's his offer, if we go along with Rittenhouse?"

"Our Welfare Reform Bill. Says he's got the votes to put it through or kill it. *Guarantees* either result."

"Forrest says we've got the votes."

"Ravenswood claims to have some potential defectors in his pocket. Hell, the bill barely passed the House. One or two votes either way in the Senate could make the difference."

Bob curled his lower lip. *Two-and-a-half years of work down the tubes, he thought, and a key campaign promise that'll kick us in the ass again next fall.* Out loud he said, "We'd better think about this, Jon. We've got a dual opportunity here: get a major bill passed and get the Court seat filled easily. Two boffo achievements within our grasp, and no need for damage control."

"I've thought about his offer."

"What did you tell him?"

"'Thanks for the call, Quentin. I'll think about it.'"

"Well, OK then. As long as we're simply dismissing important matters out-of-hand—"

"Excuse me, Mr. President," a female voice came over the intercom. "Judge Hernandez is on line three."

"Thanks, Katherine. Tell her I'll be with her in a minute."

Bob rose to leave. "I'll be in my office if you need me for any other crisis you're planning to create."

Jon glanced at his watch. "Why don't you go home? Anne and I invited the Hallsteads and the Jacobs to join us in our box tonight at the Kennedy Center. Anne somehow learned that Aida and Sarah are balletomanes. The Australian Ballet is in town."

"It's only a mere coincidence that both their husbands are on the Senate Judiciary Committee, I suppose."

"Come to think of it, they are. See you in the morning."

Jon picked up the phone and pressed the intercom button. "We're finished for the day, Katherine. Go home."

"Thank you, Sir. Good night."

He pushed the blinking light on his phone. "Glory?"

In her Pasadena chambers, Gloria shoved aside the draft of an opinion her clerk had left for her earlier and pulled at the snaps on her black robe. "Hi. I just got back and read your message. I have an answer for you."

"Do I have to ask what is it?"

"No. That is, yes. What I mean is," she took a deep breath, "I am honored to accept your nomination for the Supreme Court vacancy."

"That's great!"

"I talked to Anne this morning. She thinks it's a grand idea. So does Ophelia. Rex even said he'd sponsor me. My only question is well, many things. I'll want to keep this house, of course, but where will I live in D.C.? What about my unfinished cases? And getting through the confirmation? And Eddie? What happens if they say no?"

"They won't. And don't worry, you're smarter than most of the people in this town. Lots of hot air and posturing here. You should know that by now. Worse even than Sacramento." Jon cleared his throat. "So, did you, uh, discuss it with Eddie?"

"Oh, like you haven't talked to him about it."

"Actually, I haven't. I think Anne did. I know he and Mike have been burning up the phone lines. But I stayed clear. It was something Mike let drop, something about my being the devil incarnate."

"Let's just say you're no longer his favorite old Uncle Jon, at least not for the time being. And I'm a selfish bitch. You know, the usual."

Jon sighed. "Thank God, it's no worse than a standard response."

"By the way, old friend," Gloria said hesitantly, "have you ever told Anne about us?"

"Sure," he shrugged at the wall. "She knew we dated, remember? Before you came to your senses and she and I met. Why?"

"You ever tell her about—?"

"No." The answer was flat and final. "I never told anyone. No reason."

"Well, someone might know."

"Oh yeah? Who? Bob? I never told him, or Ron either. Never told anyone."

"How 'bout Rona? Jenkins or Jepson or something like that. We were in the same dorm for a while in college and then she lived with me in Hancock Park while she was trying to get back on her feet after something went wrong. I forget what the problem was, something about a boyfriend I think. Anyway, she knew you. She knew both of you."

"Really? Was she pretty? Did I make a fool out of myself in front of her?"

"No, but I think she saw and heard more than I wanted her to."

Alone in the Oval Office, Jon furrowed his brow and shook his head. "Sorry, I can't remember the woman. And what difference would it make? That was a hundred years ago, and we never did anything wrong anyway. Just normal people doing what people do. I don't care what your father said. We were in love. You married Arty. I found Annie. Life goes on. Who cares? She might not even still be alive. I hate to be the one to break this to you, Glory, but we're not exactly young anymore."

"You're right about that. But still, I can't help but wonder . . ."

SIX

Friday, April 28

"Judge Hernandez, I'm not contesting the intent of paragraph three on puh-page eighty-nine, but rather Ms. Park's per-per-perplexing choice of words in line thirty-four. The English is sim-sim-simply unclear."

Gloria stared unseeing at the thick document in front of her. The window behind her desk was stuck again, so the air in her Pasadena chambers had grown stale. The airlessness seemed intensified by the incessant arguing of the two attorneys who sat on the other side of her massive desk. They vied for her decision on the language employed in a contested international trade contract.

She rested one arm on a stack of legal volumes used to research another case, and tried not to look at the short, plump barrister who refused to comprehend his opponent's views. Try as she might to put the thought out of her mind, Freddy Gartz's bulging eyes and expiratory, grunt-like wheezes always reminded her of a feisty little pug in serious need of a choker or oxygen or carbon dioxide or something.

"What's wrong with my Engrish?" Florence Park protested with an indignant air. The recently naturalized Korean-American antitrust lawyer pushed her glasses up on the bridge of her tiny, flat nose and peered suspiciously at her adversary. "Be spechific! Be prechise!"

"Excuse me, Judge Hernandez," a soft male voice lilted over the intercom.

"Yes, Terry?"

"Sorry to interrupt you, but that call you were expecting from San Francisco is on line two. You know who, of course."

Florence and Freddy diplomatically looked away while Gloria excused herself and picked up the phone. She listened for a moment, then swiveled her chair around toward the window.

"I'd be delighted to join you for dinner tomorrow night," she said quietly into the receiver, "but I'm not getting on a plane to meet you halfway. Take the 3:47 into Burbank and Alonso will pick you up at 5:00, outside in the usual place. That should give us plenty of time to have dinner at Xiomara if I make the reservation for 7:30."

She listened again and then tapped her fingernails on the chair's arm. "Fine, bring him. We can all talk it out together. But you may as well know now, I've already called and said 'yes'. No, don't start. I don't have time; I have two attorneys with me. Alonso will pick you both up tomorrow at 5:00. Yes. The Mercedes. Good-by."

Gloria cut off the call and pressed the intercom button. "Terry, no more interruptions until I've finished working with Ms. Park and Mr. Gartz."

She hung up the phone, surreptitiously kicked her shoes off under the desk, rubbed the bottom of one foot against the other, and leveled her judicial countenance at the waiting attorneys. "All right. Now, Ms. Park, about line thirty-four . . ."

SEVEN

Sunday, May 7

The maximum-security fencing surrounding Camp David, atop Catoctin Mountain in northwestern Maryland, blended in with the native trees and shrubs of the eastern Blue Ridge hardwood forest. Removed from the cacophonous distractions of official Washington, Jonathan and Anne Morgan donned cotton shirts, jeans, and Nikes to hike along the well-tended trails that were set off by pink azaleas, sweet white violets, blue larkspur, and the rosy-pink flush of mountain laurel. Only the wind's song rustled the golden silence of flowering maples, oaks, poplars, and sassafras on this cool, clear Sunday morning. Their Secret Service detail walked quietly, several yards behind and to the sides.

Later, after they had returned to the rustic presidential lodge for breakfast, Anne brushed her short, curly brown hair off her forehead and poured more coffee. Her husband plopped his feet on the *New York Times*, which laid in disorder on the coffee table, while she slipped off her walking shoes, kicked her feet up on the couch, and nestled in to his side. He moved his arm around her waist, pulled her close, and kissed her gently, then more passionately. Just as Jon nibbled on her ear and reached for her breast, he heard a rustling sound and looked up to see a young man wearing a wrinkled, oversized tee shirt and blue boxer shorts amble into the room. He yawned pointedly and settled into an overstuffed chair opposite them.

Stifling his exasperation, Jonathan relinquished his hold. Anne moved away. "Did you rest well, dear?" she asked. She pushed into the couch while Jon smoothed down the back of her shirt, just a bit too playfully. She displaced his hand. "I'm so glad you decided to join us this weekend. You looked very tired Friday."

"Oh, yeah, I can see how you'd miss my company." From years of experience, Michael knew to keep the grin off his face. He'd walked in on his mother and father too many times and in too many places to write them off as sexually decrepit. Besides, he wasn't about to move out on his own to avoid their increasingly less-discreet encounters. At twenty-seven, he knew a good thing when he had it. Being the president's son had landed him his job on the Republican National Committee, Stanford degree notwithstanding. While many of his fellow history majors scrambled for teaching positions or savaged their parents' resources for graduate studies, he enjoyed the dotage of the White House domestic staff and curried favor with his mother by staying home for "just a few more months." Now he slumped back in the chair, his brown curls still awry from the pillows, his long legs spread far apart, his arms thrown wide in another expansive yawn.

"So, did you guys catch the North-Youngblood show?" Michael closed his eyes to avoid looking in the wrong place. He rubbed the stubble on his chin and right cheek, the current look of a British actor he admired. *Why can't you two at least confine it to the bedroom?* he thought.

"Actually," Jon said, "I was hoping you'd watch it and let me know what happened." *Ten-thirty and the boy is still rumpled and unshaven,* he thought. *Why can't he at least pull on some jeans?* "Who did Alfred skewer today?"

Michael grimaced. "Aunt Glory mostly. You know how he baits his guests, but I can always spot his own agenda. He went after Carlisle pretty good—Daisy, right? Republican senator from North Carolina?"

Michael waited for Jon to nod before continuing. "I think we'd better make sure her next campaign is well funded. She thinks you walk on water, you know." He kept his tone casual and eyes half-closed, but watched his father's face for any reaction from under his lids. "She was cool at first, but then she got kind of bitchy. You know what I mean?"

Anne had settled back against her husband's shoulder, although he stiffened, unreceptively. At the mention of one of the most-watched Sunday morning political talk shows, it seemed as if Jon's entire psyche had gone on alert. *He probably doesn't even realize his arm is still around me,* she thought.

"Anyway, Alfie made some sarcastic remarks about Aunt Glory being rich, and Carlisle practically cut off his balls—politely, you know, like she used to do in court. Then she turned it around into a tribute about her honors and all that."

Mike recognized the intense blank expression on his father's face. *He's waiting for something specific. Not Carlisle, not North-Youngblood.* "Remember Lorenzo Madrid, the new guy from New Mexico?" he tried. "We did one of those fiesta-dinner deals for him in Santa Fe before the last election? Well, he picked it up from Carlisle with how twelve percent of the population is Hispanic now, and Aunt Glory impacts their pride, and she's done so much for the L.A. Hispanic community, and she's Latina, and she's got impeccable qualifications. You know, all the goodies you wanted to push. It was almost as if Peterson and Garrison had scripted it, the way Carlisle and Madrid played off each other. Alfred was damn near apoplectic. Almost bit into that flashy diamond on his pinkie."

OK, that's what he wanted, Mike realized when his father's face softened.

Well, maybe Stanford was worth it after all, Jon conceded to himself, watching his son lumber over to the sideboard for a drink of water. *At least he picked up on what was really going on.* Anne moved at his side. He pulled his arm down, started to speak, then remembered to give her a peck on the cheek first.

Well, good, he finally realized I'm here, she thought peevishly.

"So who was on Alfred's good side—I mean, the democratic side?" Jon prompted when Mike had plopped back down on his chair, his hand over the top of the glass to avoid spilling.

"Senators Fairchild and Duckworth."

Jon's eyebrows shot up. "Christine Fairchild? Really? What did she have to say?"

Mike shrugged. "Nothing good, at least not at first. She called us a bunch of elitists, said you and your cronies all had your way paved by money and contacts and public gullibility, that sort of thing. Nothing new. All the typical democratic dogma. Alfred pulled out the church thing, you know, 'cause Aunt Glory's Catholic? Like there's some kind of conspiracy between you and the Catholic Church to get her onto the Court? You should have seen Fairchild's face! Doesn't Alfie know she's a big mackerel snapper from 'Bawlmer'?"

"Michael!"

Mike shot his mother a look of apology, but mentally shrugged off the interruption. His father was still listening intently, which was all that mattered. "Sorry. Anyway, Fairchild says she doesn't think any of the forty-nine Democrats will vote for Gloria, and with her needing fifty-one yeas to get confirmed, it'll be a tight race, especially 'cause some Republicans might jump ship."

"Yeah, that's possible," Jon admitted, and began to mentally tick them off. *Ravenswood wanted Rittenhouse. Montague's got some kind of a grudge against me, and Albrecht, well . . .*

"But we're gonna fight for her, right?" Jon's eyes narrowed and Michael stopped to wait until his father's focus returned.

Anne took the opportunity to stand up. "Well, I'm sure Gloria will win them over. Now, how about our tennis game, Chief?"

"Did you want to hear the rest?" Mike asked, ignoring her.

Jon quickly cleared his visage. "Sorry, just thinking about Fairchild. Yeah, there's something about her that— Oh, go on. What about Duckworth? What'd he have to say?"

Anne sighed and busied herself getting another cup of coffee from the sideboard.

Michael wrinkled his nose. "Good old Cornell Duckworth, asshole *cum laude*. You can always count on Alabama's junior senator to bring every issue down to sludge level."

"Michael, really, that's enough." Anne turned back to them. "I don't think we need to hear anymore, do you?" she said to her husband. She set down the cup and held out her hand to coax him off the couch. "Let's go, it's getting late. You two can talk mudslinging some other time."

Jon waved her away. "Go ahead and change, honey, I'll be right with you." He looked past her to his son. "What'd he say?"

Anne reluctantly sank back onto the couch. *Great. Another "day off" ruined. What's the point of coming out here if all they're going to talk about is politics? Maybe it's time for him to move out. At least we'd get a few minutes to ourselves. Why did I push him to be here anyway?*

"Well, by then Alfie was into his—what did you call it a couple of weeks ago—his 'rousing' thing? Anyway, he started off by calling Ducks an outrageous homophobe which, of course, he is, but he certainly can't afford to admit that on national television. So our friendly Alabama senator blathers on about how the *New York Times* is a piece of shit, and where do they get off writing that op-ed piece about him being a gay hater. If you were brain dead or had been living under a rock during the last election, you might even believe it. 'Some of my best friends know people who know people who are gay,' blah, blah, blah. Boy, he really got red in the face. I mean literally! I didn't think people really did that. And Alfred's just eating it up. You could almost see the ratings' chart ticking upward in his head. Then Ducks jumps on Aunt Glory's money, but not like Fairchild, oh, no. None of that polite, she's-too-rich-for-the-little-people stuff. He goes straight after her donations— you know, the megabucks she's put into your political campaigns. Yours and St. Clair's and her other 'GOP pets.' That's a quote by the way."

"Cheap shots, Mike." Jonathan flicked his hand. "Consider the source."

Michael nodded. "But that's not the rough part."

"Do we really need to know about the rough part?" Anne put in, already knowing the answer. The two men apparently did not hear her. Michael leaned forward sharply, as if he were about to spring into action. His eyes were glued on his father, who had assumed a similar stance. Anne made a gesture of defeat to no one in particular. *I might as well have left. They wouldn't even notice I was gone,* she conceded.

"NYB is egging Duckworth on. Ducks is getting hotter and hotter. Carlisle butts in to refute and Ducks looks like he's going to burst a vein. Then Madrid says something about Hispanic pride and Alfie kicks that back to Ducks, and Fairchild cuts in about you and Aunt Gloria being old friends and, all of a sudden, the man blows. 'Friends?' he says—and this is a quote, Pop. 'Only friends? Two kids in their early twenties with hormones on high boil and dealing with the frustrations of law school? Give me a break. Or at least give them a break.' Then he throws back his scarred face and brays like the jackass he is."

Anne caught her breath, "Oh my God."

"He just kept laughing," Michael went on more calmly. "He just wouldn't shut up. Even North-Youngblood couldn't handle it. He cut to commercial. When they came back, the camera never hit Duckworth again. Trouble is, the SOB is on the judiciary committee."

Anne looked from her son to her husband. Mike was leaning back in his chair, a mixture of triumph and unasked questions playing about his lips. Jon remained perched at the end of the couch, poker-faced, the velocity of his thoughts betrayed only to her by a slight shifting between his shoulder blades. She broke the silence before he had a chance to address Mike again. "Well, politics as usual." She stood up again, this time planting herself directly in Jon's field of vision so he could not see his son's expression. "It's getting late and I'd still like to play," she said firmly.

"Shouldn't someone call Aunt Glory?" Michael prodded.

Anne shook her head without turning around. Her voice remained composed but her eyes pleaded with Jon's. "It's too early in San Marino right now. I'll call her later. Besides, I'm sure she's just as used to this kind of nasty nonsense as we are." She paused, but neither man spoke. "Someday," she went on wistfully, "we'll be back in Montecito in the home we love. I hadn't appreciated until recently the wonderful privacy we used to enjoy there. The winding lanes, the old stone walls—"

"The overgrown property lines," Jonathan picked up, "the damage from the sea air—"

"The beautiful girls, the soft sand, the great surfing," Michael chimed in.

Anne gently pulled her husband toward the door, relieved she'd managed to forestall yet another difficult moment and grateful that, for once, neither of her men had insisted on provoking a confrontation. "Will you be here when we get back?" she asked Mike as they passed his chair.

He looked up, his eyes wide and chaste. "Where else would I be?" he asked innocently.

Gloria sat in her music room and sipped freshly squeezed orange juice. At 7:15, the sun had been up for an hour in San Marino, California.

"Friends? Only friends? Two kids in their early twenties with hormones on high boil and dealin' with the frustrations of law school? Give me a break. Or at least give them a break."

Gloria clicked off the TV and blew the breath out of her cheeks. *What a boor. Jon's right, there are some incredibly stupid people back there.* She opened the French doors leading to her garden where trimmed, green yew hedges and adherent, mauve wisteria softened the old brick walls. Niches in the walls contained classic statues and intriguing busts. Miniature lemon trees, pink azaleas, and scarlet rhododendrons flourished in large terra cotta pots. Neatly clipped, low boxwood hedges bordered a path of fine pebbles that led to an oval pond located under a wisteria-covered arbor at the far end of the garden. A statue of a young, nude woman stood in the center of the pond. Water spurted outward from the nipples of her breasts.

Gloria inhaled deeply, allowing the fresh morning air and lovely, tranquil setting to calm her. She watched Celia bend over the roses and count leaves to clip the new blooms at just the right spot. *Ah, that's what I need,* Gloria daydreamed, *a simpler existence. No cases to decide, no intrigue to wade through, no idiots tearing me down on national television in front of tens of millions of people.* She stepped back inside. Gloria sighed. *I hope Anne didn't see that lout,* she went on to herself, meandering slowly around the music room. She stopped to run her right hand over the ebony grand piano that Arturo had always played so beautifully. Mozart, Chopin, Ravel . . . *Maybe I should call her. Or Jon. No, he can handle it.*

She moved down the hallway to her office. Framed photographs rested on her desk, on tables, on top of the filing cabinets: her parents with the Archbishop of Buenos Aires at her confirmation; she and her father on horseback at one of his ranches in the nearly treeless pampa of central Argentina; a honeymoon shot of her and Arturo on the French Riviera; Eddie as a little boy, gazing at Michael, as a baby in a bassinet . . .

Oh, Jesus. Eddie. What if he saw it? Maybe I should take the phone off the hook.

Before she could reach it, the telephone rang. She groaned. *That's him! I know it's him.* The ringing stopped. A short moment later, Celia knocked on the doorjamb.

"Mrs. Judge? It's that lady with the too-small car."
Thank God. "Cuffy! Hello."
"Are you all right, Gloria?" the caller whimpered.
"Of course. What's the matter?"
"Oh, that awful show. Did you see it? The one with Youngblood-North or whatever his name is?"
"Yes, dear, I saw it. Don't worry. It's all nonsense. But I'm so glad you called." *If I can stay on the phone for another hour, he can't get through.* "I was going to call you this morning. How did your appointment with that psychic go?"

Four hundred miles north, the fog was lifting from Pacific Heights. Sunlight filtered down onto Eduardo and Isamu, who sat propped up in bed, drinking their first coffee of the morning. A vista of San Francisco Bay with the majestic, red-orange Golden Gate Bridge in the distance was emerging from the soft haze through their second-floor bedroom window.

"Friends? Only friends? Two kids in their early twenties with hormones on high boil and dealin' with the frustrations of law school? Give me a break. Or at least give them a break."

"God, Eddie!" Isamu pointed the remote at the TV and hit the off button. "What a dork!"

Eduardo idly ran his left hand along his partner's well-toned, sculpted body. "I guess I ought to call her."

"Why? It would only upset her. Let it ride."

"Yeah, but she's alone. And that was pretty bad. Politics is so raunchy, and Mom's so uptight. She can't even talk about sex. I don't know how she got around to having me at all." Eduardo ran his hands through his hair, then smoothed it down. He punched Gloria's number on his speed dial. "Line's busy." He hung up and set it on auto redial.

"Come on, man, relax. She'll be OK." Isamu caressed Eduardo's upper thigh lightly. "You're still planning to go to Washington, aren't you? You can talk to her then."

"Yeah. I hate the idea, but I'm the only one left now that my grandmother is dead."

"You're really tight, baby," Isamu soothed. "We should do some of those deep breathing exercises. Here, let me."

Eddie moved forward slightly, then back. "That numb-brained redneck." He put his left hand on Isamu's smaller one, now deep in Eduardo's groin.

"The guy's a fucking jerk. Forget it. Come on, guy, it'll relax you."

Eduardo sighed and loosened his hold. Later, the two lay wrapped in each other's arms. "You know," Isamu muttered absently, running his hand gently across his lover's chest, "I could go with you if it would help."

Eddie considered the idea and then shook his head. "No, you know that won't fly. One of us has to stay here to do the presentation for the Prentice Foundation. Besides, Uncle Jon's handlers would have a fit."

"I thought your aunt wanted to meet me."

"Yeah. But later. Maybe out here. Yeah, better out here."

"Mmmm." Isamu sank a little deeper against Eddie and let his eyes wander around the sunlit room. They settled on the bedside clock. "Buddha, it's nearly eight!" He sprang gracefully out of bed and pulled on a tee and jeans. "I'm going down to Jack's on Fillmore to pick up fresh, breakfast bagels. I'll be back in twenty minutes or so. Cheer up, bambino, we've got a great day planned."

"Cheer up? I thought you were the one who's supposed to be depressed."

"I am. Actually, I'm very depressed. I just happen to be happy right now. At least I'm not anxious about being depressed."

Eddie groaned. "That's a low blow."

"You complaining or—" Isamu lowered his eyelids and slowly rolled his tongue over his lips.

"Get out of here, you brooding butterfly!" Eddie bombarded his giggling bedmate with a hail of pillows.

"Oh, woe is me," the Japanese architect mimicked in his best Scarlett O'Hara voice. "How ever will two such lovely, but screwed up boys get along?"

The combination of Isamu's clipped Asian intonation and his attempt at a southern accent made Eddie laugh, as always. In response, his willowy lover, who had slipped on penny loafers, gave him the finger. "Elizabeth thinks I've got the power to get myself together."

"With her help, of course." Eduardo stretched out languidly across the rumpled sheets. "You really love that shrink, don't you?"

"I guess," Isamu lamented. Eddie waved him away. "Get going before you make me horny again."

"Oh, shut up." Isamu reached down to muss his partner's hair, a quirk he knew Eduardo hated, before heading for the door. "Remember," he called over his shoulder. "Eleven o'clock services at St. Mary's. Then lunch with Bernie and Skitch." He came back to pose dramatically in the doorway. "Skitch is in therapy again, by the way," he said in a hushed tone.

"Why doesn't he change his name to Steve or something? 'Skitch' sounds hokey. No wonder he's nuts."

"Reservations at Campton Place," Isamu's voice floated from down the hall. "One o'clock sharp."

EIGHT

Friday, May 12

Reporters clamored around Forrest Garrison the moment he stepped out of the Senate Chamber.

"Senator Garrison—"

"Oh, Senator! Please—"

"Senator Garrison, are you disappointed?"

"Senator, Senator!"

They jostled his aide aside in their frenzy to shove in the microphones close enough to catch the imposingly tall, square-jawed, white-haired Arizona Republican's statement.

Forrest had become accustomed to media commotion after close votes on important bills. As he hurriedly made the short walk to his ornate, high-ceilinged second floor office in the Capitol building, he managed to avoid eye contact with anyone. He looked straight ahead, through thick, silver-rimmed glasses.

Presently, the crowd of journalists thinned around him, to clump up again around a senator who might answer questions.

Once away from the microphones and cameras, Forrest lessened his stride. And, when a short, reed-thin, wrinkled-faced woman approached, he stopped altogether. His face softened.

"Hey, Dolly."

"Hey, Forrest. Bad day?"

"I've had better. Damn it! I thought we had it in the bag."

"I reckoned as much, or you wouldn't of called the vote."

"Well, I'll tell you what to write in the *Arizona Republic*. The Welfare Reform Bill is dead for this session. If I'm still in charge around here after November, we'll take it up again next year."

"Calendar too full to try again later in November or December?"

"Yeah, and I guess it needs to be rewritten again."

"Six Republicans voted against it today. Were you surprised?"

"Not about three of 'em. But the other three, I just don't know."

SENATE KILLS WELFARE REFORM BILL
By Dolly Maxwell

President Morgan's Welfare Reform Bill was defeated in the U.S. Senate last night by a 52-48 vote. Six Republicans joined 46 Democrats to jettison a cornerstone goal of Mr. Morgan's first term, after a two-and-a-half year struggle between the White House and Congress. A House version of the controversial measure had narrowly passed last month.

Senate Majority Leader Forrest Garrison appeared dejected after the defeat. To his frustration, powerful Senate leaders Quentin Ravenswood (R-Ill.), Chairman of the Appropriations' Committee, and Carl Albrecht (R-Pa.), Chairman of the Armed Services Committee, voted with the Democrats.

"I'd asked for a roll call because I knew it was going to be close," the veteran senate leader and former popular Arizona governor said, "but I thought we'd win. Kyle Lambert was presiding to break a tie— if it came to that—but we didn't even get that far."

The president was eager to get his high-profile bill into law before the November election, now less than six months away . . .

SECTION II

THE HEARINGS

NINE

Norah Poole Stafford and her black-and-tan Doberman pinscher, Felix of Haverford Hall, shared the back seat of her silver Bentley. The automobile traveled smoothly on the George Washington Memorial Parkway along the Potomac River from her McLean, Virginia estate to the Hart Senate Office Building.

A soft-spoken, former attorney and Wall Street investment banker, Norah had parlayed her deft business skills into a shrewd eye for political expediency. Almost twenty-two years ago, she took over her late husband's senate chair. New Jersey Senator, Gordon Lyons Stafford, an eastern, moderate republican and pharmaceutical-fortune scion, collapsed and died almost instantly from a massive heart attack while playing golf near their stately residence in Princeton.

Now she leafed through a folder that contained background notes, probable objections, and potential pitfalls for Jonathan Morgan's latest Supreme Court nominee. This would be the fifteenth nominee she had examined as a member and, for the past four years, Chairwoman of the Senate Judiciary Committee. She had every intention of sending the president's friend to the senate floor with a strong stamp of approval from her committee. Felix, the perfect show dog, sat quietly next to her, observing the freeway action.

The moment the sedan stopped near the Second Street entrance, guards pushed through the waiting reporters, photographers, and TV cameramen to clear a path. From her control panel, Norah opened the window on Felix's side of the car and the powerful Doberman immediately thrust his head, neck, and upper chest out. Ears erect, he growled low and displayed glinting teeth. The reporters moved back.

"Sit," Norah commanded. "Stay."

Felix remained immobile on the seat, as the chauffeur opened the door and Norah stepped down the cordoned-off walkway amid flashing bulbs. She waved to the swarm of reporters, but only shook her head in answer to their barrage of questions. Once safely inside, she met an aide in the building's nine-story atrium. The monumental, Alexander Calder, mobile-stabile sculpture of black mountains and clouds stood nearby. The aide took the papers she held out and hurried ahead to the Central Hearing Room. The senior senator from New Jersey lingered to let a fellow senator catch up with her. "Grant! Haven't seen you for a while. How've you been?"

Middle-aged and balding, Grant Hallstead sat on the opposite side of the aisle from his respected colleague, but often found himself voting on the same side of the page. Now he flashed her a gleaming smile. "Couldn't be better, Senator. And you?"

"Just fine, thank you." She spoke with the cultivated Eastern reserve she'd polished at Wellesley and Yale Law. "You certainly look rested. Have you been on vacation?"

"Sort of." A wide grin crossed his face. "I've just come back from a weekend with the president and his wife. He was doing fund raisers in the Bay Area for St. Clair, and offered to take us along for the ride. He even lent us a car and driver so we could see Debbie at Berkeley."

"Well, he's a father, too. He knows how much you must miss your daughter. What year is she in now?"

"Sophomore. They make her work, but Aida had warned her about that. She still thinks all I did out there was play football. Hell, I worked my tail off." He wiped a hand across his ebony brow with a comical look. "How else would I have gotten into such a precarious position now, accepting gifts from a rival party's president just so I can check out my kid's social life without warning? You don't suppose he wants something from me, huh?"

Norah laughed. "Now, Grant, don't be silly. The president is just a nice guy, that's all."

Grant returned the laugh and slowed his pace to allow the Senate's patrician doyenne to enter the crowded hearing room first.

"She's in the building. She should be here soon," a husky man wearing a dark-blue uniform said from the floor below the dais.

Norah nodded at the guard, looked at her watch, and tapped her yellow, lead pencil impatiently. There was nothing to do but wait. They couldn't very well start until the nominee herself arrived. To pass the time, Norah played her favorite mental game, looking up and down the table and trying to guess which of the other seventeen senators on the committee would ultimately support Gloria Hernandez's nomination. The other nine Republicans sat to her right. Most of them—New York's, Yale Jacobs; North Carolinian Daisy Carlisle; Majority Whip, Bruce Landes of Ohio; Nebraskan, Paul Worthington; and junior senators, John Fitzpatrick of Rhode Island, and Texan Luke Roberts—would likely vote the party line to confirm. Morgan stalwarts—Campbell Townsend of Tennessee and Montanan Russell Marchbanks—had backed Morgan's appointees with one hundred percent regularity. Carl Albrecht, on the other hand, could be a problem. As a twenty-three-year-old marine, the Lancaster, Pennsylvania native had won the Congressional Medal of Honor in Korea, and he had recently made it clear he still believed fellow vet, Judge Markus Rittenhouse, was the best candidate for the open Supreme Court seat. Norah would have to find a way to reason with him.

Seated to her left were the opponents: Democrats who, for their own various reasons, would do their best to find something they could point to—other than partisanship—as good reason to reject the candidate.

Stanley Popowski, a Chicagoan up from the streets, was sure to take exception to Judge Hernandez's considerable wealth, as was Oregon environmentalist Sinead Sullivan. Vermonter, Derek Scott; Hawaii's Kawai Higashi; and Arkansas' Cotton Blalock, Congress' oldest elected official, would probably stick to their own party line, regardless of how much Hernandez impressed them.

Since the judge was single, female, and Catholic, she certainly didn't stand much of a chance with Bible-thumper, Cornell Duckworth of Alabama. Maryland's Christine Fairchild was very bright, very private, and very unpredictable, but would probably follow her party's leaders on this vote. However, after his weekend at the president's expense, plus other likely incentives to be proffered from the Oval Office, Californian Grant Hallstead just might be swayed.

"Will her son be here?" Yale Jacob's question came through a half-concealed yawn. The New Yorker and his wife were renowned for their late evenings at cultural events and post-performance parties.

Norah shrugged one shoulder toward the senator on her immediate right side. "I imagine so. It would look awfully strange if he didn't show up."

"Hmm. Do you suppose he'll bring his uh . . . friend?"

"Unlikely."

"Yeah." He yawned again. "I could sure use some coffee."

Presently, two burly men in dark suits entered the room and surveyed the crowd, before proceeding to the front-row seats. One nodded toward the door, and Judge Gloria Hernandez, accompanied by a more slender but hard-faced official, strolled confidently into the chamber. She headed for the modest table and chair arranged on the floor before the committee's dais. Behind her was a still empty row of chairs reserved for family members, her senate sponsor, lawyers, and aides.

Members of the press milled about in the table section. Spectators overflowed the sides and rear of the spacious room. Behind the soundproof glass of the TV booths, camera and sound techs played out an animated pantomime.

Gloria carefully smoothed the skirt of her gray suit before she sat down. She opened her briefcase and arranged her materials around the water pitcher and glass, provided as a standard courtesy. She briefly adjusted the collar of her salmon colored blouse, hoping her choice of attire would reflect just the right touch of confidence and vitality without implying arrogance or fervor. Not for the first time this morning, she drew a deep breath and tried to will her pulse to slow down.

"This way, Judge," a photographer called.

"Judge Hernandez, over here please!"

"Judge! One more for your admirers in Miami."

Gloria turned this way and that for the high-speed flashes coming from all directions. Behind her, Michael Morgan slipped into a front-row seat, followed by Eduardo and the darkly appealing Congressman Ari Bromberg, an old, Los Angeles family friend, who represented the solidly democratic and affluent Westside of California's largest city.

Suddenly, the photographers abandoned Gloria and turned their attention to a handsome, erect, gray-haired man accompanied by a slender, fair-skinned woman whose white hair accentuated her unfading beauty.

"Senator St. Clair! Over here!"

"Ms. Smythe! Ms. Smythe! This way!"

"Come on, Rex, let's have one for the old days."

"Can I get one of you two arm-in-arm?"

At precisely ten o'clock, Norah settled herself into position, pounded her gavel, and waved at the photographers. "This hearing will come to order, please." She paused momentarily, then gaveled louder. "Ladies and gentlemen, quiet please."

Gradually, the noise diminished until the only sound left was the chattering of a small group of White House attorneys in the first row. Norah sternly stared directly at them until they stopped, then softened her face. "Judge Hernandez, welcome."

"Thank you, Senator Stafford."

"In the interest of time," the chairwoman said, "I will begin . . ."

TEN

Later Thursday morning

Gloria sat back and listened as, following customary protocol, the committee members each made a brief opening statement of welcome and a few comments about legal issues of particular concern to them and their constituents. She easily caught the speakers' personal agendas sprinkled among the platitudes, jokes, and occasional self-congratulatory comments spouted for the benefit of voters back home. The more the senators talked, the more she relaxed. Almost as in court, she soon realized. Everyone's jockeying for opening position.

At length, Norah thanked the panelists, turned briefly to whisper to her aide, and then addressed the house. "It is my pleasure now to ask Judge Hernandez's sponsor to introduce her. Senator St. Clair, welcome. We are delighted to have you here."

Rex St. Clair walked to the temporary podium amid an unconventional round of applause. When the senior, California senator had left his family's Montana ranch forty years earlier, he was still Tom Malloy, a strapping young man with unruly sandy hair. Twenty-four years, a string of "B" westerns, high-adventure action flicks, spine-tingling thrillers, and two Oscars later—one for acting, one for directing—he had entered politics at the behest of several well-heeled, influential republicans. He readily won the race against an aged, democratic incumbent and had held his seat in the Senate ever since. Now, he positioned himself in front of his audience, with his customary flair, and began as if he were speaking extemporaneously.

"Good morning, Madam Chairwoman and distinguished colleagues. I am deeply honored to recommend Judge Gloria Hernandez of the great state of California to be the next Associate Justice of the Supreme Court of the United States."

He paused, fixed his gaze on Daisy Carlisle and, with a twinkle in his eye, said, "Judge Hernandez is, of course, well-known to the lawyers on this committee—by the way, is there anyone here who isn't a lawyer?" He swept the panel with a gesture, letting the laughter linger just long enough. "—for her classic text on antitrust law, which she wrote while a professor at UCLA Law School. I guess you could say she really wrote the book on business monopolies." He redirected his exuberance toward Grant Hallstead. "She didn't remain in the ivory tower, however, though Senator Hallstead and I couldn't be more proud of UCLA. Oh, ouch! Sorry about that, Grant. And of course, her sister institution to the north, the great UC Berkeley."

Rex acknowledged Grant's salute with a wink. "As you all know, of course, Judge Hernandez has had a distinguished twenty-year career on the federal bench, serving first on the U.S. District Court for Central California in Los Angeles and, for the past ten years, on the U.S. Ninth Circuit Court. She was born and raised in Buenos Aires, where she attended Catholic schools and in junior high, had the unusually good fortune to befriend my lovely wife, whom some of you may recognize."

Rex turned with a gracious gesture to present Ophelia. The chamber burst into thunderous applause as the celebrated British actress rose and took a brief bow.

"One day the two teenagers talked about their future aspirations. Ophelia confessed to having acting ambitions, which she begged Gloria to keep secret. She didn't want to upset her father, the British Ambassador to Argentina, who, by the way, would later not only object to his daughter's career, but her choice of husbands as well."

Rex waited for the laughter to die, then continued in a conciliatory tone. "Now, I apologize to these gracious ladies if this is embarrassing, but I've saved all the letters Ophelia ever sent to me." He carefully drew a blank piece of notepaper from his inner coat pocket and opened it gingerly. "Ophelia airmailed this to me from Kenya, where she was portraying Evangeline Stapleton in one of her greatest roles. Remember, the brave missionary nurse who succumbed to malaria? Well, she knew I was enduring bad reviews for my performance in a '70s, cutting-edge film. Some of you may recall *Crackerjack Cowboy*."

Groans erupted around the hall. Stanley Popowski signaled two thumbs down. Rex pointed at him. "Yeah, right. You must have been the movie critic for the *Sun-Times*. Went right over your head."

After a perfectly timed pause, Rex picked up his line on the last note of the chuckles. "Ophelia consoled me about the reviews and then went on about her undying admiration of our dear friend, Gloria Hernandez, who had recently corresponded with her." He brought the paper into reading position and said right before slipping on his glasses, "This is all you need remember of anything I say today."

He read from the bare page. "And Gloria said to me that long-ago day on the terrace of the British Embassy, 'I know you'll be a marvelous actress, Ophelia. I wish I were as sure of what I want to do as you are. I only know I want to do something that will make peoples' lives better.'"

Rex removed his glasses and returned them to his breast pocket. He carefully folded the paper and slipped it into his inner-coat pocket. The female senators appeared pleased. Cotton Blalock shifted in his seat and motioned for his aide to rub his humped back. Derek Scott belched softly and flipped a page in the thick journal in front of him.

In the audience, Eduardo wiggled in his seat. "This is just the overture, pal," Michael whispered. Eddie nodded and stifled a yawn. He'd seen Rex's performances since he was a little boy.

Gloria kept an impartial, judicial expression on her face during the rest of Rex's speech about how the two of them had met while she was a college student and he, still a Hollywood extra. She had already cautioned him to take out the parts he felt added a touch of humanity to the proceedings, such as her generous support of Catholic charities. She thought it would merely add fuel to her opponents' fire. Nobody's life can bear absolute scrutiny, she'd warned him. He had sighed and waved his arms and argued about dramatic effect but, in the end, Ophelia had taken a red pencil to the script and Rex had grudgingly acquiesced.

". . . highest rating from the American Bar Association for this nomination," Rex was saying. "She has my most sincere recommendation to the committee for confirmation to the Supreme Court." He inclined his head toward Norah. "Thank you, Madam Chairwoman."

Flashing his best Hollywood smile, he sat down to steady applause. Norah glowed at her handsome associate, thanked him for his remarks, and nodded toward Gloria. "Judge Hernandez, the floor is now yours."

Gloria did not respond immediately. Ophelia had coached her to take her time and let the moment come to her, but actually, she was having trouble getting her eyes to focus. As soon as the ovation had died down and she knew she must speak, the eighteen panelists had changed into ill-defined blobs on the dais. She couldn't remember any of the relaxation tricks her friends had taught her either. She ran her tongue around the inside of her mouth, the unappealing nervous habit Rex had warned her to avoid. She wanted to take a sip of water, but feared knocking the glass over with her shaky reach. Finally, she swallowed hard, spread the fingers of her right hand on a small copy of the Constitution she had brought along for reference, placed her left hand on her knee, and took two slow breaths.

"Thank you, Senator Stafford." To her amazement, her voice didn't crack. Encouraged, she pushed on. "My sincere appreciation goes to Senator St. Clair for graciously escorting me to all your offices during the past week, to become acquainted and converse about issues of importance to both you and me."

Gloria let her eyes scan the entire panel. The committee members seemed closer now, their shapes and faces clearly defined. "A few of you asked how I came to the United States. I only wish my story held more drama. When I was a junior in high school, one of my mother's cousins invited me to visit her in Los Angeles. Her son, Miguel, was a few years older than I and already a sophomore at USC. He gave me a tour of the campus, the beaches, and many of the other wonderful L.A. attractions. I loved the vibrancy and freedom of the city so much that when I returned home, I begged my parents to let me attend USC. At first they said no, of course. I was their only child, only a teenager—and a girl! But I persisted, and they finally gave in. Being accepted to USC was the beginning of my fulfilling life in California. I became a U.S. citizen five years later while attending Stanford Law School, which by the way, is where I first met Jonathan Morgan. I am grateful to him for this important nomination, and for the confidence he has shown in my ability to be able to serve on the Supreme Court."

Now when she paused to take a sip of water, her hand was rock steady. *I don't know why I was so scared,* she wondered. *I've spoken before larger audiences than this.*

She continued with her prepared statement, making sure she looked up now and then, especially right before the jokes. "I realize you and your staffs have been reviewing my opinions contained in my professional articles and book chapters on antitrust law and government regulations. Some of you may even have been forced to use my book on antitrust law when you were students. I hope you appreciate that I at least had the grace not to give copies of the latest edition out when I came to your offices."

The laughter and hand clapping relaxed her even further. By the time she finished the section on the pride she took in her heritage, her adopted country, and the ideals for which it stands, she felt completely at ease and in command of the moment, exactly as in court. She held up her little copy of the Constitution.

"I am prepared, if confirmed to our country's highest court, to work to the extent of my ability to decide each case presented before me and my distinguished colleagues based on the facts, governing law, established precedents, and constitutional guidelines." She glanced at Carl Albrecht, who had pushed her on a number of points in their initial meeting. "It would, of course, be inappropriate for me to forecast my decisions during these hearings on impending or potential cases and policy issues that might come before the Court."

He narrowed his eyes and stared at her. She held his gaze momentarily before continuing. "In closing, I wish to express my profound respect for the late, Justice Marianne McBride. During her tragically curtailed tenure, she established herself as one of the nation's most respected jurists—a brilliant, yet compassionate voice. To be considered for Justice McBride's seat on the Supreme Court is a unique and solemn honor." Gloria again scanned the panel. "Thank you, Madam Chairwoman."

The huge chamber remained silent, the only noise coming from spectators shifting in their seats or coughing softly. Finally, Norah looked up. "And, thank you, Judge Hernandez. Do you need a break, or would you prefer to proceed?"

"I'm fine, thank you. Let's proceed."

"Very well. We will, as usual, alternate from one side of the table to the other. I ask the panelists to confine their queries to public, not private matters, and to keep to our agreed time constraints during the open hearings. One half-day in closed session, for questions on private issues, will follow these public televised hearings and will also precede the open testimony of various witnesses on the last day of proceedings. Remember, we will all have the opportunity for several rounds of questions before the hearings are over. That said, I'll begin with my first set of questions, and Senators Blalock and Jacobs will follow."

Norah started with a discussion of landmark antitrust cases that Gloria had deftly handled and continued with a few questions about government oversight of bank and corporate mergers. The chairwoman eyed the large, black-on-white clock hanging over one of the side doors before turning to her left. "Senator Blalock, before we take a break, please proceed with your first questions."

"Thank you, Madam . . . Madam Chair . . . er . . . woman." The oldest member of Congress ran an index finger over his notes, and then pushed them aside. "Judge Hernandez, you mentioned the 'tyranny of dictators' in your opening statement. Were you or any members of your family personally affected by any radical changes in the Argentine government?"

Gloria answered the elder statesman's questions by describing her life in Argentina: her father's positions as a rancher, landholder, businessman, and board member of a major bank; and her own protected environment, away from the slums and raucous political demonstrations of her native city. *He already knows how he's going to vote*, she soon realized. *This is just for show.*

"No, Senator, my father never took me to Buenos Aires' slums," she said, repeating herself a little louder for the ninety-two-year-old's benefit.

"But you were aware, even from your protected environment, that some of the dramatic political changes in Argentina gave voice to the poor and undereducated. Isn't that a voice a Supreme Court Justice should be sensitive to? In addition to the well-paid voices of corporate attorneys and antitrust advocates, of course?"

Gloria smiled and leaned back. She had prepared for this. If he could put on a show, so could she. "To answer your first question, Senator, I became more aware of the injustices in Argentina when I moved to Los Angeles. The Argentine press was not always as free as the media in America."

"You really mean suppressed, don't you?"

"Yes, that's right. And in answer to your second question: Of course, I believe judges should be sensitive to the voices of all parties in a case and I think my record more than reflects that sensitivity."

After the murmurs finished rippling through the chamber, Cotton continued with questions about Gloria's Catholic education versus the American public schools, and her views on some form of school-voucher system for less affluent families. "What do you think of the constitutionality of those vouchers, Judge?"

"Senator, that's a very broad question about a controversial issue. Furthermore, school-voucher programs are being challenged now in the lower courts. It would be inappropriate for me to forecast my opinion on any of those cases. One or more of them may be heard by the Supreme Court in the near future."

Cotton took off his glasses. "Judge, could a state, under the federal Constitution, limit adoption rights to heterosexuals?"

Decades of sitting in judgment had taught Gloria how to hide surprise. She could imagine her son fidgeting in his seat, and almost feel him staring at the senator. She let the corners of her mouth curve upward ever so slightly. "That matter, too, may come before the Court, Senator. As I stated in my opening remarks, it would be improper for me to signal a generalized opinion on such questions."

Cotton sat back and furrowed his brow. "Excuse me, Judge. I didn't mean to press."

"Not at all, Senator."

Norah broke into the ensuing silence. "Senator Jacobs, you have the honor of being our last questioner before we take a lunch break."

The urbane New Yorker finished the morning with a return to comfortable territory. Gloria continued to maintain her position of nondisclosure on matters likely to be decided by the Supreme Court, but referred expertly to controlling precedents on the constitutionality of interstate-trade regulation, antitrust challenges to computer software manufacturers, and evolving intellectual property law relative to recent genetic-engineering cases. As the uncontroversial colloquy wore on, various media reps and spectators filtered out of the room.

Gloria's stomach growled. "Thank you Senator Jacobs and Judge Hernandez," Norah finally said. "It's now 1:15. We'll reconvene at 3:15. Please try to be on time. I'd like to finish by 8:00 tonight." She brought her gavel down twice. Within minutes, the chamber was empty.

ELEVEN

Thursday afternoon session

"So you support the concept of a wall between church and state? Even with your own excellent, Catholic girls' school education?"

"Yes, Senator Albrecht."

Gloria had spent the lunch break with three White House attorneys in Rex's office preparing for Stanley Popowski and his expected challenges to her financial standing, and now impatiently wanted the afternoon session to move on. *Good Lord*, she groused to herself, *this man's asked me the same thing three different ways. What's he up to? Just trying to run out his own time? Come on, Carl, ask me something different or give up your turn.*

"Do you consider yourself a devout Catholic?"

"I do."

"And aren't you a personal friend of Cardinal Ramon Delgado?"

"I am."

"For the record, Judge, his diocese is . . .?"

"The Archdiocese of Los Angeles."

"Yes. Correct me if I'm wrong, but isn't that the largest diocese in the country?"

"That's right, Senator." *And your point is*, she thought.

"And in your financial disclosure statement, didn't you list Catholic charities as your largest annual contribution? After the Hernandez Foundation, of course, which is another matter all together."

"Yes, they're separately funded. It's all listed."

"All right." Carl shuffled some papers. "Let's return to the church-state issue. More specifically, prayer in our public schools, as you had in your parochial schools in Argentina."

He pointed his fountain pen at her. "Couldn't government support religious activity in a nonpreferential way? Alternating a Protestant, a Catholic, and a Jewish prayer, perhaps, or a moment of silence for prayer, or contemplation at the start of the school day? We could raise the bar for our kids from the noise and confusion and alienation of their daily lives. Seems like a simple, inexpensive, non-intrusive idea to me."

Carl propped his elbow on the table and rested his chin in his hand, and his gaze held more challenge than his tone. Gloria stifled a sigh and offered her considered judgment on the motion. "Well, that might work well in your hometown of Lancaster, Pennsylvania, Senator, but I don't think it would work in the public schools of Los Angeles County. Our children speak more than one hundred languages and come from a much wider range of religious backgrounds."

Stanley Popowski leaned into his microphone. He had the look to go with the personality that others had warned Gloria about: bulldogged; streetwise; an urban-squalor man-of-the-people who had long ago learned that class envy was a vote grabber. And, he had used his meager background to mow down one wealthy Republican opponent after another, in his relentless climb up Chicago's slippery political ladder. Her advisors had pointed out repeatedly, how, in Popowski's later, state-wide races, Chicago had always come through for its favorite native son.

"Judge Hernandez, you probably know, the costs of political campaigns are going through the roof. Congress and the Court have fought over this for nearly thirty years now, ever since they passed the Federal Election Campaign Act. You probably even remember *Buckley v. Valeo*."

He rustled a sheet of notes close to his mike, cleared his throat, and brushed his nose with his thumb. "I'm only going to address two points about that ruling," he continued. "First, campaign contributions—which I'm sure you're familiar with—and second, campaign expenditures."

Norah glanced next to her, at Yale Jacobs, who rolled his eyes. Cotton Blalock folded his arms, settled back in his chair, and closed his eyes. A number of the other panelists turned to whisper to each other, or began writing on their note pads. *I guess the young, White House lawyers were right,* Gloria accepted. *Stanley will try to undermine my credibility because I'm rich.*

"So, Judge, the Court agreed with us here in Congress, on contribution limits. You know, the amount a citizen or, I guess in your case, a citizen and her friends, are allowed to give to a presidential or a congressional campaign fund. No problem there. But then it gets dicey, 'cause, as I'm sure you know, the Court threw out our limitations on campaign expenditures. Said we were tromping all over freedom of speech, flying in the face of the First Amendment." He gestured at the Republican side of the table. "Good deal for those people; lots of millionaires on that side of the aisle."

"What's your point, Senator?" Norah interrupted. "As you've mentioned several times, the judge is familiar with *Buckley.*"

"The point is, Madam Chair, if you've got enough dough, or enough friends with enough dough, you can pay your expenses through the right channels and not be corrupted, right? But what about the well-qualified candidate who isn't loaded and doesn't have big-money friends? Huh? He's screwed, isn't he? He has to pay everything aboveboard, straight down the line, no campaign committee over here and political action committee over there. Doesn't this give obvious unfair clout to rich candidates like, say, Jonny Morgan?"

"Or to incumbents?" This is what Gloria had been waiting for. She hadn't really needed the attorneys' advice; she'd been listening to and taking part in this kind of debate all her life. "I'm not going to apologize for being wealthy," she had told the three earnest young men. "I'm not God; I didn't set things up to work out that I'd have money while other people suffered. I was born into it, I married into it, and I've worked hard to earn and keep my own. Since the day I had any say whatsoever about my own property—which, believe me, as a woman, was not an easy thing to accomplish in the first place—I've done my best to use my money to help as many people as I possibly could. And I'm not about to stop—or make excuses for my ability to do it."

"You and I both know, Senator," she said now, unconsciously mimicking his stance in front of her own microphone, "that the Court, just as Congress, has wrestled with this dilemma ever since *Buckley v. Valeo*, in cases such as *First National Bank v. Bellotti*. It's bound to come up before the Court again, what with all the new campaign finance reform laws being proposed. At least half of them will be challenged in the lower courts before they're ever used. *Buckley* and *First National* may be precedents, but they're not carved in stone."

"So you're not going to comment about the obvious advantage to wealthy or well-connected candidates?"

Gloria centered her gaze directly into his eyes until he blinked and looked away. "No, Senator, I'm afraid I can't. Of course, that means I'm also not going to comment about the obvious advantages to incumbents like yourself, who have their own Political Action Committees. So I guess it works out all right for both sides."

Daisy Carlisle let out a loud hoot of laughter. Several other panelists chuckled. Norah Stafford reached for her gavel as a low undertone filled the hall, then let her hand drop. Stanley curled one jowl into a tolerant expression and waited for quiet.

"So," he began again when the snickering had stopped, "you're not going to talk about campaign expenditures. OK, then, let's get back to contributions. Judge, you've contributed to Jonathan Morgan's political campaigns, right?"

"Yes, Senator, I have."

"Presidential and gubernatorial campaigns?"

"Yes."

"How about our friend, Senator St. Clair?" He gestured at the actor-cum-politician behind Gloria. "D'you give money to his campaigns?"

"Yes, Senator," she said. "That's all a matter of record."

Stanley smiled. "Known to you and Senator St. Clair— and now to the rest of the country." He hurried on. "Have you personally sponsored fund raisers for these men?"

"Yes, Senator."

"And for other Republican politicians?"

"Yes, Senator. I wanted to sponsor a fund raiser for a Democrat once, but I couldn't find one who would take my money." During the ensuing laughter, Rex, his eye on the TV monitor, licked his index finger and made a "1" in the air. Stanley hunched over his mike.

"These fund raisers been in your own home? In San Marino? Other places?"

"Both in my home and in other public venues."

"And, of course, with fund raisers and your wealthy contacts, wow, you musta collected bundles of cash for your buddies Morgan and St. Clair."

"I'm sure you're familiar with the process, Senator."

"Hmmmm." Popowski cleared his throat. "Judge, how many fund-raising affairs do you suppose you've sponsored for Jonathan Morgan?"

"I answered that question in my financial disclosure, Senator. I'm sure you have a copy available to you." Gloria hesitated. *Oh, what the heck.* "Over the years, approximately twenty events for President Morgan."

"Twenty fund raisers! Yikes! How do I get on your list of friends? Judge," he continued, "don't you think sponsoring twenty fund raisers for a president who then nominates you to the Supreme Court smacks of cronyism?"

Before Gloria could answer, Norah brought her gavel down—hard. "I'm sorry, Senator Popowski, but I'm afraid your time is up."

"But I wasn't done yet," he said, raising one eyebrow.

Norah half shrugged. "You can continue your line of questioning in your next round if you desire."

"Well, that's all right. I think I got my point across. Even if it is pretty convenient timing."

Norah brought her gavel down again, this time hard enough to startle Cotton Blalock, who had been dozing.

"Is it my turn?" he sputtered. "Where was I? Somethin' about— What the hell's goin' on, Lucy?" He peered over his shoulder to his African-American aide with long, dangling bone earrings.

"Hush now, Boss. It's all right."

"What in God's name?"

"Shhhhh. It's OK, Boss." Lucy moved forward to rub his back.

Norah reached over and patted Cotton's hand gently while waiting for the titters running through the hall to fade. "Senator Carlisle," she said, waving in Daisy's direction, "please proceed."

Daisy brushed russet-colored bangs off her forehead, looked down the table at Stanley without saying a word, then pulled herself up, leaned back, and smiled at Gloria. "Good afternoon, Judge," she said in a soft North Carolina drawl. "Just never you mind ole' Popowski and all that cronyism slush." She winked at Gloria. "He's the pet of all those giant Illinois labor unions and the recipient of millions in campaign support through all his PACs, and those famous Chicago get-out-the-vote resources. In fact," she put her hand up to hide one side of her mouth, "I understand those loyal Windy City constituents of his get out and vote for Stanley whether they're dead or alive."

Stanley jumped to his feet. "Madam Chairwoman, I object! I don't have to stand for this crap!"

Groans, laughter, scattered boos and hisses erupted in the chamber. Panelists murmured to one another. A photographer ran to the dais, snapped a quick shot of the irate Illinois senator, and moved away quickly. A security guard rushed over to chastise the cameraman.

Norah slammed her gavel several times but it was no use. She shrugged helplessly at Popowski. "This room will come to order, please," she said meekly. Once the commotion subsided, she cleared her throat. "Objection sustained," she offered.

Stanley glowered at Daisy, who blew back an exaggerated kiss. "Senator Carlisle, please proceed with your questions for the nominee," Norah ordered.

"Certainly, Senator Stafford." Daisy folded her hands on the table, smiled at Gloria, and with the skill of a clever trial lawyer, led her through a series of questions designed to highlight Gloria's generosity and humanity, in addition to the stellar academic achievements of many Hernandez Foundation recipients. By the time Daisy relinquished the floor, Gloria couldn't tell if she were being prepped to sit on the Supreme Court or to be sainted or both. *Associate Justice Hernandez. Saint Gloria of San Marino. I'd take it.*

"In other words, Judge, your generosity to needy Hispanic students through the Hernandez Foundation, and to Catholic charities in general, is easy enough with your level of wealth." Sinead Sullivan was nearing the end of her first round and, like Stanley Popowski, seemed to be stuck on the issue of how Gloria spent her money. For her own part, Gloria had lost track of the time. She knew one thing, though: It flew when the questioner sat to her left, and dragged with the people on her right. Sinead was squarely to her right.

"Here in your financial disclosure statement, your net worth is estimated at $250 million and your foundation has an endowment of $150 million."

Gloria nodded. "Those figures are correct, Senator." She silently berated her expensively dressed, smartly coiffured inquisitor. *There simply has to be something else you want to talk about. You're not exactly renting a one-room studio apartment yourself. Money is no good unless you use it for good,*

her father had always said, and she did, as much as she could.
When had it become a crime to be born rich instead of poor?

"Anyway, here's the thing," Luke Roberts, the Texan
from the friendly side of the table was saying, "many of my
rural constituents feel quite passionately about this school-
prayer issue. They're worried their kids are gonna fall into
the moral decline they see in our larger communities, like
Houston, Dallas . . ."

Gloria listened with half an ear and tried to keep the
bleariness she felt out of her answers. The questioning had
been going on for an interminable stretch of time. Her
stomach growled. She should have eaten some of that
lunch in Rex's office all those hours ago. She shifted her
weight as inconspicuously as she could. *Oh, good heavens,*
she thought, *my bottom's fallen asleep.*

"Unnecessary and intrusive censorship, pure and
simple." Gloria wasn't sure Grant Hallstead had stopped
or merely paused. His attempt to lead her into a discussion
of using the First Amendment to defend "so-called
indecent speech" had at least gotten the proceedings away
from school prayer and her money. She perked her ears up.
After talking around the subject for most of his time,
Hallstead had finally asked a question.

"I'm sorry, Senator," she said, spreading her hands and
shaking her head regretfully, "regulated indecent speech is
being tested in the lower courts right now. As I've stated
numerous times today, it would be inappropriate for me to
comment on matters under scrutiny now that may
eventually make their way to the Supreme Court."

Grant pursed his lips. "Exactly what can you comment
on?" he began, but Norah brought her gavel down.

"I think we could all use a short recess," she said,
looking as wan as Gloria felt. "Please try to be back in here

in fifteen minutes. I'd still like to finish up no later than 8:00."

The gavel banged once more, and the chamber quickly emptied. Gloria craned her neck to look around the empty room. No one remained in the hall. Even Eduardo, Ari, and Michael had escaped. She slowly lifted herself and took a few hesitant steps. Yup, her bottom had fallen asleep.

TWELVE

Anne Morgan and Sarah Jacobs meandered slowly along the gently sloping, cantilevered ramp in the five-floor atrium of Manhattan's Guggenheim Museum. The First Lady and the New York senator's wife were perusing a new show— "Twentieth Century Italian Masters"—one day before its official opening. From the inner border of the curved incline, they had a panoramic view of the museum's ground floor where the larger sculptures stood.

Tobias Ware caught up with them as they lingered in front of a bold, oil painting. "I'm back. Had to fix the lighting of a painting on the fourth floor." He sighed. "A disgruntled artist objected to our spotlights and the shading effects." He rubbed his chin and stood back a little. "Don't you adore this canvas?" He gestured widely at the painting of a young man asleep on a raft being steered down a river by two giants. "I think it's one of Sandro Chia's most powerful pieces. I've always wondered where the giants are taking him, and why. One of my colleagues in Rome thinks they represent anxiety and denial, which their young passenger temporarily escapes by sleeping. But his respite will be fleeting at best." Ware jerked when a cellular phone beeped from his suit's coat pocket. "Sorry." He listened and frowned. "I'll handle it. Just don't let them, you know." The museum director quickly stuffed the compact device back into his inner coat pocket. "Please excuse me, ladies. This shouldn't take long."

He sighed again. " A problem with an installation on the ground floor. Two Italian sculptors arguing over a space."

Muttering to himself, Tobias rushed down the ramp. The two women looked at each other and burst out laughing. "That man needs pep pills," Sarah said. "He simply never opens up."

They moved on to the next work. "Isn't this fascinating?" Sarah pushed her glasses up. "Labyrinth With Sections." She stepped back next to Anne to examine the stark painting.

"Carla Accardi," Anne said with undisguised longing. "I love her work. I was at Richmond's a few days ago. They've got several of her smaller paintings for sale. I was so tempted to buy one, but Jon would explode if I were to bring one more piece home. We're already running out of wall space." She closed her eyes and took a long deep breath. "Oh, Sarah! I love it here!" She started to fling her arms wide, caught sight of the Secret Service people watching, and hugged herself instead. "I feel so exhilarated in Manhattan. It's like I'm home."

"Well, naturally. You grew up on the Upper East Side. Who wouldn't feel that way after D.C.? It's so claustrophobic there. I hate it. Not enough to ask Yale to give up his seat in the Senate, of course," Sarah added quickly. "But enough to get out every chance I get. It's so dirty. Everyone always snooping around to dig something up on everyone else." She shuddered. "A real one-horse town."

"I know what you mean," Anne said softly. She turned abruptly away from the labyrinth with its starkly contrasting black-and-white complex of lines.

"What's the matter?"

"I don't know. It's so strange. All of a sudden that painting started confusing me. The lines got chaotic." She let her arms hang limp and shook her head. "It's probably just me. I've been feeling uneasy for days. I can't put my finger on it."

"Is it Jon? Is he upset?"

Anne considered that. "Maybe a little on edge. The hearings, you know. And other stuff. He's taking a big chance, but he doesn't say much. No, I don't think it's Jon."

"Michael?"

"No."

"Your mom? Your dad? Anyone else?"

Anne didn't answer. She just let her head droop to the side a little. Sarah returned her gaze to the Accardi painting and when she spoke, her voice was casual. "Have you talked to Gloria since the hearings started?"

"Oh, sure, we talk all the time." Anne licked her lips. "Well, I mean, we usually do. She's been awfully busy lately, what with the hearings and all. Every time I've called the hotel—" The First Lady brushed her hair back from her forehead and fluttered her hands nervously. She swallowed hard once, then again, and a third time. Just as her eyes began to mist over, she felt a firm touch on her arm.

"Anne? Are you all right? Annie?"

Anne blinked a few times. *For heaven's sake*, she scolded herself, *pull yourself together*. "How silly of me," she said after she'd regained her composure. "You'd think I was pregnant!"

"At our age? God forbid!" They both laughed. "Are you OK now?"

"Perfectly fine. What was I going to say? Oh yes, Gloria. I haven't spoken to her since the beginning of the week. I keep getting Eddie, and we keep having arguments. Actually, almost arguments. I won't let them escalate into the real thing. I'm just afraid he's upsetting her with all his nonsense. I wish we could have talked Arturo into letting him see a really fine child psychiatrist right there in Pasadena, when he was eleven." She stopped suddenly. "I'm sorry. It's an old family concern. Eddie's really quite gifted, which could be his whole problem."

Sarah looked over the rim of her glasses. "No, I'm sorry, I didn't know. How are you and she related?"

"Oh! We're not—not really. It's just that the families have always been so close, you know." Anne's voice trailed off. She swallowed again and turned to her companion with a renewed put-on smile. "Glory and I have been like this practically forever." She raised her hand to show two crossed fingers. "Even though we moved several times—you know, from Santa Barbara to the Silicon Valley, on to Sacramento, then back to Montecito—she and I talked frequently and met as often as we could. Our sons spent lots of their vacation time together. They were practically like brothers, or at least cousins. And they both graduated from Stanford."

"Yes, of course." Sarah hesitated. "You know," she said in a soft voice, "I've been watching the hearings, now and then. Yesterday when I saw Michael and Eduardo sitting together, I was struck by how much they look alike. Almost as if they actually were . . . I mean, you said so yourself . . . they look like they could almost be . . . brothers."

Anne's eyes misted over again. The labyrinth became a blur. She rubbed her hands together. Ice cold. A shiver ran up her spine. "Oh, no, Sarah," she said. Her own voice sounded far away. "I said they were *raised* almost like brothers, not that they *are* brothers. Michael is taller and heavier. I mean, if you'd ever seen a picture of Arty—he and Jon could practically have been brothers. Similar builds and expressions. Jon was maybe two inches taller. They were already married when I met them. Of course, Jon knew them before, but Eddie was a toddler when we were engaged and then the baby died . . ." She strained to focus her eyes. *Where are those wretched Secret Service people when you need them?*

"Anne, dear."

Sarah's voice was full of concern or was it shock?

"Well, I didn't mean literally, Annie. Only a silly passing thought. I didn't mean to upset you. I didn't mean anything by it."

Anne shook her hair out and patted it back down. She inhaled deeply and put on a bright face. "I'm fine now,

Sarah. I don't know what came over me. Maybe I need some water. Naturally you were offhandedly speculating, is all. I knew that. And, I'm pleased to say, Michael and Eddie have remained good friends as they grew up." She linked her hand around Sarah's arm and steered her along the ramp. "You know what? They play off one another with their expressions and gestures. I've noticed it for years. You've probably seen the same thing with your son and his friends."

"Oh my, yes. Zack and Kenny Berman. Yale and I were scared to death they'd become comedians and do clubs. Thank God, Zack became an artist. He's living with a girl we adore—good to her mother—over in Brooklyn. And Kenny graduated NYU Law. Lost his sense of humor totally!" Sarah fanned her face with the guide Tobias had given them earlier, and quickly changed the subject. She pointed to a large display niche filled with a three-panel fresco of multicolored bricks.

"I don't know about you, but that just looks like a wall to me," the senator's wife said.

Anne's eyes were sharply focused again. The familiar work was crystal clear to the modern-art historian. "It's a famous piece by Francesco Clemente." She read the brief description. "He calls it *Fraternità*."

"Doesn't that translate into 'Brotherhood' in English?"

"I think so. Brotherhood."

Sarah's smile froze. "The colors are lovely, aren't they?" she said. "But somehow it's sort of off-putting, like he wants to block us from something, or he's hiding something beyond the wall."

"Or maybe he feels like he's been cut off on the other side," Anne said softly.

Sarah nodded too fast. She pulled up her arm and tapped her watch. "Oh, dear, it's 4:00 already. Anne, honey, I've got to leave. Remember Yale's aunt? I promised to see her today in New York Hospital. Poor dear is just coming out of a stroke. Yale's counting on me to visit and call him tonight."

"I remember you mentioning it. Of course, you have to go."

"Thanks for lunch and everything. We must do it again soon. Daisy told Yale about a charming new restaurant in Fairfax that we want to try. If it's a winner, I'll call you."

Anne waved absently at Sarah's retreating back. The Secret Service men repositioned. Anne reddened at the movement. *Sure, now they come around.*

Wandering on her own, Anne stopped to look at a dramatic oil of multiple narrow, bright-red triangles with a background of small linear and geometric shapes in subdued shades of green, blue, and brown. *Political Gathering* by Giulio Turcato, 1950. She stepped back for perspective and suddenly thought of the Senate Judiciary Committee. *Narrow red triangles . . . spears covered with blood. Gloria's. Jon's. Mike's. Eddie's . . . Oh, no.* She covered her eyes with her hands, turned away abruptly, and immediately bumped into someone.

"Mrs. Morgan, excuse me."

She broke into a relieved smile. "Oh, Tobias. I'm so glad you're back."

"My pleasure. Did you want to discuss the Turcato painting?"

"Er, uh, not really. Frankly, it doesn't appeal to me much." She looked around. "Did you resolve that dispute? I hope there wasn't a duel."

"Only a duel of words, but I've been through this before with sculptors. They have controlling personalities. We reached *détente*. However, I met a gentleman on the ground floor who would like to talk to you. He said you're friends from the past. He's waiting near the Marini sculpture of the *Horseman*. He gave me his card."

She read the card:

> Dante Manzano
> Art Critic
> *Corriere della Sera*
> Milano

Oh my God, Dante! It's been a hundred years. I was still in college. Lord, I hadn't even met Jon. Dante, of all people.

"If it's a problem, Mrs. Morgan, I can arrange—"

"Oh, no, Tobias. Thank you. It's just that I haven't seen him for quite a while." She hesitated, then swiftly made up her mind. "This is a pleasant surprise. Really. Will you please point out where . . . ?"

They moved to the inner edge of the ramp and the director pointed to the right. A man in dark clothing stood barely visible behind the large, modern sculpture of a horse with a nude, male rider gazing upward.

"Yes, yes. I see him now. Thank you." She impetuously started down the ramp, then stopped and gestured to a Secret Service agent about thirty feet behind her on the upper incline. "Phillip, I'm going to meet a friend on the first floor over there, near the horse and rider."

He nodded, spoke something into a device on his wrist, and nodded again.

"We're having a big party here tonight for major contributors," Tobias said, hurrying to keep up with Anne as she started back down the spiral incline. "I'd love to have you join us."

"Thanks, but I can't. Besides, the security would be horrendous. You don't need that headache."

Phillip sprinted to catch up. He moved between Anne and the director. Tobias stopped. Anne made a mental note to thank Tobias later as she consciously attempted to maintain a normal pace. She proceeded as calmly as possible down the final curves of the spiral ramp to the ground floor.

Please, Lord, don't let him have gotten fat or bald. Anne, for heaven's sake, what's the matter with you? He's probably married. Does my hair look OK? You idiot, you know better than to see old lovers. Ah, Tuscany . . . the most wonderful year of my life . . . did I ever tell Jon?

At the sound of her footsteps, the man looked up. She extended her hands. He took them gently in his. *He looks great!*

"Dante, you look wonderful. How many years? How did you know I was here?" she gushed.

"And you look better than on TV. You haven't changed a bit." Phillip and several other somberly dressed individuals moved pointedly to various observation spots. He dropped her hands. "The rumor about your being in the museum previewing the show before it opens tomorrow spread like wildfire. And, of course," he grinned, "your private militia isn't subtle."

Anne glanced away from Dante for the first time. Familiar faces hovered conspicuously nearby.

"See?" Dante motioned with his head. "They're up on the ramp too. Everywhere."

Anne made a face. "Never mind. Just ignore them. I'm so thrilled to see you! Same curly hair, the dimple." *His hands are so warm. I love it.*

"Lots of gray, now. But I earned every strand."

"I didn't even notice. How long have you been in town?"

"Just got here Wednesday night."

"And how long will you stay?"

"Through the weekend."

An eternity. "Gee, I wish we could talk. Do you have some time? I do."

"Love to, but what about all these guys?" He looked around. "I think there's a café in this place. Maybe we could get a little privacy." Anne's eyes searched the area. Several agents started to move toward them, but she waved them off.

"Anything here is out," she said. "They'd probably have to empty the whole place just for us." *There's got to be somewhere.*

"Well, how about outside?"

She furrowed her brow and shook her head. "That makes it tougher for my protection. We could sit in the limo, but people would gawk."

"Like the ones on the ramp?"

Anne didn't even have to turn around. After many years of being a governor's wife, and then First Lady, she could anticipate the stares of the throng looking down on them from the incline, the whispers of the spectators gathering in clusters in the ground floor gallery. Her Secret Service detail had moved in closer. Phillip was talking to someone on his cellular phone. *We'd better get out of here soon.*

"I've got an idea," she said lowering her eyelids. "Why don't you come to my place for a drink?" She felt herself trembling just a little. *Please agree.* "I've got an apartment in the Carlyle for the weekend. It's just over on Madison Avenue. I want to hear all about you."

He hesitated. "Well, OK. But what about all these agents?" His eyes swept the room. "I mean if they're with us . . . "

"It's no problem once we're in the apartment. They stay outside." She began to walk him briskly toward the door. "So darling—I mean Dante—you're living in Milan? I read your card."

"Nearly fifteen years."

I had forgotten how blue his eyes are. "And you're painting?"

He shrugged. "I just paint on the weekends. I have a family and have to make a living, you know. I write about other artists and their work."

"Oh, you're married?" She made herself keep a light tone. *Of course he's married, you fool.*

"Actually, I'm a widower," he replied quickly. "Three years now."

"Darling, I'm so sorry." She grasped his arm in a consoling gesture and felt a shiver—like a jolt of electricity. *God, I'll be glad when we're out of here.*

"Maria is gone. We had two daughters," Dante was saying. "They're both grown and living in Milan. Beautiful, like their mother. One's a designer with Armani, the other a violinist in the orchestra at La Scala."

"That's so exciting. How wonderful for them." She quivered with nervous energy. "We've got so much to catch up on."

As the warm, May air hit their faces, Anne cleared her throat, put on her public visage and consciously kept from clutching his warm hand. She slid into the waiting limousine. The small digital clock in the rear console glowed

5:00. *Oh shoot, I was supposed to call Jonathan.* Dante climbed into the seat next to her and smiled. She put the call out of her mind. "So, tell me all about everything," she said.

THIRTEEN

Washington, same afternoon

The casual spectators had begun to file slowly out of the chamber when Norah glanced at her watch: 4:00. Next to her, Cotton snoozed peacefully. His steady breathing only occasionally betrayed a slight snore. Down the table to her right, Carl absently folded and unfolded a small piece of paper into tiny squares. Sinead stared glassy-eyed at the nominee, who had maintained her confident demeanor and stamina during this entire public display. *I need dinner . . . and a drink,* Norah thought. She didn't catch the last few words of whatever Judge Hernandez was saying, but knew instinctively when it was time to gavel and move on. "Senator Fairchild," she said trying unsuccessfully to keep the weariness out of her voice, "you're next. Please proceed with your questions."

The few remaining spectators rustled in their seats. Christine Fairchild, somehow still alert and limber, pulled her microphone closer. "Judge Hernandez," she began crisply, "you, of course, recall the landmark case, *Griswold v. Connecticut*? In it, the Supreme Court attempted to justify the creation of new civil rights—rights, you may recall, not even mentioned in that Constitution you keep waving at us."

Gloria shifted in her chair. Sinead blinked several times and sat back, her lips curving upward just a bit. Cotton gently snored on. Norah held her breath.

"Judge, do you think *Griswold v. Connecticut* was correctly decided?"

Gloria hesitated before answering. She could sense Senator Fairchild's hostility even though unsure exactly what the woman was fishing for. "The Court's decision was emphatic," she finally said, "but I can't remember the exact vote. On its face, the decision struck down an old Connecticut law that banned the use of contraceptive materials to prevent conception between consenting adults. But the more important outcome was the Court's endorsement of the constitutional right to privacy."

"A questionable endorsement, don't you think, but yes, that's what the decision did. So I ask again: Do you think the case was correctly decided?"

"I certainly agree with the invalidation of the Connecticut statute. As for establishing the privacy right, well, that's settled law. It's been tested over and over."

"And apparently you would agree with all those tests, despite the fact that *Griswold* was really pretty creative? Some even say outside the Court's authority." Christine paused, looked at her folded hands, and then went on. "Do you recall the 'zones of privacy' argument in that case, Judge?"

"Yes, the justice who wrote that portion argued that penumbras—no, let's do it this way. Forget penumbras—too scientific. That kind of language even baffles most lawyers." Gloria smiled at Christine, who returned a cold stare. "The justice who wrote that part of the majority opinion argued that shadows, or rays of meaning, extend outward from existing constitutional amendments. He reasoned, if I remember correctly, that added meaning could be found in those rays. In other words, they gave more life and substance to existing amendments, and that those additional meanings could therefore be used collectively to create 'zones of privacy' in the lives of people. I remember thinking it was a nice combination of physics and poetry."

"Wow! Physics and poetry. And here I've regarded it all along as a bunch of baloney."

A murmur ran through the chamber. Cotton's eyes fluttered open. Carl pushed aside his creased paper. The rest of the panel shifted in their seats to upright positions.

"I suppose there might be some sort of relationship between poetry and baloney," Christine continued. "Both come from creativity, wouldn't you agree? I've read and reread and reread that document you caress so much, but for the life of me, I can't find 'right to privacy' spelled out anywhere within its pages. And I'm a pretty bright person. I'd call that creative, wouldn't you? In fact, some scholars regard the Court's 'creation' of this so-called right to be nothing more than the rantings of a lunatic, a blatant act of crass judicial activism." Her voice grew louder. "Is that the kind of justice you're going to be?" she demanded. "A creative lunatic making new law instead of interpreting the words of the founding fathers?"

The panelists were all awake now, alert and energized, while the chamber buzzed with sympathetic acclaims and indignant catcalls. Norah gaveled for order repeatedly, but uselessly. Gloria turned around to confer briefly with one of her advisors. Norah's aide whispered something in his boss' ear. She shook her head and applied the gavel again. Presently, the last titters stopped.

"Senator Fairchild, you've asked two questions: one about judicial creativity and the other about judicial activism. They clearly aren't the same things. What are you driving at?" Norah insisted.

"That should be obvious, Senator," Christine answered brusquely.

"Well, it isn't to me."

"Let the nominee answer, then. I wasn't asking you."

Stafford slammed her gavel on the table. "Who do you think is running this hearing?"

Christine shrugged her shoulders and bowed slightly toward her senior colleague, before turning her attention back to Gloria. "Very well, Judge," she said in a conciliatory tone. "Let's move on. A less intimidating question. What do you like to read for enjoyment?"

Oh, no, Gloria warned herself. *She's going somewhere with this. She won't give up that easily.* "For relaxation," she said aloud, "I enjoy literary fiction."

"And your favorite authors are . . .?"

"Well, I enjoy some of America's southern writers, like Tennessee Williams, Flannery O'Connor, Truman Capote. I like William Faulkner and Harper Lee."

Christine smiled. "But what about Edgar Allen Poe? He lived in Baltimore."

"As Baltimore writers go, I prefer Mencken." *Where is she going with this?*

"Judge, you stated a few moments ago that you agreed with the *Griswold* decision."

"What I said, Senator, is that, controversial or not, it's settled law."

"A decision," Christine pushed on, "that laid the groundwork for *Roe v. Wade.*"

"Also settled law, Senator." *Oh, sneaky, Senator. Very sneaky.*

"Judge Hernandez, do you ever read the Bible?"

"Senator Fairchild, why do you need to know?"

Christine ignored that. "Judge, do you recall the Ten Commandments engraved on stone tablets and given to Moses by God on Mount Sinai?"

Gloria dropped into her dispassionate judicial bearing. "Yes, but what's the point?"

"Are you familiar with the Fifth Commandment?"

"I believe so. What are you trying to learn, Senator?" she snapped as if talking to an errant cross-examining attorney. "Let's get on with this."

Christine's eyes fixed on Gloria's and held them fast in the massive, tomblike stillness. "The Fifth Commandment from God states: Thou shalt not kill."

"Omigod!" Daisy Carlisle slapped the table with both hands. "Too heavy, darlin'," she drawled. "It's just too darned late in the day for theology."

"What? Speak up, Daisy!" Cotton barked. He leaned forward, stared to his right at the North Carolinian, and pressed his right ear forward. "How the hell did we get on penology? I thought we were talkin' about that damn fool *Griswold* case. Stupid opinion, if there ever was one, damn blasted muddled reasoning. Penumbras, for God's sake! Idiot that wrote that one shoulda been horsewhipped. Taking bits of the First, the Third, the Fourth, the Fifth, the Ninth, and the Fourteenth amendments and stirring 'em in an iron caldron, bringing the whole blasted thing to high boil. Then served his ungodly goulash up as a contrived right to privacy—which don't exist and never did—and we've had heartburn ever since!"

The room erupted in laughter and scattered applause. Norah didn't even bother asking for quiet. Encouraged by the disorder, several photographers rushed forward to get shots of Blalock, who beamed for the cameras. At last, Norah pounded her wooden plate and the room settled down.

"Senator Blalock, you are such a dear man," Daisy cooed.

"Well, thank ye, Senator. Now let's get back to Christy's questions about penology."

"I hate to interrupt this laugh fest." Sinead pitched her voice through the microphone so fiercely even Derek Scott jumped. "But Senator Fairchild was exploring the constitutional right to privacy and its later implications. Theology, Senator, not penology. With a *T* not a *P*."

"OK, girl, I can hear you. You don't have to shout!"

"Indeed," Norah echoed. "However, Senator Fairchild, I'm afraid your time is up."

"But, I was interrupted. You owe me five more minutes."

"I don't owe you or anyone else anything, Senator," the Chair responded coolly, looking down her patrician nose. "If we want to get out of here before 2:00 AM, we'll have to move on. Senator Marchbanks, your round, please. And when you're done, we'll break for a roll call in the Senate

Chamber, after which, I'd appreciate you all returning promptly so we can start today's final session promptly at 6:00 sharp. Senator Scott, you'll be up first, so please be prepared. Then Senators Townsend and Worthington, and we'll finish for the weekend. OK?" Norah brought her gavel down twice. "Senator Marchbanks, you have the floor."

"You stood your ground with Fairchild very well, Judge, although I can't tell what's eating her. Do you two have some sort of history?"

Gloria sat in Rex's office during the hearing break, trying to relax. Eduardo stood behind her, straining to push his thumbs into the tight muscles of her upper back. "Let go, will you, Mom?" he said, bracing his legs. "I'm massaging concrete here."

Gloria flexed her shoulders and attempted to consciously loosen the tension. But it was no use. "A little of Isamu's wine would help tremendously, right now," she started, then stopped. "I'm joking," she reassured the two horrified attorneys on loan to her from the White House. "Just a joke."

"Do you have some kind of history with Senator Fairchild?" one of the young lawyers asked again. Gloria tried to remember which one he was, Seth Greenbaum or Ned Broderick, not that it mattered. Both seemed equally young, efficient, blond, preppy, and earnestly humorless. She started a responsive, perturbed sigh, and Eduardo leaned over and kissed his mother's upturned face, and effectively covered her sigh.

"No, no history," she said, gazing into her son's eyes with undisguised gratitude. "Maybe she just doesn't like me. Maybe she thinks I'm a fallen-away Catholic. Maybe she doesn't like my son because he's—"

"—Just too hip for ninety-five percent of the people in this city," Eddie blurted. He winked at Ned.

Seth flashed a cautious glance at Ned, who adjusted his regimental repp tie.

"Maybe she's jealous of my relationship with the president."

"Maybe anything," Eduardo offered, leaning forward again to rub her shoulders gently.

Ned Broderick shifted slightly on his chair. Greenbaum averted his gaze with a nervous twitch of his right shoulder.

"Who knows, Neddie, with someone like her?" Eduardo shrugged. "She's pretty uptight, if you ask me. Probably doesn't get out much, if you know what I mean." He lowered his eyelids. "You must know the type, Seth. Withered on the vine."

The two somber young men apparently did not. They exchanged confused glances. "I was telling Howell and Jock, the other guys on our team, that the turn with Russell Marchbanks went well," one of them said.

"Is Jock the one with curly brown hair? In glen-plaid?"

"Yes, Mr. Hernandez."

"Oh, yes," Gloria interrupted. "Senator Marchbanks is a real gentleman." Gloria patted Eduardo's hand. He gave her shoulder a final squeeze and sat down on one of the half dozen, small-yet-luxurious chairs Rex had spread around his office, turning the stately room into a comfortable haven. He leaned his chair back on its rear legs to stare at the ceiling.

One young man said, "He's not a lawyer, you know. He's a farmer or something."

The other young man corrected his associate. "A rancher. A self-made success."

"Farmer, rancher, so what? What's the difference? They both ride horses."

"All gentlemen know how to ride horses." Gloria was getting tired of refereeing these bright young men Bob Peterson had sent to help her. "What do you know about the next questioner? Senator Scott?"

"Derek Scott," the second attorney said. He flipped open a notebook to show her the name. "Forty-five-year-old bachelor."

Eduardo sat up. "Really?"

Gloria shook her head at him. He leaned back again. "Divorced or never married?" she asked.

"Never married."

"Maybe he's gay," Eduardo muttered to the ceiling. His mother shot a sharp look his way, but he kept his eyes fixed on the swirling pattern above his head.

"Could be," lawyer one said. "We don't know. Keeps to himself. Except for one hobby." He paused, "Bird watching."

"Ha!"

Gloria ignored her son and closed her eyes. "Now I remember Scott. Very thin, very serious. Reminds me of a long-distance runner." She opened her eyes. "He has a peculiar, almost toneless voice. I remember. Lovely, colorful framed Audubon prints all over his office. A radical contrast to the man himself, who barely said twenty words during our visit. Rex had to fill in the time." She turned to Eduardo. "He's so good at that." Eddie nodded.

"He's no fool," attorney two warned. "He's got a real thing about the *Roe v. Wade* decision, just like a lot of the other panelists. Hates the implied privacy thing. Thinks the decision was bogus and the justices were out of line." He turned to Eduardo. "And that has a lot of implications, as you know, Mr. Hernandez."

Eddie raised his eyebrows but didn't respond. Gloria cut in quickly. "So Derek Scott favors the equality argument: Women are equal to men until they're pregnant. Then we're more equal."

"Yeah, he's big on equality law, but bigger on privacy in his personal life."

Eduardo returned to his entrancement with the ceiling. Gloria rolled her eyes at him and turned back to the two somber young attorneys. "OK," she said crisply. "That's very helpful. I'm sure Senator Scott and I will live through the next thirty minutes. Anything else? Will he explode as Fairchild did? Will he quiz me about prayer habits, as

Albrecht? Will he reproach me for having a wealthy father, as Popowski?"

"Never," the effete duo said in unison.

"He probably won't even look at you most of the time," the first one went on. "He prints all his questions neatly on a legal tablet, never shows any emotion, and barely ever takes his eyes off his notes. Oh, and by the way," he added, "Scott was a justice on the Vermont Supreme Court."

Well, that's nice to know, Gloria thought. *They couldn't have told me that first?*

"And," the other one continued, "he's big on environmentalism. He'd kill a multimillion dollar construction project to save a single gnatcatcher any day."

"Well, then, he can't be all bad."

"And if it comforts you, Judge," the other hurried on, "the final two questioners are both Republican, both good friends and supporters of the president. You shouldn't have any trouble with either of them."

"Thank you." Gloria stood up. "You know, you two have put in a lot of work. Why don't you call it a day?" She showed the pair to the door and eased them through it. "Thank you so much for all your help," she said as they tried to protest. "Good night, now." She closed the door gently behind them and leaned against it in relief. "So helpful."

Eduardo chuckled. "Yeah, I can tell. I ought to take off, too. You sure you're going to be OK without me here? I can cancel—"

She waved him off. "Don't worry about me. What can Scott do besides utterly destroy my chances? Go, have a good time. I'll be fine."

"At least you're keeping that positive attitude." Eduardo kissed his mother lightly on the cheek and put his arms around her waist. "I'll be with Ari and Michael. If you need me, just call the FBI or the Secret Service or the CIA or the army. I'm sure they'll be able to track us down."

"Look, honey, I'll be fine. Anne's in New York for the weekend, and Jon doesn't want to eat by himself, so I'll just grab a bite with him."

"Oh, right, a casual potluck at the White House. What are you bringing?"

They both laughed and she pushed him away. "Go, have fun, stay out of trouble."

"OK, Mom."

"Oh, and don't get back too late."

"OK, Mom."

"And don't drink, Eddie. Please."

"Yes, Ma'am, Your Judgeship Honor Ma'am."

"Get out of here!"

Eduardo disappeared down the hallway. Gloria checked her watch. Ten more minutes to relax. She sank into one of Rex's overly comfortable chairs and concentrated on thinking about nothing.

FOURTEEN

Friday evening

Forrest Garrison rushed into the Oval Office at 6:37 PM. "Sorry I'm late. There's a mob of demonstrators outside. My driver got diverted by capital police."

The president shrugged. "That's all right. I don't know who tips them off whenever *Roe v. Wade* is going to be brought up in confirmation hearings, but it never fails. Gloria and Derek Scott sparred over Court abortion rulings this afternoon. How about a drink?"

"Sure, why not?"

"The usual?" Bob Peterson poured a double Glenfiddich Special Reserve and soda for the senate boss.

"Thanks." Forrest raised his glass to Jonathan and took a seat next to Antonio Avalos on one of the wing-backed sofas that flanked the president's and his chief-of-staff's chairs. Dan Mendelson fidgeted on the opposite one.

Bob settled himself next to Jonathan and flicked his hand at Antonio. "Why don't you begin?"

Tony set his Diet Pepsi aside. "We've had a really wild reaction from the Hispanic media. They're not only backing Hernandez's nomination, they're urging her quick confirmation. The mainstream press in Florida, Texas, New Mexico, Arizona, and California has shown solid support, too. I taped part of Randolph Searle's panel show yesterday. I think this woman, Cecelia Cervantes, could be a big asset in those key states this fall, regardless of how the confirmation goes but, in the meantime, I got in touch with her people this morning, and we've got the go-ahead to use some of this footage to rouse public opinion right now, if it comes to that. I've done a first edit to get rid of the extraneous, but it isn't exactly broadcast quality yet." He pointed his remote at the VCR. Bob and Jon looked away from each other to avoid smiling. Tony's idea of "not broadcast quality yet" would probably fare well on any talk, news, or magazine show around the world. Presently, a pretty, effervescent Latina bounced onto the screen.

"I am so delighted and so proud and so happy. And so vindicated! Judge Hernandez's nomination is a gold-plated boost for Latino collective pride, and so long, long overdue. President Morgan could not have picked a better candidate, especially now, at a time when our ever-expanding economic clout is a bigger force than any political maneuverings could ever be."

Cecelia Cervantes' presence seemed to leap off the TV. As she bent forward toward the camera, sparks of energy prompted her every gesture and expression.

"We're on a roll, my friends. Our part of the population is exploding, and I'm not talking about our brothers and sisters coming up across the borders. We have the families, we have the businesses, we have the hottest part of a burgeoning middle class, we have thousands and thousands of college-educated Latinos buying more and more goods and services. We are the future! And it's high time we were represented in our country's most hallowed halls.

"Do I care that Hernandez has money? Of course I care! I care for the positive. Do you think Hispanics have no money? More and more of us are getting more and more of it all the time. You can't hold us back. We're taking our rightful place in a country that is and has always been, rightfully, a part ours."

"Whew!" Bob threw his hands up as if to ward off an irrepressible force. "Please tell me she's one of ours."

Tony's grin stretched from ear to ear. "Republican all the way. Businesswoman, English-literacy advocate, Hispanic-pride celebration organizer, you name it. With money. And *muchos* contacts in the Hispanic media world. And, gee, maybe even a desire to go places in the political world—what do you think?"

"I think we've tied our wagons to worse in the past," Forrest said, ambling over to refill his drink. "I think somebody ought to scout her out for the future. Not this election, obviously, but how about the next one?"

Bob tilted his head at Dan, who nodded and made a note in his scuffed suede-bound book. "Nice work, Tony," Bob said. "I'm not sure where we can use it, but I'm sure you'll think of something. Dan, what else do we have?"

Mendelson flipped back a few pages. "Same show, Gustavo Montaña, Democrat from East L.A."

"Congressmen don't vote in the Senate," Tony protested.

"No, but he's a rising star in the Congressional Hispanic Caucus, which is backing the nomination."

"Tough spot," Forrest put in. "He's got to endorse her for his people and oppose her for his party. He's lucky he isn't a senator."

Bob tapped his pen. "So what did he have to say?"

"Just about what you'd expect. Just what Forrest said. He can't exactly endorse or oppose, so he pretty much stuck to the old 'we'll have to see what she says' line."

"Any real influence?"

Dan considered before answering. "With public opinion, I'd say absolutely. With anybody on the committee, I'd have to say no. With somebody in particular on the floor for the roll call, that I don't know."

"Find out." Jon's voice, flat and dispassionate, issued from his reclining position in the oversized leather chair. Bob picked up the cue and turned to the Senate Majority Leader.

"How's it look in the Senate so far, Forrest?"

"If we'd voted this afternoon, assuming a couple of defections from our side, she'd probably have lost."

Tony couldn't stop his face from falling. Dan just looked tired. Jonathan opened his eyes. "Defeated? Are you getting hassled about her money, or is it Winslow?"

"Oh, a little of both. A lot of the usual stuff." Forrest took a last swallow of scotch before putting his glass down. He held up one hand to count off the fingers. "Political reasons. Democrats payin' us back for defeating Judge Winslow 'cause they say he was more qualified for the Court than some of our guys that made it—all the same stuff. And then there's the Hispanic vote."

"Gloria is Hispanic," Bob offered.

"Right. And she's one of ours, and the Democrats consider Latinos their very own. So they're thinkin' we're trying to cut in on their territory and we'll make big-time inroads into that gold mine of support if we even try to get a Latino on the Court. Ya know, we've gotta keep all the Hispanic backing we've got to hold California." He paused to look directly at Jonathan. "And they've gotta grab most of our Latino voters to take California back and away from us."

Jon nodded. Forrest accepted the refilled glass Tony held out, took a big swallow, and wiped his lips with his left wrist. He tugged at his right ear and closed his eyes. "Where was I? Oh, yeah. Embarrassment. He held up another finger. They wanna clobber you, Jon. Money, cronyism. And they're still gloating about killing our big Welfare Reform Bill last month. And don't forget," he went on, looking around the room. "Some of 'em just hate her. Rich bitch and so damn smart and the immigrant thing. Ya know, typical crotch complaints from the men who're afraid of girls that're smarter than they. . . . err . . . women. Sorry." He took another long swig on the glass. "Let's see, then there's the Catholic thing. Ya know, the stale, votive candles in darkened sanctuaries, suspect priests and their altar boys. Hay-Soose!" He suddenly sat up. "You should hear the BS goin' on about that. You'd think she was being examined for Pope. Smoke out the chimney and all. Who the hell cares?

And the other thing . . ." He hesitated, narrowing his eyes in thought. "Shit. There was somethin' else. What the hell? Damn it, for some reason it's not comin' through." He held his forehead momentarily. "Oh, yeah." He waved the glass. "One more of these, huh? Skip the soda."

Tony glanced at Bob, who nodded. He poured another double scotch and delivered it.

"Thanks, son." Forrest held the amber liquid up to the light for a moment. "Last night, we got a new monkey wrench in the works. Raven Sanderson had a bash, up at her Georgetown estate. Usual crowd, plus—and here's the thing—five Democrats sittin' on the Hernandez fence. And, Raven somehow got old man Kirkland there. He spent the whole night goin' on about how he wants to be the one to write the opinion that overturns *Roe v. Wade* before he hangs up his chief-justice robe. Then he tells anyone that'll listen that he's not about to sit still for some damn woman who ain't gonna help him do it!"

No one spoke for a moment. Finally, Jon sat up. "It certainly is nice to have such a pretty and informative secretary—"

"—Whose dates happen to get invited to the most interesting parties," Forrest slurred back, a grin smeared across his face.

"Still," Jon shook his head and said, "it doesn't make any sense. Raven's been a liberal, forever, and a big women's rights supporter. Hell, if a democrat had nominated Gloria, she'd stand behind her all the way. You'd think she'd be more interested in her pro-choice stance than her party affiliation."

"Oh, hell, Jon," Forrest threw his hands in the air, "it's the old politics-'n-sex thing. Raven figures if Gloria loses, it'll throw votes to her buddy, Don Abbott, who she thinks is your worst, November nightmare." He paused. "'Course she's right, ya know. He was a lousy governor and now he's a piss-poor senator, but he's just about the best campaigner in the country."

Forrest cleared his throat and went on in a perfectly lucid tone, the scotch seemingly evaporated. "That smooth-talking, good-looking Kentucky crook. As phony as a silver penny, but just perfect for the TV cameras. I've seen him do his dirty work. Sniffs out anybody's slightest flaw, then exploits it like hell—on every show, on every network, and every cable station. No integrity, no mercy, no class."

Dan had almost inched his way off the couch. "That seems like a stretch to me, Forrest. Voters care more about their wallets than Supreme Court politics."

"Well, sure, but the economy's not an issue these days. It's just fine. And that's the whole point, Dan." Forrest was sitting up perfectly straight now, as apparently sober and in control as if he were speaking from his senate podium. "They've gotta find something on Jon, and they don't have much. But, an important appointment—as to the Supreme Court—with questionable, personal implications? Sure it's a stretch, but I've seen that SOB Abbott do heavy damage with a helluva lot less."

Bob waved his hand. "Back to the sex, Forrest. What's that about?"

The majority leader set his glass aside and cracked his knuckles. "Remember the Rex St. Clair thing?"

Bob shook his head.

"You don't? OK, look. After her last old man died, Raven was worth about sixty million, give or take a few, and she wanted somebody pretty on her arm. Bottom line: She wanted Rex. Respected, rich, handsome—the whole shot. And a movie star. And a widower. So what does she do?"

He paused, not for effect but for another swallow of the smooth, single-malt scotch. "Well, she almost ropes him, that's what. She's got him totin' her around to every fancy restaurant, and opening, and Broadway show, and shindig all week long for months. What she doesn't know, though, is that he's also pond-hoppin' to London every weekend to bang Ophelia Smythe. And we all know how that turned out."

"I remember the headline well," Jon recalled. "Monday morning, front-page banner with colored pictures across the entire top fold. 'Rex and Ophelia Married!' You'd think they'd discovered how to wipe out the common cold or turn paper clips into gold."

"Yeah, well Raven lost it. That's the real bottom line."

The president and his three advisors looked at each other then back to Garrison. Dan spoke up. "I don't get it. What's any of this have to do with the confirmation?"

"Weren't you paying attention at the hearings?" Forrest stared at the befuddled faces. "St. Clair's intro? He even made a big deal out of it." The others blinked back at him. "Oh for Chrissakes, fellas, get with the program. Ophelia Smythe and Gloria Hernandez have been best friends since childhood. Raven is throwing her money at all those buyable Democrats just so she can rub St. Clair's face in the shit. It's revenge, pure and simple. And she's not above letting a little of it filter down to a few for-sale Republicans, either," he added with a grimace.

Jon narrowed his eyes. "Like?"

Forrest looked exasperated. "Like maybe Carl Albrecht. Not that he'd associate with her directly, you understand, but he's pissed about Rittenhouse. And if a particular bill of his happens to get a show of future support from a couple of senators with IOUs to Ms. Sanderson . . ."

Jon let out an annoyed grunt. "Christ! Something so major and we've gotta put up with all this nonsense, because some old society broad gets cuckolded. What's next?" He shook his head quickly. "Forget it. What about her other guests? Besides Kirtland's rantings, any real damage done?"

The scotch haze had apparently caught up to Forrest. He looked down for a moment and ran his tongue around his teeth. When he spoke, it was as if to himself. "Let's see, Blanche was there. St. Antoine. I'm havin' lunch with her tomorrow at the Willard. I'll see what I can find out." He looked up. "After a few martinis, Blanche loosens up, ya know." He closed his eyes. "Who else? Oh, yeah." His eyes shot open. "Wait! Blanche already told me, today on the phone. Those guys on the fence? They're still there. I figure we can reel in a vote or two from that bunch. But," Forrest shook his finger at Jon, "she's still pissed at you for not picking Chloe Doubilet. They're old friends, ya know, gummy as pecan pie slathered with hot fudge. Both from proud old New Orleans families; same college sorority; and later, classmates in Tulane Law School." He clasped his hands tightly. "Bonds too tight to break. No way will Blanche vote with us. Don't even ask me to try."

Jon waved it away. "No problem, I understand. I'd probably vote against Gloria, too, if I headed up the other side of the aisle and was mad at the president to boot. On the other hand," he added, "you can tell those birds on the fence that I'm in a generous frame of mind presently. You know, Senator, any special projects in their states that could use some discretionary presidential funding."

Forrest nodded, as the others—taking their cue from Jonathan's discreet gesture—stood up.

"It's 7:30, folks, time to give this a rest." Jon turned to Bob. "Anything else?"

"Just a couple of things to finish up with Dan in my office," Bob answered, while steadying Forrest, who had lurched precariously to his feet. Jon displaced Bob by slipping his hand under Forrest's arm.

"Come on, old man, I'll walk you to your car. By the way, Bob," he said over his shoulder, "Anne's in New York for the weekend, so Gloria's joining me here for dinner. We'll be upstairs if you need me." He motioned to Tony, who fell into step on the other side of the senate's top dog.

"Using the Lincoln tonight, Sir?"

Forrest shot Tony a mixed look of irritation and appreciation. "Sure. My chauffeur, Lucius, is one helluva driver."

Bob motioned Dan to follow him through the opposite door. They moved, without talking, toward Peterson's

office, just steps away from the oval seat of power. Dan
lifted his eyebrows as Bob closed the door behind them.

"This won't take long," Bob said. "You've been watching
the hearings when you have the time, I know, same as I.
You've seen the president's son sitting next to the nominee's
son in the front row." Bob saw the immediate understanding
in his subordinate's eyes and nodded.

"I think two days of affirming White House solidarity is
long enough," Bob went on. "Have Mikey kept busy, maybe
a few stumping trips. Talk to somebody on the committee.
Nothing too far, maybe Baltimore, Richmond, Wilmington.
I don't want the cameras to catch the two of them sitting
next to each other again."

Dan nodded in complete agreement. "I'll take care of
it."

———

Christine Fairchild scooped up the light brown, striped
tabby that greeted her at the front door. "Hi there, Molly.
Did you miss me?" Christine nuzzled her absently, while
leafing through the envelopes her housekeeper had left on
a white wicker table: *Washingtonian*, VISA statement, Saks'
summer catalogue. "These can all wait, little fluff." She
dropped the mail back on the table and used her now free
hand to scratch the back of her pet's head. "So what have
you been doing all day, hmmm?"

Molly huddled closer, as a harsh rumble of thunder
sounded against the windows. *Thank God she's declawed,*
Christine thought, *and I got home just in time.*

She checked the clock on her fireplace mantle: 8:30.
Molly hopped down and scampered across the thick-piled,
pale-gray carpeting. The voicemail readout blinked, "3."
She hit the buttons—speaker and mem 7—and then
punched in her password and listened to the first message.

"Chrissy, hi, it's me. I got the package,
intact, although Sister Crispina wanted to have
it x-rayed before I opened it. She's probably

already reported it to Rome. She's going home
to see her family in the fall. Only five more
months. Is it a sin to wish she'd retire? Don't
answer that. I'll talk to you later. Oh, did I
mention I love it? And you, too."

A broad smile crossed Christine's face. She reached
reflexively to return the call, then dropped her hand. *He'll
be at that benefit in Annapolis. Sure am glad he liked the cordless
massager. Maybe it'll relieve some of his tension.*

A crackle of lightning and more window-rattling
thunder prompted her to rise and part the drapes, slightly.
Street lamps softly illuminated the rain as it spattered off the
Wisconsin Avenue pavement. Three stories below, a woman
under a large, black umbrella followed her leashed and
soaking-wet yellow lab, which poked along the sidewalk a
few paces ahead of her. She abruptly tugged the dog to the
entrance porch of Christine's condominium building when a
municipal bus splashed by. Across the street, a man sat in a
gray Saab sedan. *Isn't that the same man who parked there last
night in a blue Volvo? He's got the same dark hair and pointed
chin.* She shook her head. *Oh, Christine, you've been watching
too many movies,* she chastised herself. She watched, as he
finally turned off the lights. *He's not getting out of the car
tonight, either—if it's the same guy.* She hummed nervously, let
the drapes close, returned to her desk and punched "play"
to hear the next message.

"Hello, Senator Fairchild. This is Eileen,
calling from Doctor Bernstein's office. I
called the new prescription into your
pharmacy this morning, so it should be
ready for you to pick up and start, this
evening. Doctor says you can take another
pill if it doesn't help you within forty-five
minutes. You shouldn't have any side effects
with this one, but if you still feel groggy in
the morning, doctor wants you to call her
right away. Otherwise, we'll see you on June
eighth, 4:00 PM."

Christine grimaced. *Great. Another experimental drug, probably. Why don't any of these things work for me? I should probably use mama's old remedy and knock myself out with a small flask every night.* She made a note on her desk pad: "O'Brien's/new Rx." She punched "play" again.

> "Hey, Chris, it's Blanche. Look, honey, I just got off the phone with Sinead. Poor thing, she's frantic! Rory—you know, her older one?—had to appear in that dreadful juvenile court again yesterday for marijuana possession. It's enough to break his poor mama's heart. She likely mentioned it to you quietly, during the hearing for that California judge. But, this is so cruel, I can hardly fathom it. Sinead's ex-husband, who's not much of a Christian himself, is threatening to take the poor, ravaged woman back to court for custody. It's outrageous. You think he can manage that boy any better'n her? Well, I doubt it. He's just some sort of lowlife from out there in Oregon, which I've heard is just like an asylum anyhow. Well, I reassured her we'd come up with something. So call me, sugah. My other line's flashing. Might be Sinead again."

Again Christine started to reach for the phone and stopped. Instead she wrote: "Call Blanche re: Sinead" on her note pad. Blanche was right. She had just spent the day with their mutual friend and colleague. She wasn't really up to another rehash of the acrimonious divorce proceedings, let alone one more go-around of armchair psychology about why paternal infidelity is always so hard on teen-aged boys. Christine didn't have any teen-aged boys, nor had she ever had to abort a fetus or make the decision to put a child up for adoption, as did too many of the women she knew. *Look at all the wonderful things I've missed out on,* she thought ironically.

Another roll of ear-splitting thunder startled her out of her reverie. Molly, curled up on a nearby armchair, raised her head quickly and looked at her mistress. "It's just the rain, little fluff," she purred to the cat.

So if there's nothing to worry about, why am I so uneasy? she wondered. *Probably the rain. Maybe a nice soak in the tub.* She shivered at the piercing whine of an emergency siren passing below. *Must be on their way to the Georgetown ER. I'll never get used to it.* She rose and parted the drapes a little. The ambulance had passed. Another city bus lumbered by in the steady rain. The gray Saab was gone.

FIFTEEN

Under a starry sky, weekend revelers filled the bars, bistros and cafés of the exuberantly hip, Dupont Circle neighborhood. The earlier rain showers had come to an end. Casually dressed pedestrians chatted and laughed. They ignored the two young men in snug black tees and jeans who stood conversing quietly outside Barnaby's, one of the city's more popular jazz clubs. The smaller one spoke softly to his taller partner.

"I can piss off Hernandez. No problem," he said. "He's an easy mark, short fuse. But we gotta be fast. If we get separated, you know who to call?"

"Yeah, the usual."

"Right. Camera set?"

"Sure. I'm ready. How many pit bulls?"

The small man fidgeted with a pair of Coke-bottle glasses as he looked around. "Five or six. I know one's out back and," he gestured with his head, "two went inside with 'em. That's one, leaning against the limo at the curb. I figure the guy across the street, with the smoke, is another. But, could be one more just mingling out here with all these people walking by."

The tall man nonchalantly followed his friend's gesture. "You got a plan?"

"They come out, I move in fast and close, and start pushin' the fag's buttons. I figure he blows first, then the prez's kid. Best case, there's a brawl." He pulled two heavy-looking rings out of his pocket, displayed them to his confederate, and slipped one on the middle finger of each hand. "Fightin' starts good, you move out and start shootin' with the telephoto. Remember, faces. Faces!"

"Faces. Got it."

The tall man stepped back about ten paces into the shadow of a darkened bookstore, started to light a cigarette, and thought better of it. He carefully fed the unlit stick back into the pack and slipped it into his jeans pocket.

At 1:12, a husky, black-haired man in a dark gray suit emerged from Barnaby's, looked around, and nodded to the Secret Service agent leaning against the shiny black Cadillac. A short moment later Eduardo Hernandez and Michael Morgan came through the front door, followed by Congressman Ari Bromberg and a well-built man in dark gray.

"Damn it, Mike!" Eduardo was saying. "Why'd we have to leave so soon? I'd hardly started my drink. And I liked the horn player."

"And I told you, there's a better group in Adams Morgan in one of those clubs."

"Which club?"

"I don't know. We'll find it when we get there. Besides, that was your fourth. Gimme a break."

Michael and Eduardo had stopped in a face off. Ari, walking between them, seemed startled to see their almost interchangeable visages. He looked from one to the other, then abruptly clutched his groin. "Gotta go," he mumbled to no one. "Thank God we gotta driver." He stumbled toward the open back door of the limo, where yet another dark-suited man waited for the five men to progress down the club's old, brick walkway.

"Hey, Eddie! How many times your old lady have to fuck the prez to get on the Supreme Court?"

Eduardo swung his head in the direction of the sound. A small man in thick glasses was hopping and weaving, less than two feet away. One of the dark-suited men quickly moved between them.

"Hey, Eddie. Did you hafta go down on Mikey boy as part of the deal?"

Michael started to dive toward the heckler, but another dark-suited man grabbed him.

"Or, Mike, do you just do it with Edoowahrdoe for fun?"

Ari Bromberg, pushed to the floor of the limo's back seat by his sentry, huddled into a ball to hide his face. Another agent struggled to get Eduardo into the car, while two more grabbed at the taunting little man.

"Hey Eddie!" The short man bobbed and ducked, staying just out of reach of the agents, whose attention was primarily focused on their charge. "How's he taste? Better'n the queers back in Frisco? Do you and your old lady compare notes?"

With a sudden burst of rage, induced further by the alcohol, Eduardo shoved the agent in front of him, sending his protection sprawling and Michael tumbling backward. He swung, but the scamp bobbed away at the last moment. Michael, struggling to get on his feet, was hampered by his own attempts to kick away his guardians.

"Hey, Eddie! How's about a new taste treat?" The taunter ripped open his Velcro-fastened jeans, fondled his penis for an instant, then darted forward to land a solid punch on Eddie's chin, and a second below his left eye. "*Sucio puerco!*" Eduardo roared and lunged toward his tormentor. His swing caught the decoy's face and sent him spinning across the sidewalk. Blood gushed from the little man's nose. He made a show of pawing frantically for his glasses that were knocked off with Eduardo's blow.

As soon as he saw his partner hit the ground, the tall photographer ran out of the shadows into the middle of the street and began shooting.

The agent rushing from across the street hesitated only long enough to determine that the man had a camera, not a gun.

The paparazzo kept up the volley of flashes as he followed the agent into the scene of flailing arms and legs.

Flash! Eduardo's face—chin slashed, puffy left eye.

Flash! Michael, his crotch soaked, his eyes wild, fighting his defenders.

Flash! The bleeding heckler, whimpering piteously for the camera.

Flash! Eduardo thrown against the limo door, a defiant grimace on his face, then Flash! Shoved into the back seat.

Flash! Two agents helping the disheveled decoy into an unmarked Crown Vic that had just screeched to a halt behind the caddie.

Flash! A close-up of the inciter's twisted frames and shattered thick lenses.

Flash! The gleaming Cadillac and big Ford swerving to avoid the photographer who had retreated into the middle of the street again to catch the wide-range shots.

Flash! The faces of club musicians, patrons, and pedestrians watching in stunned silence as the two cars sped into the darkness.

SIXTEEN

Saturday, May 20

Jonathan Morgan sat alone at the dining table in the White House residence. His eyes skimmed rapidly across the *Washington Post*, his head shaking slowly, as he read. He stopped when a dignified, middle-aged waiter entered the room.

"More coffee, Sir?"

"Thanks."

"Anything else, Sir?"

"Uh, no thanks." Morgan checked his watch: 10:30. He turned the paper with a casual flip. "Foster, have you seen Michael yet?"

"No Sir, I haven't seen Mr. Michael this morning." The long-time, White House servant hesitated, then smiled. "That's a handsome tie, Mr. President. Is it new?"

"Oh, thanks." Jonathan glanced down. "Yes, it's a gift from an old friend. She—. Oh, I almost forgot. I've a meeting downstairs at 11:00 with the secretary of state."

"Yes, Sir. I was just about to remind you. I shall keep the coffee warm, though, as I expect Mr. Michael will be dropping by, and he stops in the kitchen, first thing."

Morgan didn't respond. He knew as soon as Mike did arrive, there would be a confrontation. The moment Foster left the room, he turned the paper back over. "Unbelievable," he said out loud. "How could they?"

He looked up at the sound of slurping. Michael leaned in the doorway, barefoot, bleary-eyed, and wobbly in a wrinkled, oversized tee shirt and his tight, vintage 501 Levi's. He held a steaming mug of coffee with both hands.

Good, I hope you feel as lousy as you look, Jon thought. *God, what a mess. I ought to slap you silly, but you probably wouldn't even feel it. This all comes from the Sinclair side. Anne and her alcoholic cousin Charley.* "Michael," he began. His voice broke. He started again. "Michael Sinclair Morgan—"

"You've seen the papers."

"Everyone from the Canadian border to the tip of Florida has seen the papers." Jon stopped talking. He did not want to start a senseless argument with this hung-over slob. He feared he might kill the boy. *And how would that look in the papers, huh? 'President mows down own son, blood spews across White House as errant idiot tries in vain to escape.'* The thought was enough to squelch his anger, at least for the moment. "Christ, Mike," he started again, this time able to control his tone. "It's the lead story." He tossed the paper across the table. Michael shuffled over and peered down at the banner headline.

FIRST SON AND NOMINEE'S SON IN DUPONT BRAWL.

It was all there in three, front-page pictures: a straight-on of him and Eduardo; another of them struggling with Secret Service agents; a side view of him being pushed into the limo. He turned to page four: a frontal shot of Eddie's swelling eye and bleeding chin; the heckler sprawled on the sidewalk reaching for his broken glasses.

"Shit."

"So what happened?"

"Well . . . the fuckin' Secret Service screwed up!"

"Secret Service screwed up, my ass!" Morgan exploded. "What do you think was going on? You were set up, for Christ's sake! Are you seventeen? Do I have to put you on a leash? Or lock you up on the third floor of the White House like President Creighton did with his loopy brother?"

"That obscene little asshole. This is all his fault." Mike shoved the *Post* across the table at his father. Morgan threw it back.

"Like hell it's his fault. I got the whole story from Jason Lemakis this morning. God, Mike, you guys should be mature enough to handle this shit by now. I'll tell you how to handle obscene little hecklers. Walk away from 'em. Ignore 'em. They're worthless garbage. Now the whole damn world knows you got suckered."

"You shoulda heard the things he was saying. Opened his fly, practically shoved his pecker in our faces. Called us faggots. And you shoulda' heard what he said about you."

"Who gives a shit what he said?"

"Yeah? Well, he said you fucked Aunt Gloria and that's why she got nominated."

Jonathan snapped his mouth shut. Michael's eyes widened.

"Shit, don't tell me it's true. You screwed Aunt Gloria? Christ, Dad, how could you? What about Mom? Does she know?"

Jonathan didn't answer. *My own damn son*, he thought. "I won't dignify that cheap accusation with an answer," he said through clenched teeth. "For God's sake Mike," he hurried on, "you've humiliated me, you've humiliated your mother, you've humiliated your Aunt Gloria, and you've humiliated Ari and his parents. Lord, Irving and Jenny must be appalled. Not to mention my entire administration."

"Oh, yeah, right," Mike spat back. "Well, let's talk about my Aunt Gloria. You had dinner with her, right here, last night, didn't you? What else did you do?" When Jon didn't answer, he jutted out his chin and stared directly at his father. "Just what did you guys do last night, Dad?"

Jonathan got up and returned Michael's stare, his own chin jutting out in mirror reflection of his son. "I have work to do," he finally growled. "You might consider taking a shower and, while you're about it, scrub off some of your filthy attitude." He stomped out of the room.

Michael watched his father's retreating figure. He picked up the *Post*, looked at the front page again, rolled it up, and flung it across the room, shattering a table lamp.

Foster rushed in at the sound. He stopped abruptly when he saw Michael standing alone, face crimson, jaw set, fists clenched.

Foster cleared his throat. "More coffee, Sir?"

Michael drew a deep breath and let it hiss quietly out through his clenched teeth. He straightened his shoulders, tightened his abs, and turned to flash his public smile at the waiter. "I'm fine, Foster." He gestured him off with a wave of the hand. "Just a typical Morgan family discussion. Excuse me. I have some things to take care of." The first son turned and stomped out of the room—looking just like his dad.

By 10:00 Saturday morning, Bob Peterson had gathered the president's closest legal and political advisors in his spacious brick colonial in Herndon, Virginia. Beverly, his politically savvy helpmate, had arranged a spread of pastries, donuts, coffee, and fresh orange juice in Bob's mahogany-paneled, commodious home office.

"I talked to the president this morning at 8:00. We've got security on the Four Seasons. No one gets up to, much less past, the door. The word is he's sleeping. Judge Hernandez is unavailable for comment. Tony will have something for her by the evening news—very noncommittal, all motherly concern. San Francisco has been alerted. The Secret Service will pick him up at the plane and deliver him to his front door. We've arranged round-the-clock protection for Eduardo and his lover until the roll-call vote is over, with backup from the San Francisco Police Department."

Forrest, looking refreshed and alert despite the previous night's binge, had been first to respond to Bob's call, bringing extra copies of the *Post* with its front-page fiasco. Ben Carothers, the president's personal counsel, had given up his regular 9:00 AM tee-off time and parked his white Cadillac Seville behind Forrest's black Town Car in the tree-lined, semi-circular driveway. Ron Jordan had pulled in last in his gunmetal gray Range Rover.

"Commercial flight?" Forrest asked, licking sugar off his fingers.

"Has to be. We don't want it to look like we've spirited him away."

"I warned Gloria about having him with her," Ben put in. "It's not enough that he's openly homosexual—which, I suppose, could have worked to her benefit if he'd handled himself right. The man's a loose cannon. Another dangerous incident like this could doom her nomination. She should have told him to stay in California in the first place."

"And how would that have looked?" Forrest's eyes were filled with pain. "Here she is, nominated for the highest court in the country, and no family shows up to support her?"

"It would have been easier to explain, than having to clean up after this," Ben grumbled.

The argument stalled while Ron had a coughing spell. Bob took advantage of the interruption to take charge of the meeting. "Done is done. Eduardo will be on a red-eye to San Francisco tonight—fewer passengers, less press. Let's deal with damage control. Dan Mendelson just spent a week out there with the P.I. we used on that Belgian ambassadorial appointment last year, the one that tipped us off about our potential nominee, then, having served time for real-estate fraud. Eighteen months in minimum-security prison."

Peterson shook his head and flipped open a leather-bound notebook. "Hernandez lives with his business partner, Isamu Narita, architect. Native Japanese. Educated at Berkeley, U.S. citizen since 1993. They met at a fund raiser for the Asian Art Museum, best estimate, three years ago. They jointly own a residence in a prime location in Pacific Heights. They have an office on Montgomery Street in the financial district. Hernandez acts as chief financial officer of their business, Hernandez and Narita Properties, Ltd. He picks the real estate—Nob Hill, Russian Hill, Pacific Heights—and Narita directs the rehabilitations. Buy, restore, and sell. All legit so far as we can find." Bob looked up and grinned. "Paul says they prefer gay subcontractors, but are open-minded enough to give a few talented straights a commission now and then."

"That's damned decent of them," Ben groused and took a gulp of coffee.

Bob flipped to the next page. "Both have plenty of inherited dough invested in stocks, bonds, and municipals. Some of their portfolios are jointly owned; others are separate. They've got joint personal checking and savings accounts at Wells Fargo, and business accounts at Bank of America. Eduardo gave Narita two-hundred shares of Microsoft a couple of months ago, apparently as a birthday gift. Narita immediately transferred ownership into both names. If they're not monogamous, they're at least pretty tight."

Ben helped himself to another cup of coffee. "Anything else? Business problems? Social problems?"

Bob ruffled through the papers. "Everything we can find about the business is on the up and up. They spend their pocket change on the usual: house, furnishings, clothes, and cars. They give a lot to various arts' organizations. Hernandez is on the board of the San Francisco Ballet. Narita's a board member of the Asian Art Museum. So they've gotta pony up some major bucks for that."

"Outwardly respectable," Ron rasped, coughing into a handkerchief.

"Oh yeah, and they buy paintings, uh . . . mostly emerging Bay Area artists." Bob pulled out a separate, photocopied sheet from the back of the notebook, read it, closed the tablet, and let out a deep sigh.

"Uh oh," Ron said. "I don't like the sound of that sigh. What else? Police records?"

Bob shook his head. "They're clean. The FBI search didn't come up with anything, either."

"Pedophilia?" Ben asked. The silver-haired Establishment lawyer shoved his glasses up on his forehead.

Bob made a startled face. "No, nothing like that. No evidence of anything with children."

"Not gay activists? No nude photos of them lying around anywhere at a Gay Pride parade?" Ron pressed. "That would provide a fascinating human-interest angle to some people, like about twenty right-wing fundamentalist groups that are working the phones to certain nervous senators, trying to scuttle—" His last words were lost in another coughing spasm. Finally, he took several deep breaths and slumped back in his chair. "Excuse me."

Ben held a cup out to Ron, but the attorney general waved it away. "Worse in the mornings. I'll be fine."

Bob waited a beat, and then went on. "We can never know every detail, of course, but Paul is pretty thorough. He hit all their known spots, talked to everyone from bartenders to civic leaders. Couldn't find anything untoward socially. Just this." He held up the photocopied sheet.

Forrest gasped, "My God, a piece of paper!" He screwed up his face. "Don't keep us in suspense, Robert, what does the damn thing say?"

Bob sighed again. "Only that young Hernandez is in treatment and on medication for recurrent, incapacitating anxiety attacks and that his bedmate is in treatment and on medication for severe clinical depression."

The room was quiet for a moment. "Meaning," Forrest said slowly, "that neither of them should ever drink alcohol, which is something they must both know. So last night's mess was either deliberately planned on his part, or he was set up, or," he swallowed hard, "the man himself is just not that bright." He looked around the room.

"Like mother, like son?" Ben asked.

"Let's hope like *father*, like son," Ron said.

Forrest reflected on that for a moment. It struck home. Vivid memories savaged him, as the picture of his son's cold, white body in the Phoenix morgue flashed through his mind. The brutally stark police report. He thought, *if only I'd paid more attention. He needed me. The clues were so damned obvious.* Forrest passed a hand across his eyes and reached for a drink, but his hand came up empty.

Bob noticed his friend's despair. *God, how stupid of me,* he thought. "Can I get you a scotch, Forrest?" But, he didn't wait for an answer. His mind raced as he got up to pour the drink. *How long since Tyler died? Four, five months? All those rumors, none proved. I shouldn't have had him come today.*

Forrest accepted the double portion of Johnnie Walker Black Label, gratefully, and took a large gulp, then another. He inhaled deeply, expelling the breath noisily. "Hernandez's sex life hasn't made it to the front burner in the hearings yet," he said, suddenly composed once more. "I think they'll probably tiptoe around it, try to sound her out on privacy rights instead of gay rights directly. Hell," he added wryly, "no one in Congress, including the gays, wants to deal with gay rights. They're more than willing to leave it to the Supreme Court, which doesn't want to look at it at all. Whenever a case gets that far, they bounce it right back to the lower courts and the state houses. The topic has all the popularity of broccoli. The Court got so badly burned with *Roe*, they're afraid to make any more sweeping civil-rights decisions."

The other three men nodded their agreement, the conversation momentarily stalled. Finally, Bob rapped his knuckles on his chair arm. "Well, I think you're right. And considering the notoriety he's just gained and the amount of backpedaling he's going to have to do out there on the West Coast, I think maybe we can exert a little pressure on Hernandez to do any drinking at home for the duration, if he simply has to indulge."

"Yeah, maybe," Ben agreed. "But in the meantime, I think we should be ready. If someone decides to use Eduardo's sexual orientation as a wedge issue, it could hurt us. I mean, realistically, the rebels have to be having a field day over this thing. Too bad it's a slow day for news. The next time I see Marge Norris, I'll tell her to rein in her front-page editors. I mean, if this weren't a set up, I don't know what is. You'd think she'd know better. They certainly had to call her first to run this shit in headlines!"

Ron shrugged. "Of course, Gloria can hedge on the gay-rights' issues or refuse to answer, like she's been doing on other hot cases in the lower courts," he said. "But I'm concerned that civil rights aren't really her strong suit. I think she should have some help, just in case. She's really at her best in antitrust and regulation. If they delve deeply into gay rights—anything without major precedent—she's going to need serious backup."

"Yes," Ben agreed, "but after all, nobody can be expected to have every case memorized."

"You're the trial lawyer here, counselor," Bob said. "Wouldn't that tip her hand? You know, suddenly having an expert sit beside her?"

Forrest answered first. "It's not unprecedented. And the roll call's going to be close. I don't have the votes yet. Anything you can do to help sway the fence-sitters . . . "

Ben put his coffee cup and saucer on the serving table before looking around at each of his colleagues. "Listen," he said, using a summation voice. "Either give her the best help you can or withdraw the nomination. We can't just sit by and watch her get slaughtered. It was never the best call to begin with, but now we're committed. If she goes down because she's unprepared, we'll be the ones with egg on our faces, not her. I can think of at least six Democrats, offhand, who are probably dancing for joy this morning and thinking of all the ways they can dig up even more dirt. Perception! Perception can kill us."

"You've got a point." Bob turned to Forrest. "What do you think?"

The majority leader had rested his chin on his hand while Ben expounded. Now he spoke as if far away. "Nothin' wrong with a powerful defense against people like Duckworth and Scott. Sullivan and Popowski can get down and dirty too, if circumstances call for it. And Fairchild's on the committee. Christine's hard to read. Kind of a smoke screen 'round her at times. But Gloria can't bamboozle her. Too damn sharp. Hallstead got pretty miffed about our *señora's* fancy footwork the other day." He leaned forward slowly and looked Bob Peterson directly in the eyes. "I think we've gotta get her some better answers pretty damn fast."

Bob winced, but nodded. "Any suggestions? Who can we get?"

Ben didn't hesitate. "Hugh Graham, of course. Professor of Constitutional Law over in Charlottesville."

"Hugh is perfect," Ron agreed emphatically. "He's probably one of the two best legal experts on privacy, in the country. Roland Bronson from Ann Arbor is the other, but I don't think we could get him. I talked to him a couple of weeks ago. He was on his way to L.A. to argue a huge privacy case. He was looking at five, six weeks, at least."

Bob quickly hefted the pros and cons in his mind. "OK," he announced. "Ben, get Graham. Tell him I'll send a limo over to Charlottesville, if he'll come. He can stay at the White House."

"I'll call right now." Ben stood up. "If it's all right with Hugh, Ron and I will meet with them in your conference room tomorrow and Monday." He turned to Forrest. "Can you persuade Norah to reconvene Monday afternoon, instead of morning?"

Forrest leaned back in his chair, his glass empty, and his face once again relaxed and smiling. "No problem, fellas. Consider it done."

SEVENTEEN

Saturday, May 20

Isamu Narita sat in lotus position on a low, cushioned table in his meditation room and gazed out at the darkness of San Francisco Bay. Dressed in a sheer, mid-calf kimono, the slim architect could barely detect two large ships pass each other in the distance, their running lights twinkling off the black water under a radiant, full moon. Making himself very calm, he sensed—rather than actually heard—the choppy waves beating against the pillars of the Golden Gate Bridge. A light breeze wafted through the open windows.

Isamu let his gaze drift to the luminous digital numbers shining from across the dim room. 10:13. 10:14. He closed his eyes and tried to compose himself once more. He opened his eyes. 10:16. When the phone rang, he forced himself to unfold slowly and carefully, before walking to the next room.

"Hello. Isamu speaking."

"Issy? It's me."

"Oh, thank God." Isamu clutched the handset and sank to the floor. He leaned against the Japanese sandalwood chest that held the phone's base. "Where have you been? Are you all right? I've been calling all day! What's going on? What happened?"

From his third-row, first-class seat on United 225, Eduardo drew a ragged breath. "It's a long story," he said in a soft voice. "They blocked all my calls, so the press couldn't get in. I'm airborne now on a red-eye, the guy assigned to me is in the head. I'm coming home. I'll give you all the details when I get there."

"But are you all right?"

"Yeah, I'm fine. Except my face is a mess, and my mother's been reading me the riot act all day, and I can't get through to Mike, and I've had storm troopers practically following me into the bathroom all day."

"Why didn't you call?"

"I told you, they were blocking my calls. Except for mom, which I almost wish they had."

"What did she say?"

Silence.

"Eddie, what did she say?"

Nothing.

"Eddie? Are you still there?"

Then, Isamu could hear strangled sobs coming from the receiver.

"Eddie, Eddie, it's all right. Come home, I'll take care of you."

"I'm fine," Eduardo choked out. "I'm fine. She said . . . she said . . ."

Isamu wiped his own eyes. "Forget it. I don't need to know. Just come home."

"My flight's due in at 12:12. Look, the guy's coming back from the john. I've gotta go. Don't worry about picking me up. They're gonna bring me home."

"I'll be waiting. With champagne. I can't wait to see you. Just get here, OK? Hey, I had dinner with Troy tonight at Fleur de Lys. He's got a new plastic surgeon boyfriend—and a new nose. He looks great."

"Troy?" Eduardo's voice changed. "You had dinner with Troy?"

Isamu laughed with relief. "He's beautiful! So beautiful, you can't believe it!"

"God, I can't wait to get back."

EIGHTEEN

Sunday, May 21

Ben Carothers and Ron Jordan had requested one of the peripheral tables in the softly lit Lafayette dining room of the Hay-Adams Hotel, which lay directly beyond historic Lafayette Park, located across from the White House. Dignified Washingtonians used the Italian Renaissance-style hotel to meet, dine, and deal. Their waiter had faded away from the table as soon as he'd delivered their cocktails, having perceived they were not yet ready to order dinner.

"All things considered, I think it went pretty well today, don't you?" Ben peered at his companion over the top of his martini glass. He'd resisted the urge to loosen his tie while the waiter hovered, but now, after almost finishing his drink in a single gulp, he unbuttoned his collar and inched his tie down ever so slightly.

Ron leaned back, one arm draped over the extra chair he'd pulled around from the side for just that purpose. He absently ran a finger around the rim of his bourbon on-the-rocks. His eyes looked glazed, his face haggard. "I don't know how many more of these inane crises I can take," he said, ignoring the question Ben had asked, for the fourth time. "It's one thing for the judge's son to get drunk and create a scandal. It's another to purposely bring in counsel that rubs her the wrong way."

"But I think we got it worked out by the end."

Ben's eyes begged for validation, but Ron was too tired to care. It had been too long a day with an inordinate amount of contention. Yes, the attorney general and president's counsel had managed to create peace between the two potent personalities by the time they called it quits, but it had been an uphill battle throughout the morning and, in the end, they'd had to settle for, at best, an uneasy diplomatic truce.

"I'll let you know what I really think," Ron said, tasting his drink. "I think the best thing we've done in the last forty-eight hours is to put that man on a plane and get him the hell away from our candidate. Lord save us from misguided family and neurotic children. If it weren't for him, I don't think she'd of had her dander up so high, and then maybe she wouldn't have started out by telling Hugh just what she thought of his scathing op-ed piece about the Ninth Circuit Court in Saturday's *Post*. Talk about adding insult to injury. Do you think the front-page editors ever confer with the editorial page staff of that publication? And then, of course, he just had to counterpunch with an equally acid critique of her ruling in *Drew v. CHP*. Not exactly your typical match made in heaven."

Ben couldn't help but laugh. "Ah, yes, but that's why we make the big bucks, now isn't it? Because we always figure out how to snatch the old man's ass out of the fire." Ben held his empty glass out in salute. Ron clinked his still full one against it and downed the contents. The waiter magically appeared, set down refills, scooped up the empties, and evaporated into the background.

"You know," Ben mused, well into his second martini, "I told Bob to get rid of him, up front. I don't particularly care about his sexual preferences or orientation or whatever it is, but I suspected he was a loose cannon all along. I'm just sorry I was so right."

Ron started to answer, but got caught up in a rasping cough. Another diner's raucous laugh rang out from behind.

"What idiots! This'll knock the Morgans off their high horses. They ought to lock their kid up, and that judge's misfit, too!"

Ron narrowed his eyes at Ben, who merely raised his brows and shrugged. "That fathead is a Democrat, no doubt." He gave a short laugh. "They'll let damn near anybody in here these days."

The attorney general took another sip of his drink, then leaned over to fish around in his briefcase. When he straightened, he drew something from a large manila folder and pushed it across the table. "While we're on the subject, take a look at this."

Ben glanced at the eight by ten image of four young men in swim trunks. He shrugged again. "So?"

"It was taken by a freelancer from L.A. out at Congressman Bromberg's place in Malibu. Last August or September, I think." Ron glanced around the room before he leaned forward. "This is Isamu on the left of the judge's son, Eddie," he said, pointing. "That's Mike between Eddie and Ari, right? Take a good look. See anything interesting?"

Ben sighed, pulled his reading glasses down from the top of his head, and picked up the photo to study it closer. "What exactly am I looking for?"

"Look at our two party animals. Notice how they're about the same height and build? Mike's a little huskier, but not much."

"Yeah? So?"

"So? So look. Look at their faces."

Ben sighed again and tossed the photo upside down on the table. "Yeah, I noticed it in the *Post*. I noticed it at the hearings. I noticed it on the CSPN broadcast of the hearings. I was hoping I was the only one who noticed it. Guess I'm not."

"And you've got lousy eyes."

The two men nursed their drinks in silence for a few moments.

Finally, Ben put their thoughts into words. "It doesn't matter who has noticed what. We can't let this get published. I'll have to talk to Tony. Or better yet, Dan."

Ron waved the hand that held the drink, cursed, and dabbed the spilled drops on the tablecloth with his napkin.

"We already gave the photographer thirty Gs for the full set."

"Negatives?"

"Yeah. Everything."

Ben considered that. The waiter, sensing his moment, zoomed in, took the two men's orders, and retreated. Ben leaned across the table. "Still, we'd better keep our eyes open. There are a lot of photographers in L.A. And a lot of people who don't have lousy eyes like mine."

"Yeah." Ron sighed deeply, painfully. "I really don't know how much more of this I can take."

———————

Anne handed her suitcase and coat to her personal aide without breaking stride, as she hurried along the corridor toward her son's room. She knocked quietly on the closed door and slipped inside. "Mike? Are you awake?"

The light on the nightstand snapped on. The digital clock glowed 11:47. "Hi, Mom. Kind of late getting back, aren't you?"

Anne crossed the room to sit on the edge of the four-poster bed. She took Mike's chin in her hand and turned his face right and left. "They said you were hurt. A terrible brawl, the papers said. You look OK."

"Only my pride's hurt, Ma, nothing else."

Anne let her hands drop into her lap. "Tell me what happened."

Mike sank back into bed and gestured helplessly. "I don't know. I guess Dad's right. We were set up. Eddie'd been drinking . . ."

"Michael! He's not supposed to drink, you know that."

"Yeah, I know. He only had a few, mostly wine. I figured, what could it hurt? Besides, I'm not his mother."

"But with the hearings and everything—"

"I know. So, anyway, this little creep comes up and starts taunting us, and Eddie got pissed and took a swing at him."

"He threw the first punch?"

That stopped him. "No," he said slowly, going over it in his mind, "I think the creep did. Yeah." Michael sat up. "That little bastard started the whole thing, all the way around!"

Anne shook her head. "It doesn't really matter. Was he as hurt as he looked in the papers?"

Mike lay back. "I don't think so. Ari was out of it all together."

"Ari was there?"

Mike laughed. "Yeah, but he was so plastered, he just fell into the limo. Nobody was really hurt bad."

"What about the man Eddie attacked?"

"He didn't attack anybody!"

"Calm down."

Mike shrugged and settled into the bedclothes.

"Was the man badly hurt?"

"I don't think so. But you'd have thought Dad was the one in the fight. He was livid."

Anne shook her head and kept shaking it. "Michael, Michael." She sighed. "We have the election coming up. Your father's most important bill this year just got defeated. Your Aunt Gloria is in the middle of a tough confirmation hearing. Grandpa is starting to fail. Souci quit—"

"Souci quit?"

"—And I've got a million things to get ready for the convention. Couldn't you try to help? At least, by staying out of trouble?"

He reached up and patted Anne's arm. "Don't worry, Mom. It won't happen again. Everything's going to be all right. Have you seen Dad yet?"

"Oh, he's still in a meeting downstairs. Something about Germany."

"Well, don't worry. Go on, get some sleep. 'Everything will look better in the morning.' Remember?"

Anne smiled down on him, half comforted, half dismayed at how grown up her "little boy" was. "I remember. Good night, sweetheart."

"G'night, Mom." He reached up to switch off the light and Anne slipped out the door. She walked calmly down the hall to her room.

NINETEEN

Monday, May 22

A bevy of photographers rapidly snapped pictures of Gloria Hernandez as she made her way to her place before the judiciary committee for day three.

Yale Jacobs slid into his dais seat in the Central Hearing Room of the Hart Senate Office Building. "Am I late?"

"You can't be too late," Carl Albrecht said, leaning across the open space between them. "The lady chairman isn't here yet. Speaking of which," he gestured toward the nominee and the conspicuously empty seats in the row behind her, "neither are the stars of last weekend's famous fistfight."

"Wait a minute." Additional flash shots caught Yale's attention. "Whoa! That guy's new."

"Is that who I think it is?" Carl finished for him. Albrecht widened his eyes. "Jesus, it's Hugh Graham."

Yale whistled softly, "Hugh Graham III, you mean. The biggest of the big guns on the right to privacy." Yale lowered his reading glasses to scrutinize the white-haired man who followed Gloria into the room. Graham stood ramrod straight, dressed in an expertly tailored charcoal gray suit, apparently unfazed by the photographers' excessive attention. He seated himself directly beside her at the examinee's table.

"I've heard he costs a fortune. Morgan must be worried."

"Or careful."

Albrecht grunted and Jacobs stifled a smile. *Maybe it's time for you to worry, Carl, old buddy.*

Presently, Norah came around the end of the panelists' table, shaking hands and dropping comments as she progressed. She finally settled between the two men. "Anything happening I should know about?"

Carl pointed. "Just your friend in the White House sending in the heavy artillery."

She looked. "Oh, that," she said offhandedly. "I knew Hugh was coming. Why do you think there's an extra chair at the table? Is everybody else here?"

Christine Fairchild leaned toward Derek Scott, who busily reviewed his notes, and whispered, "So, we've got the famous Professor Hugh Graham. Morgan's obviously rattled after that mess on Saturday. What do you suppose he's up to?"

"Trying to save her confirmation, I imagine," the drab man answered without looking up. "Probably knows they don't have the votes. What better white knight than the best-selling author of *The Struggle For Privacy*? And a savvy trial advocate besides. Not that it'll help her much," he added.

Norah checked the clock and scowled. 2:05. She gaveled for order. "Good afternoon." The din grew, rather than lessened. She employed her wooden hammer once more, louder and slower. "Good afternoon." The chamber fell silent.

"Ladies and gentlemen, it's already late. I will cut five minutes off my own time, for I'd like to get started." She waved at the photographers. "No more pictures until the recess." They retreated, and she continued in a more congenial tone. "Good afternoon, Judge Hernandez."

"Good afternoon, Senator."

"And welcome to Professor Hugh Graham, who, from the comments I've heard coming in, apparently needs no introduction." Graham stood to acknowledge the polite applause and scattered murmuring in the hall.

"Mr. Graham will serve as additional counsel to the nominee," Norah said without further explanation. "Now,

Judge, I'd like to begin by picking up where we left off last
week, exploring the notion of privacy in a general way.
What is your understanding of personal autonomy?"

Hugh told me this would be coming, Gloria thought, as she
leaned over to the microphone. "Senator, personal autonomy
is the concept that an individual has the constitutionally
guaranteed right to choose a lifestyle for him or herself, with
certain limits as to government interference. For instance, a
person could lead a hermit's life on his or her rural property,
but could not produce explosives in that setting to blow up a
government building. In other words, personal autonomy
means privacy but with limits."

"And can you distinguish that concept from a 'protected
sphere' in one's life?"

"What's she up to?" Sinead Sullivan asked Stanley
Popowski softly.

"Typical Stafford. She knows what's coming, and she
wants the upper hand."

"A protected sphere as a protected area," Gloria was
saying. "For instance, the means through law to defend an
unpopular minority from oppression by a majority."

"Like ethnic or religious minorities?"

"Yes. The idea is to prevent the majority from utilizing
state powers, such as referendums or state legislation, to
regulate or even persecute people who, they, the majority,
dislike."

A slight undertone ran through the far reaches of the
chamber. Norah waited for the murmurs and whispers to
subside before continuing. "All right. Now, let's get into
the more intimate parts of life. What are your feelings
about secrecy?"

Gloria spread her hands, palms up. "I feel, as I'm sure
you and most of the panelists do, Senator, that the secret
realms of anyone's life should be as free as possible from
public intrusion."

"But are there limits to these components of privacy?"

"Necessarily, yes."

"And Judge, I take it, you would be a staunch defender of these privacy rights as a member of the Supreme Court?"

Gloria made brief eye contact with Hugh, who rubbed the right side of his nose. Then she nodded slightly to the Chair. "Yes. With reasonable limits."

"Thank you, Judge. I've used all of my time. Senator Jacobs, please continue."

Laura Jordan gently massaged her husband's back as he sat doubled over, coughing. Although he had crushed out his last cigarette in the St. Francis Hotel's cocktail lounge years earlier, the rotund San Franciscan still bore the curse of a chronic cough and, now, some shortness of breath. Finally, he straightened up. "Sorry," he murmured for the umpteenth time.

"What did Doctor Lindholm say?"

"Oh, he ordered more x-rays. Says they didn't see any change in the radiology office. Says my lungs still look a little dirty in the bases and over-inflated. Now Doc's calling it 'chronic bronchitis,' says the spring pollens might aggravate it. He set me up to see an allergist."

"When?"

"Wednesday, I think. Don't worry about it." Ron reached up to pat his wife's hands. "And I'm only going to give you three more years to stop rubbing my shoulders like that."

They had been sharing a bottle of Cakebread Cellars Chardonnay before dinner, until his coughing fit interrupted their evening ritual. Even though Ron had promised his old friend, Jonathan, that he'd serve the full term at Justice before returning to his lucrative private practice, neither he nor Laura intended to live in Georgetown any longer than necessary. Nevertheless, they had lovingly restored the Federal-style row house they'd chosen to spend their government time in because, as Laura put it, "After thirty years of marriage, I want it the way I want it." They both agreed that getting Gloria confirmed would be one of Ron's last major campaigns. He planned to resign right after the election so they could spend the Christmas season together with their children and the new grandchild, in the Bay Area.

Jordan took a sip of wine. "There, that's better." He sank back into the couch. "This stuff may not cure my cough, but even Lindholm admits a little booze won't hurt me. Didn't I read somewhere it might prevent stroke?"

Laura rolled her eyes but her smile was lovingly indulgent. She had realized early on that her husband ascribed to the "glass is half full" approach to living, in more ways then one. "Do you want to watch Searle?" she asked, already knowing the answer.

"I didn't have a minute this afternoon to see the hearings and I have to see Jon in the morning," he said, his face full of apology. It was another long-standing contention between them and just one more reason to leave government life and return to San Francisco. No matter how much time Ron put in at the office on the West Coast, he had always left his work there, when he came home to her. It could never be that way in Washington.

Randolph Searle filled the screen while Laura settled back on the couch, her husband's head cuddled in the crook of her shoulder. *He's eastern and conventional to the core*, Laura thought, *but preferable to that egomaniac, North-Youngblood.*

"With me tonight are Mark Malone of the *Washington Post*, political historian Charlotte Vickers-Waugh, and political analyst Joey Lucarelli. Mark, let's start with you. How do you think Judge Hernandez fared today in lieu of her son's involvement in that weekend brawl?"

Laura only half-listened as the three panelists danced around each other, trying to make political hay out of what had essentially been a totally uneventful hearing session. She had left C-SPAN on all over the house as she went about her day. There had been the expected questions about privacy early in the afternoon, when she'd been trying to decide to what extent, if any, she would participate in Republicans For Choice. Ron had been gone all yesterday smoothing the way for the judge with that new attorney Ben had brought in, and had come home satisfied but exhausted. Apparently, it had been worth it, though, because as the panel hammered away at her over First Amendment rights of the press—while Laura re-potted an overgrown azalea—the woman had stood her ground pretty well.

"—best and, to me, more revealing comments were about the declining civility of the media and its intrusiveness into the lives of public figures and, even worse, their families," the *Washington Post* Pulitzer Prize winner was saying.

"You mean like her son's private life?"

"Yeah."

What a horror that must be, Laura thought, absently running her fingers across Ron's slightly balding pate. *It isn't bad enough to have your son lose control. Now the poor woman has to deal with everyone in the country knowing and talking about it.* Laura shuddered and thought of San Francisco. The program droned on.

"I've watched the judiciary committee question nominees on *Griswold* quite often," Malone was saying. "Here you've got this 1965 decision overturning an old Connecticut law that forbid married couples to use birth control contraceptives. An 'uncommonly silly law,' as one of the justices called it, which I don't think anyone would disagree with. But what really made *Griswold* a landmark case was the Supreme Court's willingness to endorse another unlisted right with full constitutional support. And here's the thing. A new civil right—the right of privacy—a privilege never even mentioned in the Constitution, was born in the *Griswold* decision. Creativity where there's only supposed to be applicability. Legislating instead of judging. That's the key. And that's why the judiciary committee always focuses on *Griswold*."

"So the senators try to gauge a nominee's enthusiasm for that kind of judicial creativity?"

"That's right. The buzz words are 'judicial activism.' Comes in two flavors: liberal and conservative."

"And what flavor do you think Judge Hernandez might be?"

"Plain vanilla."

Laura carefully shifted her weight to let her husband's head drift down to her lap. His lids drooped at half-mast. *He's falling asleep with his eyes open again,* she realized. *How does he do that?*

In the shelter of his wife's arms, Ron Jordan absorbed every word of hearings-rehash emitting from the television, even as his focus glazed over and his breathing became slow and steady.

"She fundamentally agreed with a woman's right to choose, even though she claims she would have used an equality argument instead of a privacy argument. So here's her problem, now. She's pro-choice, despite her Catholic upbringing. Some senators may fear she will also ignore her church's anti-homosexuality stance. That's a big question. We don't know how she feels about her son's gender preference." Malone hesitated. "But, back to abortion. A review of her judicial record shows she's been consistently pro-choice. Remember, if she gets confirmed to the high court, she could change her pro-choice stance depending upon the case. It's happened with other justices on abortion and other issues. It could happen again."

"So maybe that's why there've been thousands of demonstrators outside the Capitol and the Supreme Court since her confirmation hearings began?"

"Well, I can think of a couple of reasons. You've got pro-life and pro-choice advocates going back to *Roe* and its descendants, who know Chief Justice Kirkland wants to see *Roe v. Wade* overturned, before he retires to Florida. Those activists are dying for someone on their side of the fight to be elevated to the high court. The Chief needs only one more vote to sink *Roe.* Makes both sides very nervous. And the demonstrators sense that her confirmation vote in the Senate will be close. They don't want their senators to forget they'll be watching the vote very carefully, and will remember how the senators voted when they go to the polls this fall. In key states like Ohio and New Jersey, for instance."

"Would we be facing this likely close vote if the president had gone with Judge Rittenhouse or Secretary Hayward?"

"Considering all of the circumstances, you have to know, Mr. Morgan and his advisors are worried about losing this battle. So, sure, I'd have to say, politically, the president would be better off now with one of those men. Either could be easily confirmed, after all this."

"I think Judge Hernandez would be a more interesting addition to the Court than another cut-to-fit male judge." It was a new voice and Ron let his mind grope around until it placed the speaker: Charlotte Vickers-Waugh, a frequent White House dinner guest and the Landauer Distinguished Professor of American History at George Washington University. Every time they met, she tried to dazzle him with her encyclopedic knowledge of past presidents and their families. Jon had confided that she'd asked for his authorization to write his biography. He'd also confided that his wife didn't much like her.

"Either Judge Rittenhouse or Secretary Hayward would be more of the same. I think we all feel—or at least a 51 percent majority of us feel—that it's time for a change."

Ron let his attention drift as Vickers-Waugh went off on one of her famous digressions, expounding on the scandals former presidents had withstood and overcome with their families, their friends, their servants and, it seemed, even their livestock. His mind started to relax as his lids began their final descent toward being closed. Suddenly he brought his consciousness back from the edge of sleep. *No, don't let it go to Duckworth's Sunday morning innuendoes, please.*

"Simply old friends. Just friends. OK?"

OK. Good. If I can only get a few hours sleep tonight without the damn cough keeping me up. I wish I could just sleep here. I never cough when she's holding me.

"This is where their problem comes in, 'cause it's gonna piss . . . er . . . uh, anger gays who traditionally support Democratic candidates in urban areas."

Ron's eyes snapped open. He knew that voice: Joey Lucarelli, former senior political advisor to President Timmy Butler who had been defeated in his re-election bid by Jonathan Morgan. The young, edgy, three-hundred-pound author and MSNBC commentator was smiling into the camera. He used the practiced, man-on-the-street style Ron had spent hours analyzing before the last presidential election, looking for an Achilles' heel. He'd never found one, and the race ended up close, albeit decisive.

"I'm seeing that Democratic senators may have to hold their collective noses and ally with those Republicans who are beholden to the religious right to defeat her in a close roll-call vote."

"Sounds unlikely to me."

Joey Lucarelli's face took on the mien of erudite seriousness that Ron knew he had cultivated for his popular course in political philosophy at Georgetown. A shiver of terror ran down the attorney general's spine.

"I predict someone's gonna hit her with *the* landmark privacy case," Lucarelli was saying with exaggerated wide-eyed earnestness. "The *really* big one. 1986. *Bowers v. Hardwick*." He winked at the camera, "Stay tuned."

In the supposed haven of their Georgetown abode, Laura Jordan watched helplessly as her husband once again crumpled into a prolonged coughing fit. *Oh, what I wouldn't do to have this wretched election over*, she thought. *I just can't wait to get out of this dreadful town.*

TWENTY

Monday, May 22

Jonathan had rushed into the dining room at 8:00 expecting Anne to call him on the carpet for being late, but no one sat at the table. Now, having accepted a lame explanation for why his son was not around and having offered an even poorer one for his own tardiness, the President of the United States of America picked at his salad and inwardly squirmed under his wife's disgruntled gaze. "So how was New York?"

"The museum opening was wonderful, if that's what you mean."

Jonathan wasn't exactly sure what he'd done wrong, but he felt pretty sure it was at least a two-dozen roses mistake. He ran the possibilities through his mind: birthdays, anniversaries, her mother, the hearings, their son—bingo! "Have you seen Michael since you got back?" he asked, trying to keep his voice casual.

"Oh, Jonathan," Anne said, putting her fork down with enough force to make it bounce. "How could you let this happen? Do you have any idea how he feels now? He thinks you don't trust him at all."

"Well, I don't." It was out before he could stop himself. "For heaven's sake, Anne," he pushed his chair back from the table and ticked off his fingers. "He let his best friend drink, when he knew he shouldn't; he let himself get duped into a brawl; he fought with his own security detail;

and he looks like a half-wit in the press. How am I supposed to feel?"

"He's only a child."

"He's a fully grown man who acts like a child."

"He looks to you for validation."

"Well, he doesn't have it."

"He's done a lot of good work for the committee. One of their best fund raisers. Very popular with young voters. Poll after poll shows he's been great for you."

"Then let *them* support him for a while."

They ate in prickly silence. Foster cleared the salad plates and served the chicken. Anne toyed with the skinless breast under its low-cal sauce. Once they were alone she whispered, "This looks terrible. Couldn't we order in Chinese?"

Jonathan let himself breathe easily again. He hated arguments with his wife. *Approval for that indulged brat, my ass. When the hell will he grow up for Chrissakes? Cabinet members, senators, heads of state . . . all amateurs compared to Annie on her high horse.* "Why don't we slip out for an ice-cream cone later? What the heck, we could tool around a bunch of lighted monuments in the convertible, top down, of course. Give the Secret Service heartburn. After all, we're 'the first couple.'"

Anne suppressed a smile. *God, I wish he'd be that adventurous.* "Will you talk to Michael? Please?"

Jonathan bobbed his head in agreement. She had won again. "If that's all you want, Annie."

"That's all I ask."

"Well, I'm sure it'll all blow over in a few days. Meanwhile . . ." He took his wife's hand.

Gloria Hernandez padded around her suite at the Four Seasons Hotel, Georgetown, in robe and slippers. She had returned to her set of rooms late after dining with the St. Clairs and Fitzpatricks in the hotel's restaurant. The peaceful, shaded view of the softly lighted Chesapeake and Ohio Canal and its towpath hadn't been enough to throw off the strain of the day's questioning that had put her in a fidgety mood, though. Every time she settled into a chair, she suddenly thought of something else she had to jump up and do. Sleep was obviously out of the question.

Kate Fitzpatrick, a vivacious preservationist, had apparently sensed Gloria's discomfort earlier in the evening. Kate had tried to calm her nerves with humorous anecdotes of the former Supreme Court justice and pioneer environmentalist who had championed the canal's restoration and, incidentally, written the controversial right-to-privacy opinion in *Griswold v. Connecticut*. Kate and her Republican senator husband, John, had no doubt meant well, but Gloria wasn't one to beat a subject to death. She'd heard quite enough about *Griswold* all yesterday and today and knew, well enough, that she'd probably go around that same block many more times tomorrow. When the phone rang at 10:30, she was still up and pacing. Let it ring, she thought. I don't think I can take any more cheering up. After six times, though, she reluctantly answered.

"Hi, Mom."

Gloria's shoulders drooped at the sound in Eduardo's voice. *Oh, please, child, let's not go over it again.* "Eddie, dear, how are you?" she asked tersely, hoping to forestall another round of who's-to-blame. "So thoughtful of you to call here at 10:30. But I am still awake."

"Have you seen the papers?"

Lord, what now? "I scanned the local papers, the *Post* and the *Times*. I didn't see anything new, but then I mostly looked for pieces about my confirmation. Did I miss something?"

"Oh, God, Mother, that stuff is so old. I'm talking about the article about me!"

Gloria searched her mind. She vaguely remembered Ben Carothers stopping in during one of the hearing breaks to warn her of rumors about a tabloid article, something about Eddie and Michael. What was it he'd said? She shook

her head. "Look, Darling, it's been a long day. I didn't read
any article, but whatever it said, just let it go, OK? Politics
is like this. You know that. All lies and innuendo."

"What? What are you trying to hide? You and your
friends know all about this stuff, don't you? I can tell when
you're trying to cover."

Suddenly, she remembered what Ben had said. "A
nonsense piece about Eddie and Mike being more than just
old friends. We weren't fast enough to squash the story, but
don't worry, Tony'll handle any fallout."

"Eddie, I'm not covering up anything."

"You've known about this for a long time and never
told me. God, women can be so deceitful."

"Eddie, Eddie." She planted herself in a chair, forced air
into her lungs, closed her eyes, and blew the breath out.
"Look," she said, her voice now as calm as she wished she
felt, "we'll work this out. Whatever it is. We'll get through
this crisis."

"I'm already nauseated. God, my hair might fall out."

"What? Your hair?"

"It's everything I don't know, that's what it is," he
whimpered. "I can't take this kind of deception. You know
that. How could you not tell me?"

"Tell you what? Eduardo, for heaven's sake. What in
the world are you talking about?"

"God, I'll be thirty-one this year! Just thirty-one! My
whole life is still in front of me and now, and now . . . breast
cancer!"

Breast cancer? As if a fog had instantly lifted, Gloria
suddenly pictured her son on the other end of the line, a
continent away—his armpits soaked with sweat, his eyes
squinted against threatened tears, his upper lip curled.
"Breast cancer? You don't have breast cancer."

"Oh, how do you know?" he half wailed, half sobbed.

"Now, Eddie, I want you to think about this. Really. Do
you feel a lump? Did what's-his-name find something? Do
you have any nipple discharge or bleeding? Does your
breast hurt or do you have chest pain anywhere else?"

Eddie caught his breath. "No," he admitted. "No lump that I can feel. It's hard to tell. I mean, I've got great pecs."

"Yes, you do."

"And none of the other stuff, either."

"So you see."

"But there was this *big* story in the *Chronicle* from the UCSF Medical Center on male breast cancer." His voice began to rise again. "And their youngest patient is thirty-one years old. Thirty-one! Don't you get it? Don't you see the connection?"

"I see a panic attack, sweetheart. That's what I see. Nothing else. Have you taken your meds today?"

"That doesn't have anything to do with anything."

"Yes it does, Eddie. You know it does. Have you been drinking?"

"No, Mother." His voice immediately dropped into snide. "It's a little early, don't you think? I just got home from work. Isamu is just now fixing dinner."

Well, irritated is better than anxious. "That's good. Look, no drinks tonight, not even wine. You're having an anxiety attack, I promise you. That's all this is. You don't have breast cancer. Go take your pill. Do it now. I'll wait." She heard him curse, but the phone suddenly muffled as if it had landed on something solid. He was gone for less than a minute.

"OK, I took the pill, but it didn't work. I'm still scared to death."

"Oh, come on, *mijo*, you know it doesn't work like that. It'll take a few minutes. Let's both take a few easy, deep breaths."

"I never thought it would end this way," he moaned. "Why me?"

"Eddie, listen to me. Eddie? Eduardo!"

"What?"

"Listen to me. Are you listening?"

He sniffed. "Yeah."

"OK, look. You don't have breast cancer. I'm willing to bet you a new silver Lexus coupe that you don't have breast cancer. This is just panic, pure and simple, from not taking your meds on time and having too much alcohol over the weekend."

"Yeah, sure."

"Is it a bet?" She had noted the time when he got back on the phone; now she checked her watch again. *Another few minutes and the pill should kick in.* "Don't you remember? Two years ago? You read something about testicular cancer and you had a panic attack about that, too."

"Dad died of cancer, Mom."

"I know, dear, but Dad smoked like a chimney for forty years and died of lung cancer. You don't smoke. And your friend doesn't either, does he? You take care of yourself. You eat right, you jog, you swim, you go to the gym."

Gloria spent the next ten minutes talking to her son about nothing important and checking her watch. Slowly, the panic and tears edged out of his voice and a confident tone returned.

". . . closed the deal with just the preliminary set of drawings. I think we've really got a winner with this new concept."

"I'm glad to hear it. And you sound better. How are you feeling now?" Gloria shook her head and walked to her bed.

"Oh, better. And a little stupid. Sorry I called you in such a frenzy. And with everything you've got to deal with there, too."

Lying in her hotel bed, her slippers off, her conversational invention worn out, Gloria let her eyes drift closed. "That's all right, *mijo.* I think you wore me out enough that I can finally go to sleep. Just remember to take your meds, please."

"I will. Oh, and the silver Lexus?"

"You didn't win the bet, dear, but you know what? I feel generous." She yawned, "Pick it out, send me the bill."

"Thanks. And hey—don't let 'em wear you out. That's my job."

She gave a short laugh. "Good night, *mijo.*"

"*Buenas noches, Mama.*"

TWENTY-ONE

Tuesday, May 23

Claire Baldwin waited near the elevator that serviced the private residence. Presently, the doors opened and Jonathan Morgan stepped out.

"Good morning, Sir," she said cheerfully.

"Morning."

"Here's today's schedule."

He scarcely glanced at it as he walked with Claire, his personal aide. "You've got the call arranged to Ken Ashworth?"

"He'll be in his office between 2:30 and 3:15 this afternoon. I confirmed with his secretary this morning. I put the transportation bill we passed in April on your desk, just in case. Nearly $5 billion for discretionary spending."

"Good. Kenny wants three more bridges for Wyoming."

On their way down the hallway, Jonathan stopped to poke his head into an office. "How's it coming, Andy?"

Andrew Grunwald was a scholarly looking man badly in need of a haircut. He glanced up from between recent copies of the *Congressional Record* balanced precariously on stacks of manila folders and thick dot-matrix printouts. Open sections of the morning's *Washington Post* and *Times* were scattered on the floor nearby. When he saw the president, his hand darted to his rumpled, olive-poplin Brooks Brothers' suit, possibly in search of the repp tie that had somehow gotten caught under his shoulder. He peered at the president through small, wire-rimmed glasses.

"Morning, Sir." He gestured vaguely at the white marker-board behind him, where a large "13" had been poorly erased and covered by a faint "12."

"No change since late Friday, I'm afraid," he said. His apologetic voice barely carried above the undertone of his staff working the phones. "Half my crew was out sick the last two days with that bug that's going around, and it seems like half the Senate took off, too. Couldn't reach a soul all weekend. The good news is we're pretty close to getting Martindale and Ashworth."

"Don't worry about it, we'll get 'em. You're doing fine. Keep up the good work."

The leader of the free world moved down the hall once more, his aide almost trotting to keep up with him. A chunky man in a gray, pinstriped suit raised his hand in greeting as he approached from the opposite direction. "Morning, Sir."

"Morning, Eric. Where's the Dow this morning?"

"Up fifty-seven and rising, last I checked, approximately fifteen minutes ago." The Commerce Department economist answered briskly, never breaking stride. He continued over his shoulder as they passed. "Earnings came in better than forecast at Alcoa, G.E., and Intel."

Jonathan's secretary stood waiting to follow the president and his aide into the Oval Office. "Good morning, Mr. President, Claire. Mr. President, Bob Peterson would like a couple of minutes."

"Have him come in now." The secretary placed a cup of coffee—cream, no sugar—at Jon's right hand before she exited. In one practiced, preoccupied movement, he retrieved the hot beverage, sat down, and scooped up the papers Claire had set directly in front of his chair. "What's the group? Where?"

"National Association of Realtors, 10:15 at the Hilton."

He nodded. "Fine. They like short talks and good news about interest rates. Let's tell 'em I hope rates get notched down soon. And allow thirty seconds for a standing ovation."

"I'll put it in. Fifteen minutes?"

"Too long."

"I'll edit."

He turned his attention to the folder of legislative bills that awaited either his signature or veto. Claire retreated to the couch that faced the inner door and began marking up the realtors' speech. The door leading to the outer hallway opened and Bob Peterson strode in. "Good morning, Mr. President."

He turned to Claire. "Please." He nodded toward the door.

Claire gathered up her things and scurried out, headed for the desk next to the president's secretary, letting the door close behind her. Bob handed a tabloid-sized newspaper to his boss. "It's this week's edition of the *Galactic Scribbler*. A useless piece of crap, but you know how it is, people look at it 'cause it's free."

The banner headline read:

BROTHERS, LOVERS OR FRIENDS?

Reliable Washington sources have confirmed there is more to the Michael Morgan/Eduardo Hernandez relationship than meets the eye— although plenty meets the eye . . .

Between the front-page, full-column story beginning on the left side and its continuation down the length of the right-hand column was a side-by-side blow-up photo of Jonathan's and Gloria's sons, obviously taken at some point in the confirmation hearings when one had leaned over to hear the other.

The president and his chief of staff remained silent for a protracted moment. Finally, his shoulders sagging, Jonathan broke the ice. "Anything libelous in the copy?"

"Of course not. Innuendoes, suggestions. It's got your basic satirical spin; just enough to raise the public's hackles, vacuous enough to escape legal action. Typical *Scribbler* fare. The problem, of course—"

"—is that it'll get picked up by the mainstream," the president finished. "They live on rumors these days, damn the consequences. People who've never heard of Supreme Court confirmation hearings will just eat this stuff up." He slammed the paper down. "Damn."

"I'll have Tony obfuscate." Bob looked at his watch. "It's 9:50. He can address it in his noon press briefing. It'll make the evening papers and TV. We've gotta squelch this junk."

"No."

"Jon!"

Jonathan groaned. "Oh, all right. I just hate giving it credence at all." He stabbed at the intercom. "Claire, how's the speech going?"

"I've sliced out two, maybe three minutes."

"Good enough. I'll read it on the way to the hotel."

Bob stepped up as Jon headed toward the outside door. Claire, seeing their faces, stopped in the doorway and backed out of the office for another moment. "Jon, are you OK? Anne called Beverly last night. If there's anything we can do . . ."

The most powerful man on earth hesitated for a split second. "Thanks, but there isn't anything to be done. I don't know what's going to happen. I just know it was time to take this chance. Hell, I still think we can get her confirmed."

Bob Peterson watched his best friend straighten up and step purposefully out the door, followed by Claire and the waiting security detail. He stood listening until the limo pulled away, its police-escort's sirens blaring. Then he turned and walked to his office, filled with his own thoughts.

TWENTY-TWO

Tuesday, May 23

Gloria settled behind the highly polished mahogany table and adjusted her microphone to a comfortable level. Now in her fourth day of hearings, the spectators, media reps, ever-present photographers—even the panelists—had become somehow less intimidating. She and Hugh Graham had figured out how to stop shadowboxing and get along. The line between her friends and foes on the committee had been clearly drawn. More relaxed than she ever expected to be sitting in this room, she realized, with a maternal start, how much last night's phone call with Eduardo had helped put her at ease. *And why not?* she thought. *They're just like children, asking intrusive questions and pouting when they don't get the answers they want. If I can get him through one of his attacks long distance without having to call an intervention team, I should be able to deal with this bunch of bickering adolescents sitting right in front of me.*

"Judge Hernandez, if you're ready."

Gloria turned her attention to John Fitzpatrick, as he asked the first set of questions. True to the loaded hints he had dropped over dinner the previous night, the Senate's youngest member limited his queries to separation-of-powers doctrine and the constitutional authority of Congress to formulate and implement tax policy. *We might have rehearsed it over coffee,* she thought, half grateful, half amused.

"Thank you, Judge. That's all I have," he concluded.

"And thank you, Senator, for keeping us on time for a change," Norah said. She gestured to her left. "Your turn, Senator."

Cornell Duckworth worked his mouth for a moment, glanced at a note card, adjusted his pale yellow-and-blue paisley tie, and finally looked at the nominee. Gloria returned his gaze, eye to eye. "Morning, Judge."

"Good morning, Senator."

"Since we started these hearings, we've been talking a lot about *Griswold, Eisenstadt, Carey,* and *Roe*—landmark Supreme Court cases, ya'all agree, that either set up or perpetrated precedents for this so-called privacy right we've been battin' around." He leaned back in his chair and spread his hands. "Now, my good neighbors up here on the Democratic side of the table look at this privacy thing as the Court overstepping its bounds, and using somethin' that don't even exist as an excuse to push through all sorts of fanciful rights concerning contraception and procreation— matters that rightly belong in the Lord's domain."

Gloria drew a long breath but kept quiet, unlike the spectators. The Alabama senator fingered the vertical scar on his forehead, allegedly the result of a college barroom brawl, and shuffled through a thin deck of three by five cards. At length, the mumbles subsided.

"So," he picked up, "with that in mind, maybe you remember how the Court refused to extend the 'privacy right' in another landmark case, *Bowers v. Hardwick.* You 'member, doncha? The one where they finally came to their senses and said, 'No, for once we're not gonna say to hell with the Bible,' the one where they said homosexuality is just plain wrong!"

This time the mutterings didn't stop until Norah applied her gavel.

"I do remember the case, Senator," Gloria broke in, as Duckworth started to speak again. "However, I don't remember it in quite those terms."

"Oh, really?" Duckworth folded his arms across his chest, his smirk an open challenge. "Well, why doncha tell us what terms you do remember it in."

To Gloria's right, Hugh Graham folded his arms in conspicuous mimicry of the inquisitor. Gloria kept her expression placid. She and Hugh had been over this case many times, each discussion prompting the memory of the moment when she had discovered Eddie was gay. It had been nearing twilight in San Marino, when her son and a Stanford friend went out to the secluded pool. The senior classmates hadn't noticed her standing at a second-floor window as they caressed each other, slipped out of their swimsuits and . . . She'd never mentioned it to either Eddie or her husband. Now she forced the image from her mind once more and recounted the circumstances of the case with perfectly controlled judicial intonation.

"In 1982," she began, "Michael Hardwick, a young Atlanta bartender, was charged with breaking the Georgia anti-sodomy law when a police officer observed him performing oral sex on another man in Hardwick's bedroom. The ACLU, which had been searching for a test case on the law, offered to defend Hardwick through the trial process. The Eleventh Circuit Court ruled against the Georgia law because it concluded Hardwick's fundamental rights had been violated, since his activity had been private, beyond the reach of state law, and was therefore protected by the United States Constitution. The U.S. Supreme Court agreed to hear the case because other federal circuit courts had ruled that such private-sodomy cases were not protected by the Constitution. They reversed the Eleventh Circuit Court's ruling."

Duckworth wore a triumphant glow. "They reversed the Eleventh Circuit Court's ruling," he repeated. "Five to four! Made it clear that nowhere in the United States Constitution does it say homosexuals have the right to have oral sex, even in a private setting. The Georgia law was upheld, and so were all the similar laws in other states.

That's 'settled law,' as you like to say, isn't it? Homosexual sodomy ain't right and it sure as shootin' ain't legal!"

"Senator Duckworth," Daisy Carlisle interrupted. "I know you have serious intentions, but as a practical matter, consenting adults are generally not prosecuted for nonpublic violations of sodomy laws."

"Sure! 'Cause there's usually nobody around to witness 'em doing it in private!"

"I'm talking about consenting adults, gay or straight," Daisy persisted.

"She's right, Senator. Really," John Fitzgerald jumped in, "come on, now, we're all adults here. What's the big idea? Is it your intention to establish a federal law forbidding sex throughout the country except for men and women using the missionary position? Georgia may criminalize sodomy, but most other states don't. Some have laws against anal-genital sex but not oral-genital, some just talk vaguely about 'crimes against nature.' Some states outlaw sodomy by gays but not by straights. In one state, sodomy's fine if you're married, criminal if you're not. It's called freedom. Different strokes for different folks."

"Well, now, that's just the point!" Duckworth's response was buried amid the rumblings of the spectators and the outbreak of arguments on the panel. Norah gaveled for order to no avail. Presently, she put her mouth directly in front of her microphone and projected her voice through the cavernous hall. "This chamber must be silent before we proceed. And any photographer taking pictures during questioning will be ejected from the room." She glared at the retreating offender, and then swept the room with a fierce scowl until the noise subsided to a tomb-like peacefulness. "Thank you. Senator Duckworth, you still have the floor. Please continue with your *Hardwick* questions. I know this is one of your favorite fund-raising issues."

Cornell glared at the chairwoman before lurching forward to address the junior senator from Rhode Island. "It's no surprise there's state-to-state differences on sodomy law, Senator Fitzpatrick, 'cause lots of God-fearing Americans are appalled by it, no matter who does it or how it's done! You're not old enough to know this, but until 1961, the filthy act was outlawed in all fifty states." He quickly turned back to the nominee. "Judge, is sodomy a criminal offense in California?"

Gloria frowned. "No, Senator, not if the act is performed between consenting adults in a private, nonpublic setting."

"So it's legal if it's in private. When is it illegal?"

"Well, Senator, 'between consenting adults in a private, nonpublic setting,' would clearly mean that any other act of sodomy would be illegal. For example: It is illegal to force sodomy on anyone. It's illegal if performed on a minor, even if the minor consents—the participants must be adults. And it's illegal in any public setting, as is any kind of sexual act." She glanced at Hugh, who inclined his head slightly. "Those are the scenarios I recall. I'd have to check the legal literature for any others."

Duckworth spread himself over the table. "So if I understand you correctly, Judge, two homosexual men can commit sodomy, long as they're consenting adults and they're in a private setting, like, say, a bedroom. Is that right?"

Norah cast a warning look around the hall to quiet the ensuing whispers. Sinead Sullivan put her hand over her mike and mouthed to an aide.

"The answer is yes, Senator."

"The answer is yes. OK. So here's the $64,000 question, Judge. Do you agree with that law?"

The hush of the audience was almost palpable.

"It's settled law in California, Senator. I cannot comment further."

"Confound it!"

Duckworth slammed his hand on the table, sending papers flying to the floor and startling Cotton Blalock into an alarmed curse. Norah gaveled a half dozen times, but shouts and catcalls continued to fill the room. Finally, Norah motioned to the security guards, who began moving about the room to quiet people, individually.

"Judge," Duckworth spat, "I'm losin' all my patience with you! You're an individual! You're a citizen! You're a mother, for cryin' out loud! You've gotta have some kind of an opinion. Do you agree with the California law that says two fags can have oral sex anytime they want, as long as no one's lookin' or not?"

"And I'm losing my patience with you, Senator," Norah interrupted sharply, bringing her wooden mallet down with a smack. "Your time is up!"

"What?" Duckworth bristled.

And suddenly, jeers emanated from the room: "Unfair. Queer lover. Bleeding heart hippie. Lefto pinko."

"Point of order! Point of order!" Norah stood up to point out individuals, as spectators and panelists jumped to their feet in protest. "Eject that photographer!" she commanded. "Clear the well! Remove that man! Clear out anyone spouting foul or obscene language."

Security officers charged around the room, jerking their thumbs here and there to expel the offenders and motioning people back into their seats. Finally, the hall settled into an expectant silence. Sitting up very straight, Norah Poole Stafford swept the chamber with an aristocratic glower and gaveled once more. Satisfied at last, she turned to her right and smiled graciously. "Senator Landes, your questions, please."

"Actually," the balding Ohio Republican began in his bland Midwestern tone, "I'm more interested in setting the record straight at this point than asking any more inflammatory questions. Judge, I commend you for not compromising your position to answer my good friend Senator Duckworth's question. After all, *Hardwick* was narrowly decided. Why, after weeks of fighting with himself, the justice who cast that one, all-important vote to uphold the Georgia statute, said he would have voted differently if the defendant, Mr. Hardwick, had been prosecuted and sent to prison under the law. Imagine going to prison for having sex in your own home with another consenting adult. Cruel and unusual punishment,

that's what it would have been and, by God, it flies in the
face of the Eighth Amendment. I say the Constitution
screams 'No!' Besides, Georgia's own supreme court struck
down the anti-sodomy law in 1998. It violated the state's
constitutional protection of privacy, spelled out for all to
see. OK," he said, his voice calming. "That's all I wanted to
say. Who's next? Senator Higashi? Kawai, I'm giving you
my time."

"Thank you, Bruce."

Gloria took advantage of the subsequent exchange of
pleasantries and rubbed her eyes. When the gentlemanly
Hawaiian senator stated that he wondered if the privacy
right could be extended to include both heterosexual and
homosexual marriage, she let the clock run while she
consulted with Hugh Graham. Then Gloria looked up to
Kawai Higashi and said, "Senator, I expect the issue of
homosexual marriage will be tested several more times in
the states, just as it was in Hawaii—where the voters, the
legislature and the courts concluded that now is not the
time to approve such unions."

"You're referring to our 1998, state constitutional
amendment that limits marriage to opposite sex couples?"
Higashi replied.

"That's right, Senator."

"Well, OK, but what do *you* think about gay or lesbian
marriages?"

Gloria smiled and shook her head. "Senator Higashi,
both you and I know that's properly a legislative issue. I
have no constitutional authority to make law."

The Republicans tossed her another bone when Russell
Marchbanks, the non-attorney from Montana, questioned
her. Gloria felt well equipped to handle his inquiries on
natural resource law, restraint-of-trade litigation, and the
death penalty. But then, the questioning returned to the
Democratic side, and her apparent foe, Maryland Senator
Christine Fairchild.

"Judge Hernandez," Christine's face was as unreadable
as before, yet Gloria sensed a fierce hostility she could not

quite put her finger on, "please tell us your understanding of the word 'family.'"

"Family?" Gloria hesitated. "From the legal perspective, the family is a social group, a fundamental part of society. I think of family in terms of relations, of course. Mothers, fathers, spouses, offspring, grandparents, aunts, uncles, and cousins."

Christine considered the answer. "Fair enough. Would you say this fundamental society unit, as you put it—from a legal perspective—has values?"

Hugh whispered something. Gloria nodded. "Yes, I suppose so. You're no doubt talking about the unit's principles, its standards."

"That's right. OK. We've got a unit with principles. And from your point of view, you say that means a mother, father, and children, is that correct?"

"Well, traditionally, yes. Today, of course, things have changed. We have different, more diverse families now. Single parents. Childless couples. Grandparents raising grandchildren."

Christine nodded thoughtfully. "Different families. Diverse families. Like couples of the same sex?"

"Or different sexes. Couples of the same or opposite sex forming a partnership and living under one roof. Obviously, the definition of 'family' has been extended to include the evolution of life as we know it today."

"Let me be absolutely sure I understand you." Christine folded her arms on the table and propped herself on them. "A gay or lesbian couple living under one roof, forming what the media likes to call a 'domestic partnership,' you call that a family?"

Gloria folded her own arms on the table and propped herself on them. "By contemporary standards, yes. I would have to call that a family."

"Couples with no hope of fulfilling the primary goal of marriage: procreation. Couples that undermine the traditional values this great nation of ours was founded on. You call that a family?"

"For whatever reason, if they're living together, providing the comfort and security of helpmates to each other and sustaining a monogamous relationship, then, yes, in today's world by today's standards, I'd call that family."

The two women stared defiantly into each other's eyes, until Daisy could no longer stand the tension. "Well, glory be! We're back to the old church-and-state separation question! Give us a break, Senator Fairchild. You're sounding more and more like my ex-husband and his 'wife's place' nonsense. This is Congress, not a church or mosque. Neither religion nor the legislature has the right to dictate the primary goals of marriage. Good heavens! If it did, you and I'd be barefoot and pregnant right now! Face facts, woman. Half of all new marriages terminate in divorce; one out of three kids is born out of wedlock. We've got enough fatherless homes to fill a quarter of this country."

"And regardless of your feelings about homosexual practices, Senator," John Fitzpatrick broke in, "gay men rarely produce illegitimate kids, and account for a minuscule fraction of those divorces."

Norah tried to wield her authority when the panel burst out in yet another heated debate, but it was Carl Albrecht who brought order to the room. "Judge Hernandez!" he shouted above the clatter. "Judge Hernandez!"

The noise dwindled.

"Judge Hernandez," Albrecht began again.

"Yes, Senator?"

"Judge, are you proud of your family?"

"Senator Albrecht, what kind of question is that?" Gloria bristled, the fire rising in her chest. "Naturally I'm proud of my family. How dare you ask such a thing."

Norah picked up her gavel once more, but Carl made a slashing motion. "Well, Judge, I'll tell you. I dare ask, because I'm confused. First you say you're Catholic. Then you state that two men living together can constitute a family, a decidedly anti-Catholic stance. You won't discuss your family, about which there have been many questions, both in and out of this chamber, but you claim you're proud of it, anyway. So now I ask you, Judge, which is it? Are you really Catholic, or do you just pay off the Church expecting that will offset your religious obligations? And if that's the case, can this panel expect you to do the same thing on the Court? You'll do what you please, damn the conventions or expectations of the judicial system? You can't have it both ways. You can't say you adhere to one of the strictest sets of rules on earth—and Lord knows, you Catholics have rules for everything—and then turn around and claim the right to pick and choose which of those rules you're going to disregard. So I ask again, which is it, Judge? I think that's what we all want to know. It can't all be true. Which one's a lie, the religion or the family?"

In the barely restrained stillness of the Central Hearing Room, Gloria did not even attempt to hide the fury in her eyes or the deep, highly audible breath she took before she answered. "Senator Albrecht," she said, letting the ice surface in her voice. "Allow me to clarify my 'stance,' as you put it. Yes, I am Catholic. I believe in God, in the sanctity of the Church, and in the teachings of Jesus Christ. I also believe in the Constitution of the United States of America, which states I am free to enjoy my religious beliefs. But I am not free, either as a private citizen or as a court official—at any level of the judicial system—to impose those beliefs on anyone else, except, perhaps my own minor children. Therefore, I state again: In the context of today's society, for the purposes of the *law*, Senator, not for purposes of my life or the hierarchy of the Church, the definition of 'family' has had to be restated to include groupings previously considered outside the norm. As far as my own son is concerned," she struggled to calm herself, "I have brought him up to adhere to the fundamental principles of Catholicism, which foster, among other moral precepts, the traits of fairness and tolerance. I love my son, dearly. I am very proud of who he is and what he has accomplished in his life. And I do not see how any of my beliefs or attitudes in any way contradict each other, or would interfere with my abilities to render fair and informed judgment on the Supreme Court."

The hush lingered only a second or two before spectators, panelists, and even some of the media people burst into applause. Daisy rose to her feet, as did Norah, Yale, John, and a number of people in the audience. Carl's mouth hung slightly open, until an aide nudged him, and he sheepishly joined the ovation. Christine, who remained in her seat, clapped hesitantly, surveying the chamber without moving her head. At length, she eased back in her chair and let her hands drop in her lap. As the cheering died down, she tilted her face slightly and gazed at the nominee. Finally, she folded her arms across her chest and smiled, ever so faintly.

TWENTY-THREE

Tuesday, May 23

It must be almost midnight by now. Christine lay awake with her eyes closed, determined not to check the clock again. She gently reached down with her left hand to stroke the sleeping ball of fur curled up against her thigh. Molly responded with a soft purr. "Nothing wakes you, does it, little fluff?"

At the sound of the muted beep, Christine quickly tapped "talk" on the cordless phone she'd kept perched on her right shoulder in anticipation. The small, tawny cat shifted position, pushing in even further against her leg. "Hi."

"Sorry I'm late. Were you asleep?"

"No, of course not. How did the meeting go?"

"Like usual. Too long. The Bishop dreams of a new monumental cathedral we can't afford. Maybe he'll be lucky enough to go to L.A. when he moves up. Poor Father Donust, who never asks for anything, really needs a new roof at St. Timothy's. It was pouring last time I gave mass there. Buckets all over the place. Fortunately, I was on key that day and he's got a devoted following."

Christine snuggled further into her pillow, momentarily upsetting Molly, who stretched to show her displeasure, then fell back to sleep. "I'm sure you handled it well."

"It's why I'm the kingfish." The warm, quiet voice on the other end of the line paused. "So, how did it go today? Did you ask?"

"I asked."

"And?"

"Just what we thought. I don't see how I can vote for her. I don't know how she can call herself a Catholic."

"I don't see how I'm going to make it until Thursday. Why can't you come up tomorrow?"

"You know why." Christine rolled on her side. Molly flopped off the bed, shook herself, then jumped up again to settle on the other side of Christine's legs. "I have the hearing all day, that dinner . . ."

"But you don't even want to go to that dinner."

"I know, but I have to. I'll be stuck at the Mayflower till 8:30 at the earliest. I wouldn't be able to get there until after 10:00 sometime, and you know how Crispina is."

The other voice sighed, a great, desire-laden expiration that made Christine press the phone closer to her ear and stroke at the sheets with her free hand. Molly pounced at the movement, then rolled over to let her stomach be fondled for a few seconds before she reflexively scratched Christine's hand away with her back paws, hopped off the bed and disappeared into the living room. Christine continued stroking where the cat had been. "Are you going to be able to get to sleep?"

"I've poured some wine. Father Virgil got a new shipment this afternoon. The wine cellar's his pride and joy. How about you?"

"I have those new pills the doctor ordered for me. She assured me they'd do the trick. Maybe she got it right this time."

"I wish I could relax you enough to sleep."

Christine lay silent, a single tear trickling down onto the pillow. *I wish . . . I wish . . . .*

"I guess we'd better hang up."

"Will you call tomorrow?"

"How can you ask? You know I will. Christine, you know if I could—"

"Don't say it." She rolled over on her side, rubbing her wet cheek against the sheets. "After all," she said, trying to sound brave, "according to Judge what's-her-name, we're a type of family, too. Anybody can be a family. Damn the commandments. Damn the Bible. Damn the Church." Her voice trailed off into tears. She buried her face in the pillow, the phone clutched tightly against her head.

"Oh, Chrissy."

"I'm sorry," she sniffled.

"No, I'm sorry." The voice on the other end cracked. "I don't know why we keep doing this to each other. We have to stop this. This is madness."

"I won't drive up Thursday."

"You have to come up Thursday."

"Don't call me anymore."

"All right."

"No. Call me."

"You'll come Thursday?"

"I'll be there. Call me tomorrow."

"Try to get some sleep, my beloved."

Christine smiled into the receiver. "I will. Take care of yourself."

"I'm going to hang up now."

Christine waited. "Hang up."

"I'm going to. Are you OK?"

She nodded at the darkness. "I'm all right," she whispered. "Call me tomorrow."

"I can't wait to see you Thursday."

"Stop talking. Just say good night and hang up."

"Good night."

Christine tapped "talk" and watched the little light go out. "Good night, my prince," she whispered into the darkness.

TWENTY-FOUR

Wednesday, May 24

Daisy Carlisle hurried through the lofty atrium of the Hart Senate Office Building after a fifteen-minute break in the hearings. *Recess is almost over and I'm gonna be late. Well, Duckworth's here, after all. Wonder where he's been all morning.*

"I'd like you to meet someone," Cornell Duckworth called, wiggling his fingers to motion Daisy over. "I'm sure you recognize the Reverend Gideon Heartfelt, president of the Christian Alliance for Freedom. One of our greatest televangelists, spreading the Lord's word to every corner of this great nation. Reverend, this is Senator Daisy Carlisle, formerly Charlotte, North Carolina's most shameless . . . er, brilliant trial lawyer."

Handsome, tanned, and impeccably tailored, the fundamentalist clergyman offered his hand. "How do you do, Senator? I'm honored to embrace innumerable Carolinians—including many prominent barristers—as a very important part of my international congregation. I assume you are a member of my flock."

His hand was cool and slightly damp. Daisy put on her sweetest smile. "No, Reverend. I'm afraid your brand of religion is just a tad too intolerant for this little 'ole girl."

Heartfelt's smile twitched for no more than a split second. "Intolerant is a rather loaded word, Senator. What you mean is, I have no tolerance for those who would inflict and even legalize sin, for those who have strayed from the path of the Almighty, or for those who are scheming to deliver this beloved land of ours straight to the doorstep of Satan! I have no tolerance for certain individuals who have already attained positions far too lofty for our citizens' good, in the exalted justice system we have, and who seek to wreak even greater havoc in the most highly esteemed court in the nation. No doubt this is the intolerance you are referring to. Lord," the reverend implored, tilting his face upward with eyes closed. "Deliver us, we pray, from this most unholy of women, this pariah, this demonic creature. I most humbly beseech you, dear Father, to give your misguided daughter, Daisy Carlisle, the wisdom and, oh yeah, the strength to deliver us all from the wrath of this nominee." He suddenly clutched Daisy's hands in his and looked her straight in the eye. "Senator, you have the power in these hands, in your superior intellect, in your strong heart to thwart this evil Los Angeles juggernaut from further destroying the moral fiber of our sons and daughters."

Daisy pulled her hands from his and blinked several times. "No doubt," she said. "Now, if ya'all excuse me." *No doubt it's time for you to pay back for all those campaign contributions from the generous reverend, Ducky Boy,* she thought as she hastened away to the Central Hearing Room. *Good luck and good riddance, Gideon. If I had to answer to supporters like that, I'd——.*

Daisy rushed into the large chamber and slid into her seat just as Norah's mallet came down to continue the morning session. "Well, since Senator Duckworth isn't here, Bruce, I guess you're next."

Gloria had spent most of the morning fielding relatively benign questions. She hadn't needed to consult Hugh and he hadn't offered any advice. Even Grant Hallstead, from whom she'd expected a serious grilling, had avoided quizzing her about privacy-right issues. Cornell Duckworth, whose interchanges she most dreaded, had never appeared in the day's hearings at all. Her stomach told her it was almost lunch time. *Just a few more minutes. Oh, Santa Maria. He's here.*

As Cornell Duckworth quietly made his way to his seat on the left side of the podium, Norah was thanking Bruce Landes for his brevity and reminding him he still had another minute, if he wanted to use it.

"Thank you, Senator," Bruce said, with a gracious wave. "I would just like to say it's been a pleasure interviewing Judge Hernandez these past several days. Her grasp of constitutional law is most impressive. I look forward to her continuing success as a member of the Supreme Court." He bowed slightly to the nominee, who returned a grateful smile.

"Well, Senator Duckworth," Norah began with a little sigh. "How nice to have you join us. I suppose you'd like to get your questions in before lunch, now that you've consented to grace us with your presence."

"Thank you, Senator Stafford. I'll just go ahead and ignore the sarcasm." Cornell directed his pleasant expression to Gloria. "Good early afternoon, Judge Hernandez. I'm sure you're relieved to have your hearing just about over." Gloria forced a disarming smile.

Cornell continued in the same cordial tone. "Now, Judge, I wanna go back to 1986, once more, when the Supreme Court upheld the Georgia anti-sodomy law in *Bowers v. Hardwick*—a decision, we all agree at this point, that dealt a severe blow to the gay-rights movement. We do all agree on that, don't we?"

"Yes, Senator,"

"Good. OK. Now, you know, the *Hardwick* opinion has been used over and over again as a precedent for maintaining a tight control over what homosexuals can and cannot do in American society. Isn't that so?"

Hugh leaned over, covered his face with his left hand, and whispered, "Take it easy. Remember, this is his last chance to control the dialogue. He'll go populist, I bet. Just stick with the law. You'll be fine."

Gloria pulled away from Hugh and folded her hands on the table. "Uh, yes, Senator, that's essentially correct. It has. That's the power of a precedent."

"OK. So what we're basically saying is, we're all—
that's you and me, and everybody here in this room, and
watching on television from at home or their office or
wherever they are—we're all living in a country where it is
not only morally, it's legally appropriate to keep this
element of society in check. Now, I'm not going to ask you
if you agree with that, 'cause I don't want to get
sidetracked."

A murmur rumbled through the hall. The Reverend
Gideon Heartfelt was being escorted to a front-row seat
that had just been vacated for him by a clean-cut looking
young man. Daisy balled one hand and rubbed it with the
other. Cornell hesitated momentarily to finger his forehead
scar, then began again. "What I'm going to ask you is this:
How do you explain, how can you possibly justify, why
should we, knowing who you are and what your family is
and what your values are, put you in a position to write
opinions such as the piece of senseless drivel handed down
by the United States Supreme Court in *Romer v. Evans*?"

"I beg your pardon?"

Duckworth's cordial facade evaporated. "Oh, come on,
Judge! *Romer v. Evans*, the 1996 landmark decision you
musta thrown a party to celebrate. Didn't you? Or don't
you remember the case?" He waved away her attempt to
speak. "Let me refresh your memory, Judge. In 1992, the
good citizens of Colorado voted in a ballot initiative called
Amendment Two. It won by a landslide. A landslide! Fifty-
three percent of the people in Colorado said, 'Yes, it's time
to stop protecting these homosexuals. Fifty-three percent of
the voting public spoke to stop homosexuals from gettin'
protected-status treatment under anti-discrimination laws
in Aspen, Boulder, and Denver. Fifty-three percent of the
decent, law-abiding, God-fearing men and women in the
Centennial State said no, homosexuals shouldn't be
entitled to state government jobs; said no, nobody should
have to rent to homosexuals; said no, nobody should have
to hire or provide public accommodations or give any kind
of special treatment to aberrant, sin-infested homosexuals!"

An undertone swept the chamber. The Reverend Gideon Heartfelt wore a broad grin.

"Judge, do you have any idea at all what fifty-three percent means to a politician, who doesn't ever get lifelong tenure in his job, like you people in the federal courts? Fifty-three percent! *Landslide,* that's what it means. Any elected official will tell you fifty-three percent is an untarnished landslide from the people. And what did the Supreme Court do? What did they do?" Duckworth's voice had grown louder and louder as he spoke. Now, in his excitement, he pushed up from his chair and hurled his arms out. "They struck it down in a six-to-three ruling. They threw it out. Fifty-three percent of all voters and they slapped them in the face. Is that what you're gonna do?" he roared. "Is that the kind of judge you think you're gonna be?"

Amidst the hullabaloo that followed, the Reverend Gideon Heartfelt leaned back in his chair, arms folded across his chest, the very picture of righteous satisfaction.

"Quiet, quiet!" Norah slammed her gavel down repeatedly, but it could barely be heard over the uproar of the crowd and the angry shouts of the panelists. By now, half the assemblage was on its feet, shouting and waving fists in the air. It took the entire security staff, plus several more officers who came running in to subdue the spectators. Eventually, everyone regained his or her seat. The hall wavered in a strained silence.

"One more outburst like that," Norah growled into her mike, "and I will have this room cleared once and for all." She waited several more seconds for her own heart to stop pounding and for the palpable tension of her colleagues to ease, before going on. "Senator Duckworth," she started.

"I'd like to answer the senator's question," Gloria broke in. Startled, Norah gestured assent.

"First of all, Senator," Gloria said, instinctively lapsing into her judicial posture of authority, "let's get the facts straight. It was a Colorado state court that blocked the amendment's enforcement, not the U.S. Supreme Court.

Then their own supreme court, the Colorado Supreme Court, struck it down, reasoning gays, lesbians, and bisexuals had been made a 'targeted group' for the purpose of denying them equal participation in the political process. Clearly, Amendment Two violated the 'equal protection of the laws' clause spelled out in the Fourteenth Amendment of the United States Constitution."

"Fifty-three percent, Judge!"

Gloria held up her hand. "Just a minute, I'm not finished. You may recall a discussion we had the other day on just this very subject, when Senator Stafford asked about 'protected spheres' in terms of protected areas. It is part of our legal system, part of our moral heritage, to prevent the majority, any majority, from utilizing state powers such as popularly voted amendments or referendums to persecute any group of people or segment of society simply because they dislike that group. That's the whole idea behind 'equal protection of the laws,' Senator. You know it, and I know it, and every court in the land knows it. All the U.S. Supreme Court did was uphold the Colorado Supreme Court's decision."

"All it did? That's not all it did!"

Gloria shrugged one shoulder. "You're right. But, again, let's look at the facts. The Kirkland court, as you probably know, gave three separate reasons for affirming Amendment Two's reversal. First, it ruled that gays and lesbians may not be singled out for disfavored treatment resulting from active hatred, even if a majority of the public hates them."

"Which they obviously do."

"May I go on?" Gloria tapped her right index finger on the table, as if waiting for a rowdy student to quiet down. "Thank you. That was their first argument. The second part of the opinion pointed out that Amendment Two had no proper legislative end. A rather salient point, don't you agree? But the most striking rationale was the fact that Amendment Two sought to make a specific group of people unequal to everyone else. I believe I'm correct in saying the Court thought we had gotten beyond that with the end of slavery in this nation. Or perhaps you'd like to bring that back too?"

"So you agree with the decision, is that what you're saying?" Duckworth panted. He didn't wait for an answer. "You know what this means, don't you?" His face was bloated with anger. "It's a Pandora's box, nothing less. Homosexual marriages. Queer lovers in our military. Sodom and Gomorrah. The very precipice of Armageddon."

Norah reached for her gavel, but the sudden outbreak from the spectators in the room evaporated as rapidly as it had come. The panelists remained quiet.

"Senator Duckworth, it's obvious to me you don't understand the central holdings of *Romer v. Evans* at all," Daisy said, when no one else spoke up.

"Who the hell asked you?"

Daisy spoke over the rising undertone, which quickly died away. "I just can't understand your wild accusations and distortions. The Court affirmed that homosexuals should receive equal treatment under the law. Well, land's sake, that's one of the founding principles of our country. And what's more, it narrowly focused only on the initiative's concerns about housing, employment, public accommodations, and state jobs. That's all. It didn't even address marriage or gays in the military. That's just your own homophobia doin' all that, sugah."

Cornell Duckworth's face turned an even darker shade of purple. "Senator Carlisle," he snapped, "if I ever need your advice, I'll be the one to ask for it—and it'll never happen. So just shut your mouth."

Wham! "That's it. We're out of time." Norah pushed her chair back from the panel's table. "Ladies and gentlemen, we're in recess until 2:00. Hopefully by then, some of us will have regained further emotional control."

"Just hold on there, Senator Stafford," Duckworth sputtered. "That Carlisle woman stole my time."

"I don't care and no one else does either. Go have lunch, Senator, or take a cold shower or whatever it is you

do to lower your blood pressure. This session is adjourned."
Wham!

Ashen-faced, the Reverend Gideon Heartfelt strode out
of the room ahead of everyone else.

TWENTY-FIVE

Wednesday, May 24

"If you're ready, Judge Hernandez, we'll conclude your public hearings with Senator Scott's questions."

The afternoon had dragged on interminably, with Gloria answering variations of the same set of questions over and over. First the Democrats would try to force her into a scandalous stance, and then the Republicans would smooth over the same area with undisguised support. The final leg of the afternoon session had started at 4:00 after a fifteen-minute break. Gloria glanced at her watch. Only 5:30. She felt as if she had been wrung dry.

"Don't give up," Hugh said softly in her right ear. "You're doing great. This is the last hurdle. Scott will probably keep playing hardball in his strange way. He's always meticulously prepared but, according to my count, we're ahead on points, so just stay alert and maintain your cautious attitude. Leave the screaming to the Republicans. Remember, I'm right here if you need me."

Gloria looked at him gratefully for a moment, before nodding to the chairwoman. "I'm ready, Senator Stafford."

On the podium, Derek Scott held a yellow wooden pencil between the index and middle fingers of his right hand, which also supported his chin. With his eyes glued on his legal tablet, he sighed, then said, "Good afternoon, Judge Hernandez."

"Good afternoon, Senator."

Without looking up, he coughed weakly, withdrew a neatly folded, white handkerchief from his conservatively styled navy poplin suit, dabbed his lips, and patted the skin below his nose. "Excuse me." In due time, he glanced at Gloria and Hugh, started to turn the page of his tablet and hesitated again. "Judge Hernandez," he finally began, "your friendship with President Morgan spans many years. Where did you first meet Jonathan Morgan?"

Oh, good grief, not again! "As I've mentioned many times in the last four and a half days, Senator, we met in Stanford Law School."

"Oh, yes," Scott lifted a page of his tablet and let it flutter back down. "You endured the rigors of law school together. Is that right?"

And I've answered this a dozen times. "Yes, Senator."

"And you both made Law Review?"

Maybe, two dozen times. "Yes, Senator."

Scott paused. "We're talking about thirty-five years or so ago now, aren't we, Judge?"

Gloria tilted her head. "That's right."

"You were a wealthy young woman from Buenos Aires, Argentina. Grew up in one of the city's most prestigious neighborhoods: *La Recoleta*. Morgan was a poor young man from Santa Barbara, California. His folks owned a small bakery, sort of a mom and pop place. Correct?"

"Y-yes . . ."

"There weren't all that many women in the law school then, were there, Judge?"

"No, there weren't. We were in the minority at Stanford."

"So, if I understand correctly, you mostly associated with the men in your class. That would be reasonable, after all."

"I had female friends, too, if that's what you're asking."

"Let's see," Scott lifted up a page of his pad, then another. "It was you and Jonathan Morgan and Robert Peterson and Ronald Jordan, right? You all went to school together."

Uh-oh. "Yes, we did."

"And I presume you all studied together? I mean, even though there was probably at least one separate dorm for women, you all did attend classes and eat and talk and study together? The four of you as a group, isn't that right?"

"We were friends, yes. I spent time studying with them, among quite a number of other people."

"Of course. Let me see."

Scott paged through his tablet. Gloria sat alert. The tightness across her shoulders began to move up into her neck.

"Judge Hernandez," Scott let the pages of his tablet fall closed but kept his head and eyes cast down, "when you were studying with these friends—Bob Peterson, Ron Jordan and Jon Morgan—did you ever send out for pizza?"

"Pardon?"

"We've all been there, Judge. A group of friends sit around rehashing wills and trusts; somebody gets hungry, makes a phone call, sends out for pizza. Did you ever do that?"

Gloria blinked several times. She shook her head. "I don't really remember. It sounds reasonable. I suppose we did."

"Who paid?"

"I beg your pardon?"

Scott waved his hand. "For the pizza. Bob Peterson was from a middle-class family, going to school on a tight budget. Ron Jordan worked part time selling shoes. Jonathan Morgan, as we know from his endless campaign speeches, was a poor boy from a poor family, up from the wrong side of the tracks—a world away from the estate he owns now in Montecito—struggling through Stanford on a partial scholarship and two jobs. Who paid for the pizza?"

Gloria stared at the senator from Vermont. The room was so quiet she could hear the soft whistle of Cotton Blalock's breath through his teeth. "I suppose I did."

Scott raised his eyebrows and flipped another two pages. "You may remember, Judge, that Mr. Morgan faced a real crisis near the end of his second year in law school. That little bakery his folks owned at the lower end of State Street burned down one Saturday night. They didn't have insurance. Nothing. Wiped out. Mr. Morgan almost had to drop out of Stanford to go home and help out. Does that jog your memory?"

Gloria was careful not to look down. "Yes, Senator."

Scott turned to the next page of his tablet. "Who paid?"

The Central Hearing Room was silent as a tomb. Bruce Landes shielded his eyes. Norah clasped her hands on the table just behind her microphone. Stanley Popowski concealed a broad grin with his left fist. Christine Fairchild inclined forward, chin resting on her right hand.

Gloria's mind had succumbed to wordlessness. After a long pause, Scott answered for her, "Señor Juan Luis Diaz, a director of *Banco de la Nacion Argentina* and, incidentally, your father, wrote two checks—one to rebuild the State Street Bakery in Santa Barbara, and the other to help Jonathan Morgan finish Stanford Law School without ever having the distraction of part-time jobs again. Isn't that correct?"

Murmurs swept the room once more. Norah looked at the wall clock, but didn't gavel for quiet. During the rising undertone, Gloria leaned over to Hugh. "How in the world," she whispered, "did he find that out?"

"Don't worry about it. He's trying to rattle you. Keep calm. Answer his questions deliberately. He's down to nineteen minutes."

Norah finally spoke up. "Ladies and gentlemen, I realize you're tired, but we're almost finished. You know I really shouldn't mention this, but I think even my Doberman, Felix, is getting tired of these hearings. He patiently rides into the city with me every workday, but I know he'd prefer chasing squirrels in McLean. Speaking of which, would you please continue, Senator Scott."

Derek Scott, who had been leaning on his elbow, shrugged and flipped another page. "Now Judge Hernandez," he paused to dab his right eyebrow and exhale, "how about studying? The records show that you outstripped our illustrious president in practically every class, earning almost straight A's, while he came in with a slightly lower grade point average."

"And?"

"Did you ever help him? I mean especially before your father came to his aid. You know, when he was working two jobs and burning the midnight oil to stay competitive with his classmates, while you went horseback riding with movie stars and got an allowance from your daddy. Did you ever help him with, say, his case summaries for Law Review? Edit his class papers? Prepare him for mock trials?"

The stillness in the chamber pushed at Gloria's throat, as a hand squeezing tighter and tighter. "I really don't remember, Senator. It was a long time ago. But, yes, I suppose we all helped each other get through the tough classes. That's what friends are for."

Scott nodded, his chin drooping almost to his chest. He riffled through several pages of his legal pad, running his finger down the center of each one before flipping to the next. "So you studied together, and you ate pizza together, and maybe you even went to the movies now and then together."

"I suppose so."

He pursed his lips. "What else did you do together?"

Norah banged her gavel to stifle the rumbling that had started to wave through the spectators. She looked sharply to her right and eyed three senators who had started to protest. "Order, please. Order."

Hugh put his hand on Gloria's arm. "Don't let him get under your skin," he whispered, his lips barely moving, his eyes remaining on Scott. "There's nothing to this. It's just his way of baiting you."

"Senator Scott," Norah said, gesturing to the dour figure, "you may continue, but I caution you: This is a public hearing, not a private examination. You might want to save some of these questions for tomorrow's closed session."

Scott nodded at the table in front of him. "Of course, you're right. I'll move on, Senator, I'll move on. Judge, how about after law school? Although your careers diverged, you and Mr. Morgan remained friends, didn't you?"

Gloria unobtrusively filled her lungs and changed her expression. "Yes, Senator, we remained friends."

"Your first job as a lawyer was in Los Angeles, I believe, as was Mr. Morgan's. Is that correct?"

"Yes."

"So your friendship continued in Los Angeles?"

"Yes. We saw each other occasionally."

"On a business or social basis?"

"A little of both, I suppose."

"Umm." Scott paused to write something on his yellow tablet. "Judge, did you ever have occasion to use your personal relationship in the course of your legal career?"

Gloria narrowed her eyes slightly. "I'm not sure what you mean by that, Senator."

"Very simple, Judge: Did your personal relationship—your friendship, as it were—with Jonathan Morgan have any impact on the remarkable number of cases you resolved to your clients' benefit, during the time both you and he worked as attorneys in different legal firms in the same city?"

The soft whisperings seemed to creep up Gloria's neck into her hair. "I don't know what you're implying, Senator," she said, enunciating carefully, "but neither Jonathan nor I ever committed any breach of legal ethics before, during, or after our tenures at Weiskoff, Barnes, and Foley, and Kaufmann and Dobson, respectively."

"I'm sure not, I'm sure not. I was just wondering. For example, in *Constanzer v. Gustafson Corporation*, which you handled for Kaufmann and Dobson, did your relationship with the president—then an attorney on the opposing team—have anything to do with your client's $15.2 million settlement—"

"No, it did not."

"—which, of course, led to your subsequent rise to partnership in the firm?"

"My relationship with Jonathan Morgan, personal or otherwise, has had nothing whatsoever to do with the course of my legal career."

"I see. So Mr. Morgan had nothing to do with your being elevated to the Ninth Circuit Court?"

Norah gaveled for order. The room quieted more slowly this time. Gloria could sense Hugh holding his breath.

"I'm not sure what you mean."

"Well, as I understand the chronology, Judge, you and the president—then a private citizen—both finished Stanford Law at the same time, both became attorneys in top-drawer, rival firms at the same time, both worked your way up from associates to junior partners to full partnerships all along more or less the same time line. Then, if I have my facts straight, Morgan veered into a succession of private business ventures, and you became one of his—what did he call it?" He searched his notes. "Ah, yes, 'consulting attorney.' You became one of his consulting attorneys, as did Bob Peterson and Ron Jordan. The Stanford four still together, as it were."

Gloria inhaled deeply and exhaled slowly. She did not speak.

"Of course, by then you were all married—to other people, naturally—and both you and Morgan had had children. Well, you'd had a child. He had fathered one."

"That's right, Senator."

"Is there a question in there anywhere, Senator Scott?" Daisy asked impatiently.

Scott lifted his head and stared at where the sound had come from as if only then, first realizing there were other people on the panel with him. "I'm sorry. Let me just move on." He went back to his legal pad. "Judge, how did it come about that Mr. Morgan appointed you to the Ninth Circuit Court in the first place?"

Norah gaveled for order. Gloria waited for space to answer.

"I'm afraid you're mistaken, Senator. Jonathan Morgan did not appoint me to the Ninth Circuit Court."

Hugh opened and closed his mouth. Scott wrote something down. Gloria focused on the tonsure-like bald spot showing on his lowered head.

"Yes, of course. President Morgan wasn't even president then, was he? I mean, he was governor of California at the time." Scott hissed and shook his head. "Please excuse my error, Judge. I detest mistakes like this one. Stupid. So stupid of me." The Vermonter dabbed at his nose, his lips, the corner of one eye. He carefully returned the handkerchief to his pocket. He fingered a page of his tablet. "But he's president now, isn't he?" Scott asked, his voice flattening out even more than usual. "And he certainly was the one to choose you for this nomination. Tell me, Judge, how did your personal relationship impact that?"

"I beg your pardon?"

Scott leveled his eyes at Gloria for the first time. "Did you petition President Morgan to nominate you to the Supreme Court?"

Gloria sat up very slowly and very straight. "No, Senator Scott, I did not."

"So you're nothing more than just good friends, is that it?"

"That's right, Senator. We're just good friends."

Scott paused to brush a white speck on the left sleeve of his suit. He scratched his scalp with the ring and middle fingers of his left hand. He studied his notes. "Judge," he said almost absently, "do you support the fundamental holdings of *Roe v. Wade*?"

Oh, good grief! "Yes, Senator, as I've stated several times before, it's settled law and I support the majority opinion of the Supreme Court's ruling."

"Do you support the concept of a wall between church and state as regards prayer in public schools?"

"I do."

"Did you see Jonathan Morgan often when you were both living and working in Los Angeles?"

Gloria hesitated. "Senator Scott, just what is it you want to know about President Morgan and myself? We were friends. We still are friends. What else do you want me to say?"

"I'm asking the questions, Judge."

"And I'm answering them, Senator."

Scott covered his mouth with his right fist for a moment. "Judge, are you a personal friend of Cardinal Ramon Delgado of the Los Angeles Archdiocese?"

"Yes, I am."

"And is the president a personal friend of Cardinal Delgado?"

Gloria didn't miss a beat. "I don't know. I know they're acquainted. You'd have to ask him if they're friends."

Scott folded and unfolded the corner of one page. "The Hernandez Foundation provides college scholarships exclusively to Hispanic students. Do you think that's fair, Judge?"

Good heavens, how can it still not be 6:00? "Yes, Senator, as I've explained before, my husband and I established the foundation to fill a need—one that has actually grown with the passage of time, I might add."

"Senator Scott, you have exactly three more minutes," Norah instructed.

"Thank you." Scott looked at his tablet, then shoved it aside.

"Judge Hernandez, is your son homosexual?"

"OK, that's enough!" Stafford broke in. "Senator, you've been asking personal questions more appropriately reserved for tomorrow's closed session."

"I'm sorry, Senator Stafford. Really, I am. Just one more thing." Scott looked directly at Gloria again. "Judge Hernandez, should you win confirmation to the Supreme

Court and the question of homosexual sodomy comes before it again, would you disqualify yourself from the case?"

Gloria kept her face and voice impassive, as if she were presiding over a trial. "I would treat the case like any other brought to the Court for consideration. I would make a judgment about recusal based on the facts of the specific matter at hand."

"But, Judge, I've just given you specific—"

"Time!" Norah applied her gavel twice. "Senator Scott your time is up."

The Vermont senator began to protest, then apparently thought better of it. The Chairwoman of the Senate Judiciary Committee leaned back in her chair. "Thank you, Judge Hernandez, for being an excellent and understanding participant in this long hearing. And despite our occasional differences, my thanks to the committee." She gestured left and right without looking, then took a sheet of paper proffered from an aide.

"Just a little housekeeping before we finish. We'll meet in closed session tomorrow morning at 9:00 AM in our usual hearing room next to my office, so we can address any personal questions any of you might have for the judge. I've booked three hours but of course, we don't have to use it all. We'll recess for lunch about noon, then return to this chamber around 1:00 for the last public session. Any individuals or representatives of public-interest groups who wish to testify for or against the nominee's confirmation may do so at that time. Judge Hernandez, of course, will not be present."

Norah looked up and down the table. "I'll be there, and I urge all of you on the committee to attend."

"I'm afraid I have another appointment tomorrow afternoon," Carl Albrecht stated.

"Your presence isn't mandatory, Senator, you know that. But I'm sure your constituents would appreciate your being here."

Cotton Blalock, who had been slumped back in his seat snoring quietly, wakened suddenly at the touch of one of his aides. "Eh? What?"

"Then again, maybe they wouldn't," Norah finished to general laughter. "Any questions? No? Good. Then we're adjourned." She banged her gavel.

"Well, you'll be on your own tomorrow, Judge," Hugh Graham said as he and Gloria stood up. "I'm confident you'll handle it well."

"Thanks, Hugh. I'm going to miss you." She took the hand he extended and turned automatically so the waiting photographers could capture the moment. The press continued shooting while first Norah, then a succession of the Republican senators came over to shake Gloria's hand and, simultaneously, pose for an expedient photo-op.

"Well, it's over," Rex St. Clair whispered, getting in a hug instead of a handshake. "Everything worked out fine in the end, just like I said it would, didn't it? And now we'll all ride off happily ever after into the sunset."

"Thanks for everything," she said simply, returning the squeeze. "I guess the worst is over."

"Absolutely. Fade scene, run credits." Rex waved his arm gallantly and sauntered out of the chamber, hand-in-hand with his wife. The photographers followed in their wake as if the two former beloved stars were a comet and the media its tail.

At length, Gloria stood alone. She let her eyes sweep the deserted hall.

Happily ever after, Rex? But what about the sequel tomorrow? And what about my leading man, who's still in danger of falling off his horse because of me? Not to mention my best supporting actor, living out there precariously in the city by the bay. She pushed the thoughts away. *I never was good at that movie jargon.* She picked up her briefcase and turned to face the panel table one last time. "Even if I fall on my face tomorrow," she said to the empty chairs, "I'll still be the first Hispanic woman to ever have gotten this far. Not a bad legacy for a skinny girl from Buenos Aires—no matter

what happens." She squared her shoulders, gave a final
judicial nod to the settling rays of dust, and strode briskly
out of the large, incredibly silent hearing room.

TWENTY-SIX

Thursday, May 25

Gloria took her chair at the small table in the oak-paneled room. All eighteen members of the judiciary committee had appeared, two hours earlier, for the private session. Here they could legitimately ask the nominee any questions they wished about the opinions she held, the attitudes she leaned toward, and the personal aspects of her life they thought they were entitled to know. Mostly, however, the elected officials filing back from their mid-morning break had spent the morning reiterating their thoughts and opinions, rather than soliciting hers.

Now, waiting with the others for three lagging senators to return from making phone calls and getting cups of coffee, she mouthed an inaudible, "Thanks" to Tennessee Republican, Campbell Townsend for the wink and thumbs up he sent her from the dais. *I wonder if he picked up that combination from Jon,* she thought.

She let her mind linger pensively on the image of a much younger Jonathan Morgan as he stood on the other side of Arturo and twisted his neck against the formal white tie required for the occasion. When he'd reached over to brush an invisible speck off the bridegroom's lapel, his eyes had caught hers, and he'd given her the same quick gesture: a wink and thumbs up. All these years later, she still felt the tinge of remorse she'd struggled with whenever she saw or even thought of the two men together. But she'd had no choice.

"Judge Hernandez, I want to thank you, once again, for your patience," Norah said, breaking Gloria's reflective trance. "I'd like to try to finish this whole thing by noon. Senator Sullivan, if you could keep it brief."

On the Democratic side of the dais, Sinead Sullivan leaned against the table with her chin on her hand. Microphones hadn't been necessary in this private chamber where no aides, clerks, press, or spectators were allowed. Each senator was allowed only one round of questions in the short session, and Senators Blalock, Hallstead, Popowski, Roberts, Fitzpatrick, and Townsend had already used up their time alternately attacking and defending the same issues they had raised in the public hearings.

Now, Sinead traced her finger along an old, smooth-edged score in the table. "Judge, we haven't seen eye to eye on a number of issues during these hearings, but the fact is, you and I have a lot in common. For one thing, we're just about the same age, aren't we? We've both been married; we're both alone now. You've got a grown son; I have custody of my fifteen- and seventeen-year-old sons. We've both had cause to be dragged over the coals by the tabloids—you for your son's escapades, me for my ex-husband's."

Gloria listened carefully and kept her eyes on the bent blonde head. She had no idea where the Oregon senator was going with this.

"We're both lawyers," Sinead continued. "We both came up during that time when, as women, we had to work much harder and be much better than our male counterparts, just to stay in the game—and even then, we made less money." Sinead's finger hovered momentarily over the cut in the highly polished oak, then returned to stroking. "Competition with our male associates has at times been intense and sometimes bitter. We had to put in more hours, win more cases, be more discreet in our personal lives. Didn't you find that to be true?"

Sinead raised her head slowly, lifting her eyes to look directly into Gloria's. Gloria did not trust her voice; she merely nodded.

"Given that antagonistic scenario," the senator went on in a slightly harsher tone, "and assuming *Roe v. Wade* were, as you say, 'settled law' back then in the 1960s when you and I were fledgling attorneys, let me ask you this hypothetical question: Suppose you had found yourself pregnant when you were still just at the beginning, still fighting for ground, still defining yourself; before you were married, when an out-of-wedlock pregnancy could destroy a career in the blink of an eye—as could a discovered abortion, for that matter, legal though it might have been. What would you have done? Hypothetically, I mean? Would you have pressured the father to marry you? Would you have taken the chance on losing all you'd built up so you could take a sabbatical, have the baby, and put it up for adoption? Or would you have arranged for a quiet abortion?"

Gloria met Sinead's gaze with a faint smile. "Did you have an abortion, Senator?"

Sinead leaned forward on her elbows. "No, Judge, I didn't," she said emphatically. "But that isn't the question. The question is would you have?"

Gloria leaned forward, too. "Frankly, Senator," she said, matching Sinead's tone, "I don't believe what I may or may not have done with my body at that or any other time is any of your business."

Sinead raised her eyebrows. "Goodness, Judge, it was only a hypothetical question."

"Goodness, Senator, my answer was not."

"All right, I believe that settles that," Norah interjected. She gestured wearily. "Senator Albrecht, next, please."

Carl Albrecht looked back and forth between the two women, who still held each other's gaze, and shuddered slightly. "I think I'll just leave that subject alone for now, OK? Judge, you've testified several times during these hearings that you're a good friend of Cardinal Ramon

Delgado, head of the Los Angeles Archdiocese, and that your contributions to the Catholic Church and its various charities amount to millions of dollars."

Gloria sat back in her chair and moved to look at the speaker. "That's right, Senator."

"You've further testified that President Morgan and Cardinal Delgado are acquainted and may be good friends."

"I've testified that I'm aware they know each other. I was not privy then, and am not now, as to whether or not they're friends, good, bad or indifferent."

"Surely, Judge Hernandez, given your long and intimate relationship with both men, you must know—"

"Oh, good grief, Carl!" Norah interrupted. "She doesn't know. I don't know all the friends of my friends, do you? What's your point, anyway? The president is Presbyterian, after all."

Carl chopped at the air. "And I'm a lifelong Lutheran. But some of my closest staff members are Catholics and good friends."

"Meaning?"

"Careful, Carl," Stanley Popowski put in between guffaws. "I've heard some of your top aides have a direct line to the Vatican."

"What's all the fuss 'bout anyway, Albrecht?" Cotton Blalock added. "You worried the Church is gonna pressure Morgan to pressure the Judge to sway Court decisions? Ain't that a pretty roundabout way of exerting influence? For God's sake, she's Catholic! I'm not gonna vote for her, but it isn't 'cause I think she's gonna call the Vatican every time she has to write an opinion. She's gotta buncha' clerks writin' for her anyhow, if she gets in."

Carl waved both his hands. "Look, I have legitimate concerns about this. Judge, isn't it true that Delgado was one of the first prominent citizens to call with his congratulations when your nomination hit the papers?"

Gloria nodded several times. "Yes, it certainly is true. And, in almost the same breath, he also congratulated me and my partner for winning the San Marino Doubles' Tennis Championship in the seniors' category. For the record," she added with a broad grin, "my partner was Saul Katz, a nice Jewish stockbroker with no direct ties to the Knesset."

Even Sinead and Christine joined in the laughter.

"All right, Norah," Carl conceded. "Go ahead, I'm finished, I know you're anxious to wrap this up for a lunch break, anyway."

"Not quite yet, Senator. We still have a couple more to go. Christine, I believe it's your turn."

"Thank you." Christine Fairchild ran the back of her index finger along her upper lip. She tilted her head to look at Gloria, out of the corner of her eyes. "Judge, I have only one question. And, again, it's rather personal, but I think it's something we've all been skirting around and I, for one, really would like to know."

"Yes, Senator?"

"Is there anything credible in the story running through the tabloids about a possible homosexual relationship between your son and the president's son, or that they might even—"

"Considering the source," Gloria interrupted flatly, "I have to wonder why you'd even ask. But since you did, I can tell you no, there's nothing to any of that nonsense. Eduardo and Michael have been friends since they were children. That's it. Period. Nothing else."

"Thank you."

The Maryland Democrat sat back. Up and down the table senators were looking restive and collecting their notes and belongings. Norah sighed loudly and pointedly. "Senator Duckworth, you're last, but, as always, not least. I suppose you still have more questions for the nominee?"

"Just a few, Senator." He returned the chairwoman's cold stare.

"Do you think you could make it brief? I think we've all pretty much found out what we need to know at this point."

"I'll do my best," Cornell drawled. "My stomach's kinda growlin'. You may have heard."

"So that's what that noise is," John muttered.

"I heard that, Senator." Cornell chuckled with the rest of his colleagues. Then he rested his hands on the table. "Judge, it's been documented in the press that your son and his *companion* live in Pacific Heights in a grand house with a spectacular view of San Francisco Bay. Says so in the *Washington Post* I got here." He held up the paper. "Reporter calls it an 'exclusive enclave.'" Cornell looked directly at Gloria, "Guess lots of social big shots live up in the Heights. Inn't that right?"

Gloria nodded.

"We've seen pictures of your son and his *companion* in the papers. Reputable papers, too, not that trashy stuff Christine was referrin' to. The *New York Times*. The *Washington Post*. The *Birmingham News*. Inn't that right, too?"

She shrugged. "I suppose so, Senator."

"Right. OK. Now here's a picture here right on the front page of the *New York Times* of your son and his *companion* taken on opening night of the San Francisco Symphony in Davies Hall, last autumn. Now, the photo wasn't taken 'cause of your son. It was taken to show off the conductor and his child-prodigy pianist. Only a twelve-year-old, and the kid goes to Julliard, see, that's the New York connection. And your boy and his, what they called 'business associate,' underwrote a major part of this San Francisco concert. Can you see this picture? Lemme bring it down to you."

He left the dais and brought the paper around the table to Gloria, who nodded. He returned to his seat.

"OK, so you agree it's a photograph of your son, and his uh, friend. Is, um, Ismoo Nar-Narit- er-a."

Kawai Higashi closed his eyes.

"Isamu Narita," Gloria filled in.

Kawai opened his eyes and bowed slightly. She lowered her eyes and smiled. Cornell continued. "Now,

Judge, you saw how the two young men in the paper look. They look pretty darn healthy in this picture, now, don't they?"

Gloria let a shade of exasperation edge into her voice. "Just what is your point, Senator?"

"Well, now, see, I'm a little confused. Here we got two young, healthy lookin' men, supposedly companions for life, supposedly only indulgin' in their perverted sexual habits in the privacy of their own home, where nobody can see them—so it's not against the law in California—supposedly everything just peachy-pie perfect between 'em." He sat up straight and his voice suddenly lost its folksy, down-home tone. "So why did they both get themselves tested for HIV last November, Judge? Huh? Why did these two theoretically healthy young men, who make up what you try to pawn off as a 'family,' get tested for the AIDS virus one month after this picture was taken?"

Lord in heaven. "Senator Duckworth—" Gloria began angrily, but Grant Hallstead threw up his arms and interrupted.

"For God's sake, Duckworth, enough of this bullshit!" he roared. "What the hell could her son's private life have to do with her ability to render justice on the Supreme Court?"

"Senator Hallstead, your naiveté doesn't surprise me," Cornell almost sneered. "But as a God-fearing Christian, I consider it my patriotic duty to expose the truth about this woman and her highhanded, un-American, godless ways. You don't know her type like I do. You came up from the poverty of Oakland's mean streets; you are enmeshed in the mistaken belief that everyone thinks and feels and acts with the same reverence for the Bible and the Christian faith and our blessed lord Jesus Christ, just as you do. Well, I'm here to tell you, Sir, that's just not so!" He slammed his fist on the table, his voice rising and taking on the cadence of a revival preacher. "Listen, one and all. Unlike our brother, Grant, I grew up with her type, I'm here to tell ya. I grew up in the governor's mansion in Montgomery,

Alabama, the son of the Camellia State's most beloved governor. In the very heart of Dixie, I grew up with the rich and the powerful, the likes of the Morgans and the Hernandezes, the St. Clairs, the Irving Brombergs, and the Ron Jordans." He paused to finger his forehead scar, his face reddened with passion. "Pharisees! Corruption! Unbridled sin! Yeah, yeah! They talk a good game, religion and all, promising school prayer with no intention of ever delivering. Yeah, they talk about virtue and character." Duckworth formed fists with his hands and clenched his teeth. "They talk religion, oh yes. But do they believe it? Do they live it? Do they walk the difficult path of the righteous? No. I tell you, No! This woman," he stood and pointed a trembling finger, "this woman funnels money to her Vatican master and her political playmates and thinks it'll save her brazen soul from damnation to the very fires of Hell!" He lowered the volume of his voice, staring down from the dais at Gloria. "But, Judge Hernandez, it's Satan who'll have the last laugh. Oh, yes. And the proof of the pudding is the very flesh of your loins, the evil pagan that come out of your womb drippin' with your own filthy blood!"

Seventeen popularly elected United States Senators sat totally speechless, their eyes fixated on the panting senator from Alabama. Christine had covered her mouth with both hands. Daisy leaned back, clutching at her chest. Derek Scott looked stunned; Kawai Higashi, confused; Yale Jacobs, haunted. Finally, Cotton Blalock broke the stillness. "Sakes alive, boy, how you do carry on. I honestly believe you've missed your callin'. You should be passin' the basket, not passin' the laws."

At the sound of Blalock's voice, Cornell seemed to come back to himself. He looked around quickly and sat down without another word. Norah raised her gavel and started to speak.

"Well, Senator Duckworth, I'm truly embarrassed for the—"

"Sorry, Senator Stafford," Grant interrupted again. "Senator Duckworth, I really have to thank you," he said slowly. "I do, Sir. I admit it. Up to the time of your psychotic outburst, I really didn't know how I'd vote on this confirmation for a whole lot of reasons. But thanks to you, Sir, my confusion has evaporated. Thanks to your repeated outbursts of outrageous bigotry, your complete oblivion to any measure of tolerance," his voice rose, "and your inappropriate religious fervor, I'm going to go on record right here and now." He slapped the table with his open hand. "Judge Hernandez, you have my vote. I support you one hundred percent."

Daisy led the scattered applause from the Republican side of the dais while several Democrats exchanged looks, nodded, or shrugged. Duckworth looked dazed. After a prolonged moment, Norah took a deep breath. "Ladies and gentlemen, I think we could all do with something to eat. Let me remind you that the next public session begins at 1:00 in the Central Hearing Room. I must emphasize once more that every question and answer heard this morning has to remain strictly confidential. This information cannot be shared with anyone. Particularly," she looked sharply at Cornell, "the media."

Norah glanced up and down the table. "Any further questions or comments? Good. Judge Hernandez, thank you once more for your perseverance with us. You are now excused from further testimony at these hearing proceedings. This secret session stands adjourned."

TWENTY-SEVEN

Friday, May 26

Anne sat at her usual place in the residence dining room. Even though Jon was often away at dinner time—and had been for years—she preferred to maintain their customary seating arrangement, the one they had so naturally fallen into when they were first married, the one Michael had grown up with. Jon's place, on her left at the head of the too-formal, too-big, curved table, was empty again tonight. Anne pushed her salad around the plate. The dressing was too sweet, the iceberg tasted slightly bitter and the thin tomato slice looked wilted. *It's always like this on Blake's night off*, she lamented to herself.

Across the table, still wearing the coat and tie he hadn't bothered to remove after his day in the office, Michael was carefully trying to scoop up the few remaining carrots and almonds without using his fingers. Finally, he pushed the plate away with a sigh. "So, Mother," he said, dabbing his lips with a napkin, "what kind of a Friday did the first lady have?"

She shot him a disdainful look. "Your grandfather was feeling better today, thanks for asking. Did you call him?"

Michael flinched. "Oh, jeez, I'm sorry, Mom, I forgot again. Hey, I know." He checked his watch. "I'll go see him tonight. What time are visiting hours over at George Washington?"

"Half an hour ago. Really, Michael, he's the only grandfather you've got left. You could show a little more consideration."

"I know. Look, I'll go see Gram. She's probably back at the hotel by now. Right after we're through here. Don't fret, Mom. Everything's going to be fine. Grandpa will get better. Everything's going to be in good shape with his ticker. Gosh, you worry too much."

When did he become so confident? "He's eighty-four years old," she countered. "If you'd seen him lying in bed in cardiac care, all those wires and blinking and beating monitors. He looked so weak and lost. Not at all the man-about-town you've known all your life."

"Oh, come on, Mom. Raymond J. Sinclair, Esquire—the smartest bond lawyer to ever stride down Wall Street—is strong as an ox. He'll pull through, just like the last time and the time before that. He's still got the old fire in his belly. Come on, lighten up. You worry too much. It's gonna be all right."

Anne smiled in spite of herself at Michael's wink and thumbs up gesture. Just like his father, she admitted to herself once again. *Don't worry, don't worry. Of course they don't worry. That's all anyone ever says to me anymore. Except Dante.* She wandered off into another world while Foster exchanged the salad plates for dinner platters and placed Lebanese roasted lamb, rice, tabuli sauce, hummus, and pita bread between them.

"Has Dad heard about the leak yet?"

"What?"

"The leak. You know, about Eddie and Isamu getting tested for AIDS? From Aunt Glory's 'private' hearing? Do you think Dad has heard about it by now?"

"Oh. Well, I'm sure he has." Anne gingerly tasted a sliver of lamb. Her face brightened and she helped herself to a small serving of everything. Michael had already piled his plate high and was shoveling in the food.

"I'll bet Bob had a fit."

"Please don't talk with your mouth full," Anne corrected automatically. "Actually, your father called me en route to someplace, I don't remember where."

"Probably San Diego. For a speech at some wireless technologies' conference. They were flying down there from Seattle after he hit up some of his old software cronies for a little, fall-campaign cash."

She shrugged. "Whatever. He said Bob had already taken care of it. He'd had Tony get Eduardo on CBS for a brief interview. You know the kind, totally orchestrated—'one statement-three questions' sort of thing."

"Yeah, I follow. Eddie did a good job. I didn't know Bob was behind it."

"Well, I guess it was the most pro-active response Bob could think of on the spot."

Mike laughed. "Yeah, you can't get much more pro-active than network news. Did you see it?"

She narrowed her eyes and shook her head. "I was at the hospital, remember?"

"Oh, yeah. Anyhow, Eddie told the CBS guy their tests were fine. Just got 'em for some kind of life-insurance physical. You know, the leak came out in last night's *Birmingham News*, right in Duckworth's backyard. What an idiot! Anyway, Eddie was real cool on TV, probably because they did it out there. He's edgy here in town, I don't know why."

"Well, I don't know why he wouldn't be, for heaven's sake. San Francisco is home for him. Washington is hostile territory. The very fact that someone would divulge such personal information from a secret meeting, in the first place, is certainly reason for him to not like it here. And he has to be careful. Medicine isn't enough of an answer to remedy his anxiety, you know. He needs to keep his stress down, too."

Mike looked sideways at his mother. "You called him, didn't you?"

She shrugged one shoulder. "I just wanted to make sure he was all right. You know how I worry, and I couldn't get through to Gloria."

Now it was Mike's turn to shake his head. "You know, sometimes I think you care more about him than about me."

"Oh, Michael, don't be absurd."

They ate in silence for a while. Foster cleared the plates and presented dessert—a warm, honey-drenched cake filled with soft cheese and surrounded by dollops of unsweetened whipped cream. Anne picked at her portion. Presently, she put her fork down. "Michael, there's something I need to ask you."

"Dad should be home around 1:30 or 2:00 tomorrow morning."

When did he start knowing so much more about his father's schedule than I? "No, that's not it. It's about all the rumors and innuendoes."

"Yeah, what does Dad call it? 'Junk journalism.' Forget it." He waved his hand in an exact impersonation of his father. "So what?"

"So . . . so, I've seen the photos. I've heard some of the gossip. I've even had friends . . . point some things out to me."

"And?"

"And Gloria's probably noticed it, too."

Michael put the last mouthful of ultra-rich confection in his mouth. "Noticed what?" He swallowed. "Sorry. Noticed what? Exactly what is it you're trying to ask, Mother dear?"

Anne steeled herself. "Michael, you and Eduardo have been friends all your life. You've played together, you've camped together, he's helped you study, you've helped him move a dozen times or more, you two drink together—which neither one of you should be doing, certainly not in public . . ."

Michael dropped his head into his hands. "Please, let's not go there again. There has to be a statute of limitations on the number of times somebody is required to say, 'I'm sorry.'"

"No, that's not it."

He shrugged and reached for her barely touched dessert. "Well, what is it then?"

"Have you . . . have you and Eduardo . . . well, have you two ever . . . uh . . ."

Michael dropped his fork, sat back, and stared at his mother. An amused grin leaped across his face. "You want to know if we've *slept* together! You think I'm *gay*? Bob Peterson's frantic half the time about how many illegitimate kids I've got running around, and you think I'm a flaming queen!"

"Oh, never mind. It was just a passing . . . oh, you don't have to be so devil-may-care. I said never mind."

"Mother," he said, still grinning, as he bent across the table to take her hand and peck her on the cheek, "I am not gay. Not homosexual. Seriously heterosexual. Completely committed to pro-choice, of course, but horny as all get-out for girls. I like women. OK?" He sat down again, pushed his chair back from the table, stretched his legs out, and folded his hands behind his head. "Oh, God, I can't believe it. My own mother thinks I'm queer. Me!"

Anne tucked her hands under her arms and looked around the room.

"And now you're blushing."

"I am not."

"OK." Michael's tone lost some of its frivolity. He sat up and propped his forearms on the table. "So now, Mom, I've got one for you."

Anne couldn't meet his eyes. They might still be laughing at her. "What?"

"I'm not gay. Eddie and I don't do it together. But I'm not gullible, either. So . . ."

She had to look up. His eyes were as serious as the new inflection in his voice. "So, what?"

"So, what's with Dad and Aunt Glory? Do you want to talk about it?"

"What?"

"Mom." Michael's voice grew hard. "I don't care that he's president. I don't care how long you've been married. I don't care that she's always been like a second mother to me. If those two are hurting you—"

"Oh, God! No. Michael, what happened between your father and Gloria happened years ago, long before you were born. Long before we got married. Before we even knew each other."

He cocked his head. "So there's nothing going on now? You're sure?"

She shook her head rapidly. "No, nothing. I'm positive. Of all your father's failings, that is not one. He does not . . . he's never . . . no." She shook her head again. "Put it out of your mind, sweetheart," she said, returning to the comfortable role of mother. "There is nothing wrong between your father and me."

"OK. Good. Well," he checked his watch, "I guess I ought to go see Grandma. What a shame he had to get sick. Down from New York for a nice visit, and Grandpa's heart acts up again."

"Yes. It hasn't been easy for her. But, you'd better call first. She might be asleep by now."

"At 9:30? Don't be absurd. That old jewel will be up playing solitaire 'til midnight. She'd love the company. I'll let her beat me at gin rummy for a few hours."

"Don't be disrespectful. And she's very good at gin rummy. I've never been able to beat her."

"Neither have I. That's why I always let her win."

Anne lifted her face for the kiss, then watched her "little boy" stride out of the room, adjusting his tie with one hand, dialing his cell phone with the thumb of his other. *When did he get so mature? He's the spitting image of his father.* Alone at the dining table, Anne let out a deep, audible sigh. "Oh, dear, that's the problem, now, isn't it?" she mused to the empty room. "He *is* the spitting image of his father. Why did Eduardo have to be, too?"

TWENTY-EIGHT

Saturday, May 27

"Miss Simpson? Hi, I'm Drew Gardner. I'll be doing the interview. I'm sure you're probably a little nervous. We'll make this as easy as possible. Did somebody ask if you wanted coffee? A cold drink?"

The slender woman stood up. She wore a skin-tight, black Lycra pantsuit with a scooped neck that highlighted her best-shaped, suspiciously store-bought feature. The ends of her long sleeves were slightly frayed, and one of the thongs on her black, high-heeled, open-toed sandals was held in place with electrical tape. She had a small black purse slung over her shoulder by its ragged strap, and used her free hand to push her thick, tawny blonde hair away from her face. "No, actually, I'm OK," she said. Only the iciness of her fingers as she shook Drew's hand betrayed her anxiety. "I've never been in a TV studio before. How does it work?"

The NBC anchorman gave her a fatherly smile and offered his arm. "Come this way. I'll show you around. This is what we call our bull room, and in here," they went through a set of double doors, "is where we'll do the interview."

Cameras on tall, wheeled platforms, hanging lights, cables of every size and color, wall-mounted televisions, and half dozen people were scattered around a small room. In the middle, two plastic swivel chairs separated by a low round table sat on an abbreviated circular rug. "Why don't you just have a seat?" Drew asked. "Somebody will be out in a minute to touch up your makeup and do one last double-check on your hair."

The woman started to sit, then jumped up again. "They won't be able to see my face, will they?"

"No, no, don't worry. Here, let me show you." Drew said something to one of the people milling around, who spoke quietly into a headset. "Just watch the monitor." He pointed.

One of the wall-mounted televisions flickered on. The woman saw herself sitting in the chair, her head replaced by a large, fuzzy black dot, her hand fluttering at her throat. She dropped it at her side. "OK, well. That's good. I wasn't really worried. I've just never done this before, you know."

"I know," Drew said absently, skimming a clipboard someone had just handed him. He looked up again and smiled. "Please relax, Rona. You'll be fine." He sat down. "When you see the red light on top of that camera," he pointed, she nodded, "you'll know we're recording. We're not live, so we'll be able to repeat and edit if you need to. In fact, if you want, we can even rehearse a little right now."

"Rehearse?"

"Just go over what you're going to say."

"Oh. Well. I'm not really sure what I should say. I mean, when I spoke to that woman on the phone, like, she said I should just tell the whole story."

Drew nodded. "That's right. The whole story, in your own words. You'll have about three minutes. Do you want to go over it now, so we can see how long the piece actually is? Don't worry," he added, seeing her alarmed face. "We can always edit it down if it runs long. Why don't you tell me what you have to say, and then we'll just kind of take it from there."

The woman settled herself into the chair. "Well, we were roommates in college for a whole year. At USC. I was

goin' for my BA in liberal arts with uh . . . astrology major,
but I never got the chance to finish up because—"
    "You and Judge Gloria Hernandez were roommates?"
    She nodded vigorously. "Yeah, only she wasn't a judge
then. She was just another sexy student like me. Can I say
'sexy'?"
    "Don't worry, we'll cut it out in the edit. Just go ahead
and talk."
    "OK." The woman paused, as if collecting her
thoughts. "Well, she got stuck with me as a roommate in
college, but we hit it off OK. And she was real generous
with her friends then. But it all changed, you know, when
she met Arty. See, after Gloria's a lawyer, and I find her
and tell her how bad off I am, she takes me into her place
in Hancock Park to help with the housekeeping. Real nice,
she was. Very big house, she coulda had a whole crew
living there, but no, she wouldn't let me bring nobody else.
Now, do you think that was fair?" she asked plaintively.
    Drew's face remained expressionless. "So what happened?"
    "Oh. Well, she was dating bofe of 'em. You know Jonny
Morgan and Arty Hernandez. 'Course, Jon was more of a
hunk, but Arty's got lots of money. His old man owned
about half of East L.A. I'd guess. But, see, Jonny's better
built and a real American. Anyhow, she off and married
Arty, but she was pretty hot and heavy with Jon, too. You
know, I really thought she was going to marry him, only I
don't think he asked her. That was the whole problem. Or
maybe it was 'cause he didn't have any money then. I
really don't know."
    "And?"
    "And, well, I saw 'em," she said triumphantly.
    The broad-shouldered, African-American commentator
waited a few seconds for her to go on. When she didn't, he
prompted, "You saw . . .?"
    "Glory and Jon, a 'course! I not only saw them, I heard
'em. You know, screwing. One night, when they'd left the
door open. They must of thought I was out with my
boyfriend or something, but I wasn't 'cause he was out

lookin' for a place since she wouldn't let him just move in
with me."

"And so?"

"And so I was standin' just outside her door. Well, I
mean, it was open, I didn't know what was goin' on but
then I heard all this noise, like the bed squeakin', you
know, so I just stopped and listened. I mean that's only
natural, right?"

She looked at Drew anxiously. He reached over to pat
her arm. "Of course it is. Anyone would have done the
same thing. What happened then?"

The woman seemed to relax at his smile. "Well, I couldn't
hear it all, see. I mean, I heard 'em kissin' and groanin', um,
you know. *You* know. And then after, they were just lying
there, I guess, talkin'. And I heard that."

"And you remember . . .?"

The woman got a faraway look in her eyes, as if she
were trying to see into the distant past. "And I remember
her laughing. 'You're a terrific screwer, Jonny,' she says.
'We oughta make you president.' Only she says it like she
could somehow make it happen, you know? And he's
laughin' too. And he goes like, um, like, 'Oh, sure, and
make you attorney general.' And she goes—and I
remember this ex-act-ly—'No, how 'bout Supreme Court
justice?'"

She leaned back and waved her arms. "Glory's always
had the luck, you know. She's got the money, she gets the
men. She thinks she's so smart. But I remember when she's
gonna marry Arty instead of Jon. He gets mad as hell,
comes over and they have a real loud argument. But then
Glory and Arty move to some big estate in San Simeon or
somethin' like that near Pasadena, and I stayed to take care
of the house. But she still wouldn't let me have my
boyfriend move in with me! It's not like she wasn't doing it
all over the place 'specially with Arty when he's hot. She
musta done it every room in the house, but nooo, I couldn't
have Sonny leave his stuff there. Oh no, that wouldn't be
proper. The little bitch. Fuckin' kicked me out for no good

reason. I didn't steal anything. And I don't know how come he had her stupid brooch and stuff when he was picked up, but he wasn't dealing, anyway, that was all a plant. I wouldn't put it past her to have done it herself." The woman wiped at the edges of her eyes. "She had no cause to do that to me. I was sooo loyal and put up with sooo much shit."

One of the men watching the discussion signaled to Drew. He nodded and gave the woman's arm another pat. "You had a tough time," he offered.

She nodded, rubbing the bottom of her nose with her forefinger. "It was that snooty Arty, that's who turned her against me," she sniffed. "Jon, he was OK. Always asked if I wanted to have some pizza when they ordered out." She suddenly stopped and craned her neck. When she spoke again, her voice had changed. "But none of that matters, not really. What matters is, she thinks she's so high and mighty now, sitting up there with all that money and her hoity-toity friends and all that stuff, but I know the truth. The truth is, she's no better than the rest of us. She's no better than me, that's for sure. OK, I couldn't marry my kid's father 'cause he was in jail, but I would have if I could. But, her, Miss Proper Perfect, what does she do? She goes and marries the rich guy 'cause he's got money and she doesn't even know if he's the father. He probably isn't. But she don't know. She don't even know which one of her johns is her kid's real father. I bet it wasn't Arty after all. I bet 'Miss High and Mighty gonna be a Supreme Court judge' got herself knocked up by the President of the United States, and now he's makin' up for it by puttin' her on our very top court."

TWENTY-NINE

Sunday, May 28

"Jon, it's in banners all over the country!"

Bob dropped a sheaf of newspapers on the president's desk. "*New York Times, Washington Post, L.A. Times, Chicago Tribune, Boston Globe, Miami Herald, Cleveland Plain Dealer.* Andy's got copies of a dozen more. Tony's people are out collecting from everywhere this morning. It's a disaster, an absolute disaster."

He plopped himself into the chair next to Jon's desk. "I don't even remember her, do you? God!" He jumped up and started pacing the Oval Office again. "Simpson, Sonny—it sounds like a bad TV script. Who the hell are these people, anyway? Where the hell did they dig them up?"

Jonathan Morgan read through the various headlines. From the *Chicago Tribune*. "'Morgan And Hernandez Caught In Lover's Tryst.' They neglected to mention it was over thirty years ago until the bottom of page twelve. The *Boston Globe* is a little more coy. 'President, Father To Judge's Son?' Well, at least they put a question mark on it. Oh, wait, I think this is my favorite." He waved the *Miami Herald*. 'Judge Gives President Son; President Gives Judge The Supreme Court.' Kind of long-winded for a headline, but it says it all, doesn't it?"

"How can you be so damn calm about this?"

Jon spread his arms. "What do you want me to do? Rant and rave and pace the floor? That's your job."

Bob stopped abruptly, looked at his friend sideways, and sank back down in his chair. "Very funny." He rubbed his hands. "OK, let's talk damage control. Do you know her?"

"Who? Rona Simpson?" Jon shrugged and shook his head once. "I have a vague recollection of a young woman who lived in Glory's house. Her name may have been Rona. But there was a cleaning lady, a laundress, and other helpers. Gloria never lacked household staff. For God's sake, Bob, it was a lifetime ago. Her name could just as easily have been Gertie or Marie."

Bob reached over for one of the papers. "According to this story, she's a divorcée who works in a Las Vegas casino, capacity unrevealed. She has one daughter—my guess, the one she had with her dope-dealing friend."

"*Alleged* dope-dealing friend."

"He was convicted, he's not alleged. Her kid lives in Maui, also in the, uh, *resort* trade."

"God, she really hates Glory." Jon leafed through the *Miami Herald* to find the continuation of the front-page story. "Listen to this: 'I just feel it's my patriotic duty to let people know they did it all the time.' Isn't it interesting how sex scandals bring out the closeted patriots? And she's so virtuous! 'How can you put somebody on the Supreme Court that's had an affair like that?' Another litmus test for judicial nominees, Bobby, my boy. Only celibates need apply. Aw, nuts." He tossed the paper onto his desk, "Anne always told me my sordid past would come back to haunt me. My fractured affair with Glory, and the fact that I cleaned the elephant yard and the gorilla pen at the Santa Barbara Zoo for a summer in high school. How's that for getting low?"

"Not funny." Bob got up to pace again and rubbed the back of his head as if trying to ease the pain. "I don't think the problem is your sex life, Jon. Then or now. I think the problem is the result."

"*Alleged* result, you mean. Possible result. Could be-could be not result."

Bob halted in front of the desk and stared at his boss. "Are you telling me you don't know?"

"I don't know what?"

"If Eduardo is your son or not."

Jon stared back at his friend. "I never really thought about it, to be honest. Why would I? The girl married the other guy. I didn't know she was pregnant at the time. I just naturally assumed they decided to have a baby right away. We did, remember? Almost as soon as Anne and I got married, we got her pregnant. Laura Anne, three pounds, one ounce, born at seven months. Died fourteen hours later."

Bob closed his eyes. "I'm sorry. You're right; I forgot. Bev and I pretty much did the same thing." He raised his hands. "It was what you did back then."

"Right. So why would I think Eddie was mine? It seems to me I had a lot of Trojan stock at the time, anyway. At least, I bought enough of 'em to feel like I was supporting the company."

Bob's lopsided grin finally appeared. "Yeah, me too." He perched on the edge of the desk. "So, how's Anne taking all this?" he asked after a moment.

"Very well, all things considered. She did ask if Glory and I did drugs back then."

"And you said?"

"I took the Fifth. She didn't really want to know, anyway. As far as the affair is concerned, hell, Anne's known about that since almost right after we started dating in San Francisco. Remember, she was a curator then at the Museum of Modern Art?"

"Oh, yeah, that's right." He cocked his head. "Does she know you proposed?"

"Sure she knows. And she knows the girl said yes, and then had to say no."

"I remember now. It was because of the money."

"No, no, you're thinking of Stan and Louise. With Glory, it was her father."

"Ah, yeah, that's right." Bob finally came to rest in his habitual place to the right of the leader of the free world. "Her father and the Church. You wouldn't convert."

"Believe me, I would have offered. But the Diazes were Latin American aristocrats and I was below their station in every way. Arturo not only came from an extremely wealthy family, but he was a better ethnic match. I had potential; he had position. No contest in the eyes of Señor Juan. I guess things turn out for the best in the long run, because if it hadn't been for Juan Luis Diaz, I wouldn't have my Annie now."

The two friends sat quietly, each lost in his own past. At length, Bob stirred. "Did Michael say anything?"

Jon groaned. "My son, the vigilante. We had another scene this morning, of course. What did you expect? He read me his version of the riot act, all mixed up with my hurting his mother and how could I invite Gloria to the White House with Anne in New York. Sounded like he was aching to write this mess up for the *Galactic Scribbler*."

"What?"

"And then he does a 180 and says he'd kill me before he'd let me make his mother into a laughing stock in front of the whole country."

"Oh, good grief!"

"Funny, that's just what I said. Fortunately Anne was there and we got the whole thing ironed out. I've never given her any cause, and she doesn't think twice about it. Of course, now the boy figures he has a club to hold over his old man's head. And, naturally, he had to call Eddie right away, who apparently had just gotten back from some dinner and was full of his own take on the thing. I guess his lover's parents are visiting from Japan to try and reel in their own wayward son, which makes Eddie very nervous." He slapped his forehead with his right palm. "Remind me again, what made us have these kids?"

"They went over it in biology. You slept through the class, remember?"

"Yeah. Well, anyway, it seems the friend's father had already heard the news and was terribly impressed that his boy's paramour might be the son of a U.S. president. A great honor, or some such thing. He told Eddie to get married right away and start making babies. I believe Mike said Eddie nearly aspirated his lobster bisque. Sprayed it on the wall."

The two old friends laughed at the image.

"The father got red in the face and Eddie told him another bottle of champagne would serve as an apology. Then Eddie quickly changed the dinner topic to Japanese temple art."

"That sounds like our boy Eddie," Bob chuckled. "I suppose we can be glad he's—" He spread his hands and shrugged. "What else can I say?" He hesitated. "Have you talked to Glory?"

"Sure, I had to. Hell, she's still my friend. And my nominee." Suddenly, he slapped his open hand on the desk. "Damn it, Bob, this is all crap and you know it. And she got so upset; she asked if I wanted her to withdraw. Like I'd walk away from her now, after all this. For God's sake, the judiciary committee sent a recommendation to the full Senate to approve her ten to eight only two days ago. Would have been eleven to seven if Carl hadn't been so stubborn."

"Yeah, but we figured he couldn't support her. So what did you say to her?"

The president's anger evaporated as quickly as it had come. "I told her no." He drooped in his chair. "Look, we've come this far. It's not over until the roll call ends, and I talked to Forrest; he still thinks we can pull it out of the fire. I mean, she can always go back to the Ninth Circuit if she loses. We both agreed on that. But the Court needs a new justice, and I don't care what Rona Simple or Sample—or whoever she is—says, or who else comes crawling out of the woodwork, for that matter. I still say she's the best one for the job. She's got the knowledge, she's got the experience, she's got the—"

"Whoa! Take it easy, Mr. President. I'm not telling you to pull her nomination."

"Sorry."

"What about it, though?" Bob asked after another lengthy pause. "Suppose you are Eddie's father."

"I'm not."

"But suppose you are."

"Well, then, hell, he can stop calling me Uncle Jon and start calling me Daddy. Why not? It would probably make Michael the happiest camper on earth. They've always been like brothers, anyway. I avoided changing his diapers just as much as I avoided Mike's. Aw, hell, he's a grown man. He's got his own assets, a thriving business, and enough money from his mother to last a dozen lifetimes. It's a little late for a paternity suit, don't you think? What difference could it possibly make at this point?"

Bob considered that. "So she's staying in the game?"

"Damn right she is."

"And you're going to continue to support her."

"Absolutely. All the way."

"And you want Tony to tell the press . . .?"

Jon laced his fingers and pursed his lips. He tapped his thumbs against each other. Finally, he looked up. "Have Tony say that we're disappointed in the media for wasting so much space on such a lame story from such a dubious source. That we're not going to dignify the accusations of this obviously hostile and vindictive creature—no, better make it 'individual'—with any statement other than what we've already said: Gloria Hernandez and I have been good friends ever since we went to law school together, and that because of the advantage I've had to closely follow the progress of her career, I now believe her to be the best person to replace the late Associate Justice Marianne McBride. And have him reiterate that I am one hundred percent behind the nominee, and that I fully believe she will be confirmed in the roll-call vote of the full United States Senate. And we have nothing else to say."

"Yes, Sir, Mr. President."

SECTION III

THE VOTE

THIRTY

Sunday evening

The Morgans had furnished the living room of their private quarters in the White House with an eclectic combination of American, Asian, and European antiques. Some of the pieces had been shipped from their Montecito home; others belonged to the presidential residence. A huge, colorful Persian rug covered most of the glistening hardwood floor in the softly lighted room where Anne and Jonathan were relaxing after Sunday dinner. Their White House servants had departed and the president, as usual, had kicked off his shoes and plunked his feet up on a footstool.

"A second date with the same girl in one week? Hmmm," Jon was saying. "Where'd he take her?"

"Oh, dinner at 1789. Seems Kim lives only two blocks from the Georgetown campus, so they could just walk over to the restaurant, I guess."

"I see." He looked at the ceiling. "So now it's 'Kim'. Last week it was Congresswoman Lawrence."

"They hadn't dated last week." Anne settled onto the couch next to her husband. "Life today is more . . . casual."

"Casual. Right. With six Secret Service agents hovering at all times."

"There are ways to get around the Secret Service. Besides," she added quickly, "Kim can handle it. I watched her on C-SPAN the other day. Charming, bright, poised."

"Is that why she's dating Mike? Because opposites attract?"

"Jonathan!"

The president tugged on his wife's shoulder. After his meeting with Bob, he'd spent the rest of the day reassuring both the key Republican and a few Democratic senators—as well as three or four carefully selected media analysts—that no, there was nothing going on between him and Judge Gloria Hernandez. Yes, he and the judge had had a brief affair back in their salad days. No, he'd never had reason to think he was her son's father, and he certainly didn't have one now. He'd never even looked at another woman since he'd married his beautiful and talented wife some twenty-nine years earlier and nothing, surely not the vitriolic sputterings of an obviously embittered woman, could disturb the most faithful and satisfying relationship he shared with her. He'd nominated Gloria Hernandez because of her background and abilities, not because of any illusory old debt or sense of guilt. Why, the whole thing was just the media running amuck as, unfortunately, was no longer unusual.

Morgan's personal spin had been all the comfort most of his supporters had needed, and his willingness to do his own stumping—along with his unguarded admission of the previous relationship—had won over all but one or two of the rest. He'd learned a long time ago that most people were more than willing to excuse a minor flaw, if only one would readily own up to it. Now, after expending so much energy and telephonic explaining, he slipped his arm around his wife's waist and tried to edge her back against him. "What's the matter?"

"Nothing." Anne flexed her shoulders a bit. "You know, Dad's doing better. I've decided to go to Connecticut, after all."

"Umm." Anne had settled uneasily into his embrace and was fidgeting as he tried to nuzzle her neck. "Connecticut, huh?"

"Yes, this Tuesday. It's only a day trip. Muffy Cheever and I are flying up early to Hartford for the opening of the Georgia O'Keeffe exhibition at the Wadsworth Athenaeum. I'm supposed to give a talk on the artist, her New Mexican milieu, and her legacy. Muffy says it's been sold out for weeks."

"Tuesday. Connecticut. Fine. That's good." Jon ran his fingertips across the soft spot on Anne's throat. She let out a soft sigh and leaned her head back on his shoulder.

"Did you know I'm the most-admired woman in a poll of Connecticut's GOP women?" She grinned. "Norah Stafford is number two. You know the group: They get out the voters, drive people to the polls and such."

"Um hum."

"And, oh . . ."

Jon stopped kissing her ear. "Oh, what?"

"Uh, I wanted to tell you. Muffy says Louis isn't sure he's going to vote for Gloria. She says he wanted oh, um, he wanted . . . Rittenhouse."

"Yes, I know. I talked to him earlier today." The president tilted his wife's face toward him, peered into her dark brown eyes, and kissed her adoringly. She made a small noise and pushed him away.

"What's wrong?"

Anne sat up, her back to her husband. "Jon," she started, then stopped. She took a deep breath. "Jon, do you suppose Norah and I could campaign for Louis this fall? We'd need transportation, support staff . . ."

"Sure, whatever you want. Is that what's bothering you?"

"Well, I was thinking *quid pro quo*," she rushed on. "You know, we campaign for him, he votes for Gloria."

Jon blinked a few times. "OK. I'm sure Lou'd love your support. So?"

"So, I've got a lot of faith in Louis Cheever. And Muffy is a dear. Such a comfortable person. Like a breath of fresh air in Washington. I really enjoy her company."

"Anne, what's this all about?"

The president's wife leaned back against his chest, but kept her eyes focused on the Marin oil across the room. "It's just that, well, she and I have been talking about maybe taking a little trip together. You know, after Gloria's roll-call vote, but before we go to L.A. for the convention in July. Just Muffy and me."

"OK."

"You know how it always is; you're so busy, and Louis is co-chair of the platform committee, and there's hardly ever any time for us to be together or have any time off or anything . . ." After coming out in a gush, her words seemed to trail off. Jon neither noticed nor cared.

"I think it's a wonderful idea," he agreed, easing her back into kissing position. "You two have so much in common. Maybe you could go to Paris or London, even Switzerland."

"Or maybe even Italy," she said from somewhere in the crook of his neck. "Muffy has . . . um, ummm . . . uh, a Vassar classmate with a . . . um . . . villa above Florence."

"Umm huh." Her resistance had evaporated. Jon slid his wife into a more comfortable position, and they fell into a familiar, breathless clinch. "Italy's nice," was the last thing he whispered in her ear before words became superfluous.

THIRTY-ONE

Monday, May 29

"Mr. President, you have no choice."

Ben Carothers and Ron Jordan sat facing the president on the winged-back sofas of the Oval Office. In spite of their secretaries having buzzed repeatedly to remind them of imminent appointments, none was willing to give up the argument before persuading the others to give in. Now Jonathan Morgan shook his head for the fifth time.

"I'm not going to do it. Why should I? Who cares? Arturo is dead, Eddie is grown up, even Mike doesn't really give a flying fig, and Anne just wants it to go away. Why stir up a hornet's nest if we don't have to?"

"But, Sir," Ben pointed out yet again, "the nest has already been trampled on the ground, and the damn insects are flying all over the place—mostly in our faces." As an old friend and advisor, he hoped his pointed formality would somehow sway his increasingly stubborn and formidable client. It had worked often in the past. It simply wasn't working today.

"No." The president rose to indicate the discussion was over.

Not to be outdone, Ben stood up as well, and looked Jon dead in the eyes.

Ron stayed seated and rubbed his eyes tiredly. "Jon, we've got to control this," the attorney general said. "No lies. No cover up. You can't make a personal phone call to every voter in the country as you did to those key senators."

"That's right," Ben cut in. "We need to get this out in the open and prove your innocence, once and for all. I needn't remind you that perception means everything in politics. Don't be deluded by the Inner Beltway's prevailing arrogance. The working woman, alone in the voting booth in Des Moines this fall, couldn't care less if a pundit such as Alfred North-Youngblood regards presidential peccadilloes as mere fodder for the Georgetown cocktail hour."

"Aw, screw North-Youngblood. As for my innocence, of what am I guilty? This is a person we're talking about, not a crime."

Ben pointed at Jon. "You've got to quash the media circus we've got going here. The Simpson woman threw a thunderbolt; now you've got to provide the rain to wash away the effects. I've talked to some paternity experts. DNA profiling is simple, essentially painless, and as accurate as anyone could ask for. If you'll just give a small sample of blood, I'll put a rush on it. We can have the results in a few days and end this, once and for all."

"No."

"Judge Hernandez and her son have already agreed," Ron said quietly.

"Who told you to ask them, in the first place?" Jonathan sat down again with an exasperated sigh. "Good grief, fellas, you can't just go around poking into people's lives like this, all these years later. How do you think Arturo's family will feel if it should turn out he's not Eddie's father? How do you think Eddie will feel? He's already got enough problems as it is. And by the way, let's not forget Gloria's emotional well-being. Do you have any idea what it's like to bring up a gifted, anxiety-ridden child like he was? And now you want to put them through all this? You realize, of course, that the fallout of this stuff will affect Annie too. And for what? It's nobody's business to begin with."

"Well, if it doesn't matter to you, Jon, think of the party. Think of the election coming up." Ben had sat down next to the president and tried to change his manner from that of an advisor to one of a cohort. "We've got an awful lot of loyal Republicans who'll take the brunt of this mess if you let it drag into the fall. We've got to nip this thing in the bud."

Jonathan's whole body suddenly drooped. "If I say yes, will you finally stop with the tired clichés?"

"My lips are sealed, Sir."

The intercom buzzed again. The most powerful man in the world groaned once more. At length, he waved his hand. "OK, set it up." He stood, straightened his tie, and buttoned the suit coat he'd left open during the debate. "Now, believe it or not, I have more important things to worry about than the paternity of a thirty-year-old independent, and I might add, highly, self-sufficient man. Just let me know when you want me to bleed into the tube."

"Don't fret about it, Jon, I'll have it arranged in the blink of an eye. That is . . . I mean . . . I'll phone the lab immediately."

"OK. Now get out of here. Both of you. Claire, what's next?"

The president's personal aide fell into step with him as he headed out of the Oval Office. "Sir, your cabinet has been waiting in the conference room since 9:30. Almost an hour."

THIRTY-TWO

Tuesday, May 30

Andy Grunwald was erasing "7" from the marker board and replacing it with a "6" when Tony Avalos appeared at his door. "Are you sure that's right?" the youthful press secretary asked, pointing.

Andy gave Tony a baleful look. "We just got Irwin, democrat from Florida," he said, with obvious forbearance. "He caved to the Cuban-Americans. I may be getting older, but I think I still know how to count."

Tony shrugged. "I wasn't questioning your competence, Andy. You know me better than that. I was just wondering if you'd included Underwood. We got an announcement from his Albuquerque office this morning. I guess he was in a bind with his Republican counterpart beating the drums for her confirmation to all those New Mexican Hispanics. He didn't want to look like an ass if she got in without his vote."

"We counted Underwood. And Vaughan."

"Who?"

"Democrat from Texas."

"Oh, yeah. I knew about him, he's up for reelection. If he wants another term, he's got to play to his own Hispanic constituency. Did you see the pictures in the *Washington Times* yesterday? All his Texas field offices got picketed. When Dan talked to him this morning, he said his Washington office had been inundated with calls, faxes, e-mail, the whole works. The Latinos are out in force behind our nominee. It's kind of nice for a change."

Grunwald had been listening with only half an ear from behind his desk, but now he looked up. "What's nice? To have your people on our side?"

"To have something in Washington we can get behind besides welfare and immigration reform." Tony watched the older man nod absently and go back to riffling through a vast data printout. "Guess I ought to let you get back to work."

He stopped at the door. "Uh, what about Martindale? The boss said he called this morning. I guess the president tried to reason with him all last week, but Martindale put him off until after a fishing trip. I heard something about the VP accidentally running across him at some lake in Idaho over the weekend, but it's only a rumor. Anyway, he's in. Did you count him?"

"The count is accurate," Andy assured him without looking up. "You boys have three-and-a-half days to tie it up."

"And nights," Tony said, wagging his index finger even though he knew Andy wasn't looking. "Don't forget the nights."

Grunwald did not straighten up, but he lifted his eyes to scrutinize the young man standing in the doorway. "Time for the president to call in some favors," he stated with precision. "And maybe pass out a few more."

Tony scanned his mentor's face fondly for a moment, then nodded. "I'll pass the thought along."

"I mean, it's up to you, Josh." Vice President Kyle Lambert and Senator Joshua Bowden were relaxing in the bar of the Congressional Country Club after eighteen holes. The vice president was buying, since he'd somehow managed to lose on a course he'd been playing skillfully since arriving in the capital. "The machinery is all set up, just waiting for us to flip the switch. I know which of those seven bills you're voting on this week are going to go through, and which ones the president will sign; we can attach the new O.U. football stadium rider to any one of them, and you'll get a bonanza of votes."

The Oklahoma Republican swirled an ice cube around in his drink with his index finger. "I appreciate the offer, Kyle. And, by the way, I'm not so sure I appreciate your throwing the game today—"

"Would I do that?"

"—but I'm going to take your money anyway. Serves you right. However, as far as the bill is concerned, well . . "

"Thousands of votes, damn-near guaranteed. Isn't that what your office said the other day?"

Josh stared at his drink before taking a man-sized gulp. He put the glass down. "The problem is, I know I'm on the hit list. If I don't come through with at least one of the things I've promised those folks, they're going to organize to get me out. The nice part is, if I do deliver, they'll work just as hard to keep me in. And I sure could use some of that campaign money you've got sewn up." He shook his head and wrinkled his nose. "But there's something about your judge that stinks. I mean, really, Kyle. All that stuff about them screwing and giggling on a sultry August night. Shit. Sounds like a bad Tennessee Williams' production, and he's not real big in Oklahoma City. Too damn decadent. If they'd at least have been engaged or something."

"That was over thirty years ago, buddy." Kyle caught the bartender's eye and pointed to both their empty glasses as he talked. "You telling me you went to Sandra's bed a virgin?"

Josh had the grace to laugh. "Sure, just like you did on your wedding night." His voice grew serious. "But I'm not trying to put one of my old squeezes on the fuckin' Supreme Court."

"And neither is the president. What he's trying to do is put one of the most respected and qualified jurists in the country on the Court. Esteemed, damn brilliant, articulate, dispassionate."

"Yeah, yeah, yeah. We all know she's all that. But she's also a stubborn, hard-to-read woman."

"Just like a bunch of your constituents, who admire a woman with guts. And you know women, pal. They stick together."

Josh sucked his teeth, grimaced, and finished his refreshed drink in one large swallow. "Yeah, there is that," he admitted. He let out a long breath. "I'll think on it, Kyle. I'll think on it real hard."

Forrest sat in his favorite, fraying, overstuffed chair amid his cherished, familiar things in his still-alien, cramped apartment in the Watergate Complex. He had thought it would help to move out of the Arlington house that he and his family had lived in all those years, but it hadn't. Everywhere he looked, something reminded him of the wife he adored, whom he'd lost to ovarian cancer only a year and a half ago, and the son he'd fawned on, who had found a way to escape from his own pain just five short months ago.

By 7:00 PM, the senate majority leader had fortified himself with two double scotches and reconciled himself to going on with the task at hand. Politics doesn't stop for personal tragedy, and he still had to bring in the votes for Judge Gloria Hernandez's confirmation to the Supreme Court. Forrest Garrison was a veteran of more senate contests, filibusters, and "tremendously important" roll-call votes than he cared to count. He knew what was expected from his party, and from this relatively young president he'd helped put into the White House. He steeled himself, picked up the phone, and punched in Nancy Osborne's number.

If it weren't for her strong feminist leanings, Forrest wouldn't even have bothered making a call to the liberal

Michigan Democrat. She had already blustered on the Senate floor about the audacity of Morgan's nominating an old, very rich ally to the Supreme Court. She then rushed on to assail the Republicans for a litany of past sins. Nancy finally concluded her verbal assault by condemning the GOP senators for their "vindictively engineered annihilation" five years earlier of Everett Winslow's reputation during that jurist's candidacy for the Supreme Court. Forrest couldn't even argue with her on the matter. He, too, had felt Winslow deserved far better treatment, and would have made a perfectly adequate associate justice. But his party had said no, and Forrest was, if nothing else, a faithful, party man. *At least Timmy Butler didn't screw his appointees first*, he thought now. Then he dismissed the thought, because a voice had responded on the other end of the line.

"Hello?"

"Hello, Senator Osborne. Forrest Garrison here."

"Oh, hi Forrest. What's up?"

"Well, I figured I'd still find you at your desk at this hour. Don't you ever go home?"

In her office on the third floor of the Dirksen Senate Office Building, Nancy laughed. "I do, but not yet tonight, I'm afraid. I just had an aide walk out in a huff yesterday morning, and my personal secretary decided to go into labor about two hours ago. I'm having a hell of a time sorting out the stuff I need to cram into my briefcase."

"The nerve of her. Doesn't she know U.S. Senate staff isn't allowed a personal life?"

"I told her, but I guess she didn't hear me. The baby isn't on the payroll yet. What can I do for you? And please, don't ask me to vote for Judge Hernandez."

"I'm calling to ask you to vote for Judge Hernandez. I think she's a brilliant jurist, an honest and forthright woman, and a voice of reason. Just what the Court needs. She'll be a seasoned moderate, maybe the new leader of the critical center of the Supreme Court."

Nancy Louise Osborne grunted. "Oh, please, Senator Garrison, I beg to differ. Another woman on that male bastion is a great idea, but not this woman. Not this woman, nominated by this man. This nomination, Sir, is an affront to all women."

Garrison refilled his glass, balancing the phone with his shoulder, as his colleague stormed on into his ear, her initial friendliness and informality gone and forgotten.

"—used her for fun and games and now wants to atone for his brutish sexism? Men are all after only one thing, Forrest. Peasants or prime ministers, doesn't matter. How can I trust this man? How can I trust any man? How can you guarantee me their sordid affair isn't still going on? How can you say with any certainty that he didn't father her child, and isn't now trying to pay her back or cover his guilt?

"Nancy," Forrest gulped half the glass, gaining fortitude with the soothing liquid, "Nancy, let's be real. This nation was founded by a bunch of guys who never let a swinging hip go by without taking notice, and it's been the same ever since. At least 'this man,' as you call him, did his playing around before he got married—and so did she. It was the 60s, remember? The sexual revolution, and I can't think of half a handful that didn't take part in the insurrection." He leaned forward in his chair as if she were in the room with him and let the harshness of the liquor edge into his voice. He hadn't risen to his current position by being a choirboy. "Here's how it's going to play out," he warned. "If you and I fail to confirm Judge Hernandez, we'll have another male on the Supreme Court faster than you can say Ypsilanti, Washtenaw County, Michigan. And," he pushed on before she could interrupt, "you're gonna have to come up with a damn sight better reason for a good fifty-one percent of your constituents back in Detroit, Flint, and Lansing, than a short-lived romance between two consenting adults half a lifetime ago, back when most of our voting public was doing exactly the same thing. I mean, it's not like they were dropping acid or shooting heroin or plotting to overthrow the government."

"Oh, I know I'll have hell to pay with hundreds of my sisters in Ann Arbor when I cast my 'No' vote Friday," Nancy shot back, her own voice getting hard and gutsy, "but, I guarantee you, Gloria Hernandez and her old flame don't have a whole lotta fans in those cities you just named. You're forgetting: It's not just that she did the deed, but that she claims to be a practicing Catholic, then and now. Just where do her morals lie, Senator? I ask you that. No, Sir, I'll take my chances with the voters. At least they always let me know where I stand."

Forrest loosened his grasp on the phone, rubbed a thumb along the rim of his empty glass, and sat back in his chair with an insouciant smile. "Well, Nancy, you've certainly made your position crystal clear. I won't be counting on your support, Friday. Of course," he added casually, "you probably won't be able to count on mine for the Edwards' bill, either, if and when I ever let it come to the floor for a vote."

A sustained silence followed. At length, he heard a quiet laugh. "Well, if that's the way it is, Forrest, then I guess that's the way it is. I suppose I should have known that bill would go down in flames if the confirmation went the wrong way for you."

"I guess that's the way it is, Senator."

"I can't change your mind? Like maybe on the merits of the bill?"

"Can I change your mind on the merits of the nominee?"

"She has no merits that I can see."

"Well, then, I guess there's nothing left to say but to say good night."

"Good night, Senator Garrison."

"Good night, Senator Osborne."

THIRTY-THREE

Wednesday, May 31

"Mr. President, Chancellor Vasquez on line three."

"Maria! How are you?"

"Just fine, Jon. Busy, but very happy. And you and Anne?"

"Same old, same old—just great. 'Course that could change since the weather is starting to get hotter and muggier here in D.C."

"Well, we're almost into June gloom out here. You know, we won't get the real heat for another month."

"Yes, I remember. I've been away from California for only a few years, you know. And I'm back on a regular basis."

In her book-lined Westwood office, UCLA Chancellor Maria Vasquez sat in front of the computer next to her phone and frowned comically at the screen. "And you never stop in to see me. I'd be hurt if you didn't keep coming up with all those ridiculous excuses, like international crises and national disasters and nonsense like that. But," she relented, "you didn't call to discuss the weather or my feelings of neglect, did you?"

Jonathan Morgan swiveled in his chair to look out the window behind the Oval Office desk. "Well, now that you mention it, no. You remember Gloria Hernandez, don't you?"

"Since we were two of only a handful of female faculty members, yes, we got to know each other well. Even if I hadn't known her, I would now. She's been on the front pages of the newspapers almost every day lately."

"Which is why I'm calling. The roll-call showdown on her Senate confirmation is on Friday, and we're still trying to pick up the last few votes. I was hoping you could help."

"Gladly, but I don't think my ballot counts in the U.S. Senate."

Jon grinned. "No, but it certainly does at UCLA. Look, Maria, I've got an idea to run by you. Remember the huge drug bust in South Central about six months ago? Violent shootout. Ten people killed just after midnight one Saturday. Does it ring a bell?"

"Sure. The biggest crack bust in the city's history. We saw the same thirty-second footage of one of the police officers being shot multiple times for over a week. What about it?"

"Well, one of the people that got killed, maybe even the one in the footage, was Jorge Garcia. A fine officer, LAPD detective. His son, Billy, lives in Ocean Park with his mom and fourteen-year-old brother. Billy's a senior at Santa Monica High; terrific grades, high SATs, well liked by teachers and his peers. He's been accepted at UC Berkeley, San Diego, and Davis. The L.A. Memorial Fund is picking up all his college expenses—everything."

"So, what's the problem?"

"He doesn't want to go to any of those schools. He wants to go to UCLA. Like his dad did. So he can follow in his late father's footsteps. So he can be a support to his grieving mother, and a solid, positive role model for his younger brother, Raúl."

"Oh, brother. Listen, Jon, you can stop selling, I get the idea. But how does my pulling strings to get him in here— if I do, and I'm not saying I just can, it's a lot more complicated than you think—how does that help Gloria?"

"Remember Rex St. Clair?"

"Of course. One of my all-time favorite actors and now, in his greatest role, Senator St. Clair has been one of UCLA's strongest allies."

"Well, he had lunch with fellow Senator Bryce Collins yesterday. Turns out Bryce is Billy's uncle on his mother's side. He's a Democrat from up in Tacoma, but he's not rigid about it. I have a gut feeling we could break the ice with him if we could get his nephew into UCLA."

"Hmmm. Hold a moment."

Jon watched two of the White House gardeners trim the shrubbery outside his window and wondered once again how they knew exactly which leaves to take off and which to leave on. The tap-tap-tap of Maria's computer keys echoed faintly over the phone line. While he waited Jon thought about the great job Maria had done in the face of many obstacles, being the first Hispanic chancellor in the UC system. Shortly, she came back on.

"OK, I got the process started. It'll take a little while. I'm going to have to make some phone calls and actually pull myself off this contoured chair and walk out of my office to consult with a few people, but hey, for you Jon, anything."

"Maria, I can't thank you enough."

"Oh, yes, you can. You can actually show up and give the keynote address at our fall convocation. You know, the one you promised to attend last year and missed."

"Look, it's already on my calendar," he assured her, making a hurried note to himself. "I've scheduled my entire weekend around it, and I've told Claire to make sure nothing, and I mean nothing, pushes it aside this time."

"Except maybe a nuclear war."

"Not even that."

"Dear Jon. You sound so sincere, I almost believe you. But I want you to try anyway, and I expect you and Anne to come to the party I'm throwing at my place afterward, too."

"Will there be a few loyal donors in the crowd?"

"*Sí, Señor*. About a hundred of our biggest."

"I'll tell you what, Maria. You get young Billy into school, and I'll dust off my best UCLA undergrad stories to regale your donors with."

Maria gave a low whistle. "Mr. President," she said, "you've got yourself a deal."

Chairman Yale Jacobs lingered in the empty hearing room, after all but one of the other members of the Senate Finance Committee had left for lunch.

Dottie "Babe" Horvath, Democrat from Wisconsin and small-town girl at heart, looked at him askance. "You can't be serious, Yale. Even if they ended up canonized, in the very distant future, as Saint Gloria and Saint Jonathan, there's still something fishy about her nomination. If we can believe any of Rona Simpson's story, it's either a payoff, the realization of a long-standing conspiracy, or an attempt to soothe the guy's conscience. I mean, why the hell didn't he choose some great Latina jurist he hasn't slept with? God, there oughta be at least two or three."

"Come on, Babe. The affair was so long ago, you were barely alive."

"Yale, please! Flattery at its worst. Keep talking."

"Why should we need to know or pass judgment on every detail of these political actors' lives?" he hurried on. "I sure wouldn't want my early indiscretions thrown in my face, would you? It's the performance on the job, not in the bedroom or anywhere else, that counts. Lord knows, some people probably think it's kind of fishy to have an elected official who rides motorcycles, wears leather to committee meetings, and spends her free time drinking beer and hanging around bowling alleys, but who's to say you're not every bit as good a senator as any of the rest of us?"

Horvath threw back her head and roared her horsy laugh. "OK, so maybe your sophisticated Manhattan neighbors consider me a hokey, old, Milwaukee broad. My constituents know I have their best interests at heart, else they wouldn't have reelected me so many times."

"Exactly. And it doesn't matter to any of them that the D.C. police get most of their discretionary funding out of the speeding tickets from that Harley collection of yours."

Babe walked Yale toward the chamber entrance and paused just inside the door. "I'll tell you what, buddy. You want my vote on Hernandez? I don't really have anything against the lady. Seems like she'd be fairly competent, if you want to know the truth. But if I'm going to buck my party, you're gonna have to kick back some. And since you've made it so personal, I do mean you." She poked him in the ribs.

"Exactly what do you want?"

"How much do you want my vote?"

Yale's face and bald head turned crimson. "I am a married man, you know. My wife's got spies everywhere."

Babe punched him on the shoulder and let out a piercing hoot. "Nothing as intimate as you're thinking, dude." She poked his ribs again—harder, this time. "Although you may not think that, afterward. Here's the deal: I vote for Hernandez, Friday—you take a little ride on the back of my hog, Saturday morning, 'less it's pouring. Honest to God, I promise I won't crack a hundred."

Yale's shoulder felt like he'd been hit with a club, and he just knew the spot where she'd been poking would be black-and-blue in the morning. "You don't come through with the vote, all bets are off," he hedged.

"Is it a deal then?"

Babe held out her right hand, but Yale shook his head. "I'm not going to shake on it, Babe. I may have to use my hand to sign something later today. But it is a deal," he added hastily. "You vote 'Yea' Friday, I put my life on the line, Saturday."

Babe grinned and clapped him on the shoulder once again. "You're gonna love it. Lots better 'n sex. And you've got nothing to fear. I've only lost two or three riders in my whole life — 'course I'm due."

In the balmy late afternoon at the Chevy Chase Club, Kyle Lambert whacked a backhand from forecourt. It barely cleared the net. His svelte opponent, Democratic Senator Caleb Dickinson, lithely ran forward and deftly returned the ball to the baseline. The lanky, muscular Texan ran back for the return shot, swung, and missed.

"Game, set, match," the trim Boston Brahmin called out with a triumphant grin on his face.

"Won fair and square, Caleb. You were just awesome today."

"Yes, for the first time, I finally defeated you. But, I had no doubt victory was at hand. I really hit my stride today."

Kyle smiled good-naturedly and patted the junior senator on the back before they gathered their gear and moved off the court. "I've thought a lot about your phone call," Caleb said later as they walked slowly to the locker room, "and this is what I think. Hernandez might be all right on the Court, but I don't see her as Chief Justice of the United States, ever. In my view, to succeed Kirkland, she'd be another one of the pack—all competent, but no leaders. And Kirkland knows it."

Caleb lowered his voice. "If she loses Friday, tell Morgan to act fast. Nominate Rittenhouse. We'll put him through easily. He's not only a leader, he's ideologically close enough to Kirkland that his confirmed placement would make the old man feel comfortable about retiring. Then say, in a couple of months, provided he gets a deal with Morgan to elevate Rittenhouse to chief justice as his replacement, the old codger bows out gracefully to coast through the rest of his life in Boca Raton. After Kirkland retires, and with Rittenhouse moved up, Morgan can play his Hispanic card for the open associate spot—this time with somebody he doesn't know personally, and everybody wins. It's sure fire, you've got to agree."

Actually, it would be, if Chief Justice Kirkland opts to retire, Kyle thought, *but there's no guarantee of that, you arrogant SOB.* Then he lied. "We've discussed that very plan, of course. But isn't Rittenhouse awfully conservative for you?"

"Well, he's ideologically to the right of me, yes, but not far. I could live with him as chief justice."

"What about *Roe v. Wade*? Everyone says Kirkland won't step down until he's found a way to trash it."

"True, but the abortion dynamic is changing. The real issue is the fact that we've got fewer abortions anyway, so it's becoming a moot point, even for the Court conservatives. Face it: The number of doctors doing them is shrinking. How would you react? They get death threats, they get picketed and spat upon, their cars get egged and worse. They put themselves and their families at risk every time they act on their convictions. As I see it, we leave *Roe* in place to soothe its backers, 'cause it's becoming irrelevant." He paused. "You know, Kyle, I think abortion moved from a privacy right to an equality right, and now it's going to end up dying as a law-and-order issue."

Kyle gave an impression of considering that, then moved on. "So bottom line, how do you think you'll vote Friday?"

Caleb stopped walking. His face had the astonished look of a man who'd just walked into his living room to see a zebra eating his couch. "Are you kidding? Didn't I make that clear? I wouldn't vote for her if she were the last judge in the country."

THIRTY-FOUR

Thursday, June 1

"Oh, don't bother, Claire, I'll help myself."

Forrest headed for the silver coffee urn and pastries arranged on a side table in the Oval Office. "Sorry I'm late again. More demonstrators than yesterday. We didn't want to run anyone down."

Jon waved the explanation off. "Tony was just telling us about the count."

Tony waited until the older man had made a selection and nodded to him before he began talking again. "Well, like I was saying, we were down to five about 9:30 this morning. Andy got confirmation that Bryce Collins is announcing for Gloria at a press conference later this morning."

"Claire, remind me to drop a thank-you note to Chancellor Vasquez," Jon said.

"It's already on your desk, Sir, ready for your signature."

"You know, one of these days when you anticipate me, you're going to be wrong," he admonished.

"Not in your lifetime, Sir," she muttered sweetly.

"Well, you can tell Andy to change it to four," Forrest said, holding his filled-to-the-brim cup gingerly, as he eased himself into a chair to Jon's left. "Louis Cheever will endorse on the floor this afternoon around two."

"Chalk one up for the first lady." Tony grinned.

Jon did not respond. His mind had segued to the unusually passionate interlude that had followed their

conversation Sunday evening. *Where has the week gone?* he
wondered. *Why's she been in such a funky mood since she came
back from Hartford? She said everything went well there. Damn!
I forgot to call her dad again. That's it, I hope.*

"I guess the question is," Dan observed, "how about
the other four votes we need for a tie?"

"I'm holding out hope for Bowden and Horvath,"
Forrest answered. "Neither has given a flat-out 'no' so far."

"The vice president said he's willing to drop a few
more games to Josh if it helps," Tony said blithely. "He's
been in an amazing slump lately. The worst couple of
weeks of his athletic career, he says."

Forrest chuckled, sipped his coffee, and sampled a
Danish from his plate. "I'd offer my services too," he said,
swallowing, "but I don't think anybody'd buy it at this
point. I've been trying to persuade Lily to come on board. I
know she'd love to see another female on the Court, but
she says she'd prefer a Native-American Democrat. Do we
even have any of those in the running?"

"Maybe I could call her," Claire offered. "I spent two
hours with Senator Bluecorn at the Smithsonian a couple of
weeks ago. We just happened to meet at the Navajo rug
exhibition they're featuring now. She told me all about
growing up on the reservation and how she worked her
way up and out. She's a fascinating storyteller. Her
grandmother used to weave rugs like the ones they have
on display."

She looked at Jon quizzically, who nodded once. She
jotted a personal line in the margin of her notes.

"Still leaves us one short to tie," Dan said. "And since
we have to figure all one hundred will be there . . ."

Heads nodded around the room, a quiet dismay
settling in the air. At length, Jon brought his desk chair to
an upright position. "Well, I think . . . I think we just might
be able to snag one vote we haven't considered yet."

Claire's pen hung poised over her note pad. "Who?"

"Christine Fairchild."

"Who?"

Jonathan grinned as Tony and Dan exchanged incredulous looks, and Claire sat stunned. He didn't often catch his super-alert staff so off guard. Forrest put down his cup and sat back with a thoughtful expression.

"You guys gotta learn to watch more closely," the president said. "Didn't you notice how she started to change as the hearings progressed? Oh, it was subtle, but it was there—a smile now and then when Gloria didn't fall for a baited trap. You had to watch her eyes. A couple of those answers must have nudged her conscience a little. You know, they're both Catholic. And I don't think they're as diametrically opposite as it seems at first glance. Forrest, give us a thumbnail sketch of your Maryland colleague."

Forrest closed his eyes momentarily as if trying to organize his thoughts. "Well," he started slowly, "you probably already know that she's from Baltimore. Democrat, liberal, dedicated. Bright, very bright. Sometimes frighteningly so."

"What does that mean?" Claire asked sharply.

Forrest shook his head remorsefully. "I think she's got one of the higher IQs in Congress. Women who can outthink me—just like that—scare me a little."

"I don't see why," she started, but the men were all nodding. "Oh, sometimes, you men . . ."

"Anyway," Forrest went on, "she's not married, at least not now. I don't know if she's ever tied the knot. She keeps a pretty low profile around here, except for political functions. My accountant is one of her neighbors, but he doesn't know much about her either. Says she's polite, but keeps to herself. There've been all sorts of rumors—shady past, female liaisons, a secret lover somewhere. You know, the usual stuff about someone who hardly ever opens her mouth except to say or ask something brilliant and who no one can seem to get next to. I know a guy who tried to ask her out once, but once was all he tried. He said he got the impression she was permanently unavailable, but why, he couldn't say." He grimaced. "Sorry, Jon, that's all I've got. Not much, but then, nobody seems to know the lady."

"Thanks, Forrest," Jon said, wagging his fingers. "Don't be concerned about it. You're right, nobody seems to know her. But I was so intrigued, we did a little quiet investigating on our own. Bob?"

All eyes shifted to the chief of staff, who had sat quietly drinking coffee the whole time. Now he set his cup aside and opened a leather-bound folder to remove a sheaf of papers. "In the course of our probe," he began easily, "we learned a lot about the senator. To begin with, you're right, Forrest, she's bright. More than bright. Three earned degrees: B.A., M.A. and LL.D., and four honorary doctorates. She got her bachelor's and master's in the amount of time it took me just to figure out what I wanted to do with my life. She was an only child, daughter of a decorated war hero: two Bronze and one Silver Star, two Purple Hearts; field-promoted five times during World War II, and killed in Germany on a classified mission two weeks before *der Führer* committed suicide. Anyway, Colonel Bradley is buried in Arlington. I wonder if she remembers him? The mother was an economics professor at Johns Hopkins, in and out of Washington as a consultant over at Treasury. The stepfather, Clifford Fairchild, was a successful businessman who doted on the mother and saw to it that his stepdaughter went to private, Catholic schools and good universities. Her IQ is evidently too high to be charted with conventional testing. She had very few friends." He looked up. "I guess she was too much for most of her peers."

Forrest nodded heartily. "I told you, she's scary."

Bob raised his shoulder. "I guess. Anyway, one night she saw Brendan O'Donnell playing forward on Mount St. Joseph's championship basketball team. They were both seventeen."

"*Cardinal* Brendan O'Donnell of Baltimore?" Dan asked skeptically.

"Same city, but a couple of years before he made cardinal," Bob said, his amusement showing in his lopsided grin. "They were in high school. In fact, they both went to separate boys' and girls' schools all the way through. They actually met on a blind double date, after which they evidently became fast friends, if nothing else. Our information is kind of unclear on what else, if anything. Nevertheless, they're still good friends."

"Senator Fairchild and *Cardinal* O'Donnell?"

Jon looked up from the steeple he'd made with his fingers. "You got a problem with that, Dan?"

"No, of course not," he said, his nervous energy almost audible in the snap of his voice. "It's just that, well, you don't think of cardinals as having girlfriends. At least I don't."

"I'm sure it's nothing like that," Claire said dryly.

"Well . . ." Bob swallowed and ran his tongue around the inside of his mouth.

Claire's eyes widened. "One of our contacts told us Fairchild was devastated when O'Donnell entered college seminary in their hometown. From what we can discern, his family was pressuring him into becoming a priest. Our contact also said he resisted making the commitment until Christine finally agreed to the idea. Why she ever agreed remains a mystery, I guess. Respect for the Church? No one seems to know. Hell, it's apparently their sacred secret." Bob paused to rub his temples. "They kept in close contact—even stayed on parallel career courses. While he was earning his B.A. in philosophy at St. Mary's Seminary in Baltimore, she zipped through pre-law at Johns Hopkins and stayed on to pick up a M.A. in international relations in record time, just so they could keep seeing each other, from what we can tell. She got her law degree here at Georgetown, while he was earning his Doctorate of Sacred Theology at the North American College in Rome. At that point, our sources tell us, she started appearing at the post office three and four times a week to mail letters to Italy. She even accompanied Brendan's family to Rome when he got ordained, and—oh, this is interesting—our informant says her face was almost impossible to read; a real strong mixture of pride and pain. This is a quote. Don't ask the source: 'I've never met another man the equal to or better than Brendan O'Donnell.'"

"But what does that mean?" Dan sputtered. "Intellectually, emotionally—not, physically? It couldn't mean—I mean—"

Forrest raised his eyebrows. "Danny boy, I've never seen you like this before. The man's only mortal, you know."

"He's a cardinal!"

"The point is," Bob said, bringing his staff's attention back to him with a few raps of his pen on the chair arm, "we don't know."

"And why should you need to?" Claire demanded. "The answer is, you don't." She glared at Dan, who bristled but did not respond.

"Claire's right," Jon interjected. "No one needs to know. It's their concern and their problem, if it is one. Bob, go on. What else do we have?"

The chief of staff cleared his throat, sent a warning look around the room, and returned to his prepared notes. "OK, let's see. She stunned her politically conservative Republican parents by becoming a Democrat and entering Baltimore politics at a local level. By that time, O'Donnell had returned home and was serving a poor urban parish. She got elected to the House of Representatives shortly before he got appointed Bishop of Pittsburgh." He scanned the next page. "Fairchild went on to snag a seat in the U.S. Senate while O'Donnell got appointed Archbishop of Baltimore. The Pope named him Cardinal of Baltimore just two years after she won re-election to the senate by a landslide. He settled into the rectory; she inherited her parents' three-story, historic townhouse on East Mount Vernon Place, just a short, four-block drive away from the cardinal's home." He looked up. "Phone records show nightly calls between Baltimore and Washington. She's seen a series of doctors for sleep dysfunction. Guess he's keeping her up at night. Or maybe he helps her drop off. In any event, info on him is a lot harder to come by. You won't find anyone in Baltimore society willing to discuss, much less condone them as a couple, but it hasn't stopped anyone from inviting the two to appear together at various fund-raising functions. They're apparently quite a draw, possibly due to the very reaction Dan has so obligingly demonstrated for us."

"Who'd of thought?" Forrest mused. "She's so low-keyed—"

Tony raised his hand. "This is all very interesting, and excuse me for being slow, but just how does it help us to get her vote tomorrow night?"

Jon answered before Bob could speak. "Well, there's a little postscript to the story," he said. "Only two members of O'Donnell's class at the North American College have been appointed Princes of the Church."

Forrest held up a finger. "Uh, who of the what?"

"Cardinals," Dan said in a husky gasp.

Jon nodded. "Right. O'Donnell was the first. The other just happens to be an old friend of mine. And a good friend of Gloria's, for that matter. Ramon Delgado."

———————

Later that morning, with all of the day's official events and meetings behind him, the president worked at his Oval Office desk. He wrinkled his brow as he speed-read through the seven amendments to a new, federal gun-control bill. "Why'd they bother writing it to begin with?" he groused to the empty room.

"Mr. President, Cardinal Delgado on line four."

Jon pushed the papers away with a sigh of relief and reached for the phone. "Ram! How are you?"

"Not bad, Jon. I was expecting your call. Our girl's in trouble, right?"

"Yeah, I'm afraid so. We could lose tomorrow. You know how I hate to lose."

"I seem to recall a tantrum or two in our younger years when the surf wasn't up to your liking. I'd have hoped you'd gotten over that kind of stuff by now."

Jon laughed. "Yeah, I did. I passed it on to Michael."

"How's he doing?"

"Good, real good. Growing up, dating girls, with nothing noticeable pierced."

From his Los Angeles rectory office, Cardinal Ramon Delgado laughed along with the President of the United States, his friend of more than five decades, since their boyhood together in Santa Barbara.

"Annie OK?"

"She's fine. Glory's hanging in there. Eddie's . . . Eddie."

They both laughed again. Finally, the clergyman got serious. "So, Jon. What can I do to help?"

"Well, Cardinal Delgado, since you asked, here's what I need you to do . . ."

THIRTY-FIVE

Thursday afternoon

Christine Fairchild drove her four-year-old white LeSabre out of the condominium's garage and headed north on Wisconsin Avenue. She soon passed the towering National Cathedral and the meticulously maintained grounds of Sidwell Friends School. By 2:55, the still-light traffic made it possible for her to maintain the posted speed through Chevy Chase. She breezed by elegant homes and well-kept lawns in Bethesda, and onto the grayish-white Capital Beltway, softened on either side by varying hues of summer green trees. In Prince George's County, Maryland, Christine turned north onto I-95 and headed toward Baltimore on the heavily patrolled freeway. She thought a gray Saab had been following her from Georgetown but, when it continued straight on the belt highway she breathed an unconscious sigh of relief.

Less than an hour later, she had entered Baltimore's drab southwestern periphery and progressed to the upgraded Russell Street. Oriole Park at Camden Yard had enhanced the area. Beyond the stadium on Paca, she reached for her cell phone to let the rectory know she'd arrive in ten or fifteen minutes. Presently, she pulled up to the gray-stone clergy house. A young priest met her curbside to help her out and to park the Buick. Up the street, a black Peugeot slid discreetly to the curb, its driver having already called the White House to report that

Senator Fairchild had arrived safely at Cardinal Brendan
O'Donnell's residence.

Christine moved easily across the dimly-lit entryway,
where impeccably clean, marble floor tiles reeked of
disinfectant. A dramatic bouquet of deep-red roses swelled
out of a silver vase sitting on an imposing, heavily
polished, mahogany side table. Their delicious fragrance
almost nullified the institutional odor of furniture polish.

She quickened her pace as a man appeared at the far
end of the hall and began hurrying toward her. Regally tall
in his black suit and white clerical collar, Brendan
O'Donnell still had the near-perfect posture, broad
shoulders, flat abdomen, and narrow waist she had been so
taken with over forty years earlier. The scattered gray
streaks in his curly hair may have betrayed his fifty-eight
years, but they were offset by his ruddy complexion,
straight nose, firm chin, and dazzling blue eyes.

He grasped her hands. "You're here. Thank God." He
bent slightly to kiss her on the cheek. They held each
other's gaze for a fraction of a second, then moved apart
and slowly walked back the way he'd come.

"I love the roses," she said, for something to say. "Your
idea?"

"No, sorry. Father Bertram gets all the credit. He had to
coax Sister Crispina into removing the religious literature
so he could put them there. I don't know how he got her to
budge." He looked at his watch. "It's almost five. Is it too
soon for cocktails?"

"I'll never tell."

A door to their left suddenly swung open with an eerie
squeak. They stopped walking. Christine restrained a sigh.
Sister Crispina Petronilla, a stocky, gray-haired, black-clad
woman stepped into the hall.

"Your Eminence," she said with reverence. "Senator,"
she bit off with barely concealed disdain. She surveyed
Christine from head to foot, her pinched face clearly
expressing what she thought of Christine's blithe, sand-
colored designer dress, its tortoise-shell buttons, bright,

patterned sash belt, and the casual summer haircut shining under a new auburn tint. The nun's eyes lingered momentarily on the violet amethyst ring sparkling on the senator's left fourth finger.

Christine had never relished Sister Crispina. She'd first met her when the Holy Father had placed a scarlet hat on the new cardinal's head in the Paul VI Audience Hall, conferring on Brendan at that instant full membership in the Sacred College. For one compressed second, the two women had shared a mutual joy. But Crispina had shown obvious dismay the following afternoon when, after a solemn mass on the front steps of the Vatican basilica, His Holiness had fitted a cardinal's gold ring onto O'Donnell's right fourth finger. Afterwards, the new "prince" had smilingly and publicly slipped his now unessential bishop's amethyst ring onto Christine's hand.

That night, alone in her hotel suite several blocks away, Christine had consoled herself over Brendan's absence with the memory of his touch, his unspoken pledge, and the certain knowledge that upon their return to the United States, their nightly telephonic intercourse would resume.

"I was just coming to look for you," the sister said to Brendan now, by way of explanation. "Will Your Eminence be leading us in evening prayer?"

He did not answer immediately. When he did, his voice had a specific gentleness to it, the kind Christine knew was forced. "Of course, Sister," he said. "Probably a little after nine. I'll have Father Virgil summon you, as usual. By the way, the roses at the entry are lovely."

"Lovely? Perhaps. But simple, natural, unadorned purity is what makes each flower special. Even a weed is one of His gifts." She held her chin up and glanced at Christine once more. "Good day, Senator Fairchild." The rectory's dour, chief housekeeper retreated through the hallway door letting it fall shut just a bit too loud.

Brendan and Christine both sighed simultaneously then burst into laughter together. "She knows when you're here," he said, taking Christine's arm and continuing down the hall. "She seems to have a sixth sense when you and I are at that exact spot."

Christine settled into a leather-upholstered couch near the unlit fireplace in Brendan's oak-paneled retreat, while he fussed at the well-stocked bar on the opposite side of the room. "I think she's got sensors under the carpet," she said. "I wouldn't put it past her."

"The usual?"

"Please."

Brendan dropped onto the couch beside her, spilling a few drops from the Tanqueray martini, which he held out. He clinked his glass against hers. "To my beloved," he said.

"To my prince," she responded, completing the ritual.

They sipped their drinks. "Not bad," he murmured. "Do you mind if I smoke?" He opened a sterling silver cigarette box, removed an English Oval, slid it into a carved, ivory cigarette holder, and lit it with the matching, silver lighter. The smoking accouterments had been a gift from Christine, against her better judgment, when he was elevated to bishop. There were so few socially acceptable expressions of love open to them.

An older priest shuffled into the library. "Good evening, Senator Fairchild," he cooed, smiling benevolently. He held his pudgy, folded hands in front of his chest, the very picture of a medieval friar. "Your Eminence, I've opened a bottle of the Cabernet Franc from that case the mayor sent you. It needs to breathe before dinner," he added, his hands waving to illustrate his point, his eyes misting in anticipation.

"Fine, Father Virgil. Thank you. Be sure to have a glass yourself." Brendan clenched his cigarette holder between his teeth.

"I always do." The cherubic cleric plodded away.

"How long do you suppose before the next habitué?" Christine asked with marked forbearance.

"Let's hope it'll be a while. So, how did it go today?"

A deep, energetic voice from the hallway interrupted. "Indians three up on the O's. Top of the tenth and our guys look bushed."

"Pray, Father Tim," Brendan called back.

The head that went with the voice poked through the open door. Short and husky, the priest strode into the study. "We need more than that. Only one out and Cleveland's hot! Oh, good evening, Senator." He gave an enthusiastic wave and bolted out of sight.

"Not that bad."

"What?"

"You asked how it went today," Christine laughed. "I said, 'Not that bad.' I didn't want to have to start the whole conversation over."

Brendan chuckled, took her glass, set it on the end table next to his own, and stretched his arm around her shoulders. She nestled against him with a release that felt like coming home. Neither spoke for a long time.

"I still haven't made up my mind," she said finally.

"I know."

"The vote's tomorrow."

"Don't be anxious about it. You'll know what to do when the time comes."

Sister Rosemary appeared at the doorway. "Did you call, Your Eminence?"

"No, thank you, Sister Rosemary. I'll let you know if I need anything."

"Senator."

"Sister."

Christine went on, as if they hadn't been interrupted. "I can only imagine what Sister Crispina would say if it got back to her that I voted for someone with Judge Hernandez's views."

"That's not your problem."

"But I wouldn't want it to be one for you. Besides, she's so, I don't know what to call it. Her son is homosexual, you know."

"So you've said, a couple of dozen times now."

This time the incursion came from Father Jerome. "Your Eminence, the electrician says we have a problem with the pulpit microphone in the main sanctuary. I just know I won't sleep . . ."

"Well, tell him to go ahead and fix it, Father Jerome."

"Yes, Your Eminence. Thank you." He hurried off.

Christine shook her head. "Where was I? Oh, yes, I'm not condemning her for the sins of her son, Brendan, I'm just saying—"

"Saying what?" the cleric mumbled. "How can we tell how we would handle such a situation? Actually, I feel kind of sorry for the woman. Who among us could bear such scrutiny? Certainly not me."

She moved against him, snuggling a little closer. He closed his eyes and inhaled deeply.

"If only she weren't so tolerant of abortion. And opposed to public-school prayer. And willing to put up with . . . those . . . things some men do with each other."

He grinned. "It's called sex, Chrissy."

"Not between men. Then it's called—"

Sister Lucy intruded this time. Was there a conspiracy, perhaps? "I think I found the perfect passage for your sermons at St. Charles and St. Edwards this Sunday, Your Eminence."

Christine buried her face in Brendan's shoulder so Sister Lucy Mengoni, a middle-aged woman with unfortunate brown hair and pronounced buck teeth, wouldn't hear her giggle.

"I thought we'd use these words from Matthew," she continued, pushing up her glasses and reading from her notebook. 'For what is a man profited, if he shall gain the whole world and lose his own soul?'"

"You don't say? Matthew said that, huh? Not bad." Brendan waited, but Sister Lucy showed no signs of leaving. "Let's use it," he finally said. "How long is the sermon?"

"About twelve minutes."

"Please cut it to nine. Gives me more time with the parishioners afterwards. And please have it on my desk by seven, Sunday morning. I'll look it over on my way to the first mass."

"Of course, Your Eminence. I've got to run," she said breathlessly. "Good night, Senator." She turned and scampered off.

"What was that, Your Eminence?" Christine joked into Brendan's chest. "Did you want to get more than two sentences out without interruption, Your Eminence? Why would you want that, Your Eminence? Could you look at my hangnail, Your Eminence?"

She was sitting up now, having pulled away to smooth down the hair he'd been twirling between his fingers and to resettle her sash belt.

"Sodomy."

"Huh?"

"The word you didn't want to say. It's sodomy."

"I know what the word is, Bren. I'm just not sure what her judicial position on it is."

"I could use another drink." Brendan pushed off the couch and walked stiffly to the bar. "I got a call from Ramon today," he said over his shoulder.

"Aragon?"

"Delgado. Out in L.A. You met him last year when he came to the American Cardinals' Dinner here."

"Oh? What'd he want?"

He returned to the couch with two more drinks. This time he was careful to hand her the glass before he tried to sit down. "He wants you to vote yes."

"Umh!" She dabbed at the liquid that had spilled down her chin when she started to speak. "In heaven's name, why?"

Brendan used his thumb to wipe a droplet off her lower lip. He licked it dry. "He's head of the archdiocese out there, remember? He's also, it turns out, an old friend of the Hernandez family. Knew the father. Baptized the son. Says he watched the boy grow up. I guess he had a number of problems when he was young. Very gifted, Ramon said. Also very neurotic."

"They seem to go hand-in-hand, don't they?"

"Anyway, he says this judge is a pillar of the Church." Brendan changed his voice to mimic one of his bishop's deep-toned pronouncements. "Generous to a fault. And done so much to help Latinos. Established a foundation. Sizable gifts of time and money. A pillar, an absolute pillar of the Church."

They both laughed. Brendan waved away the priest who stuck his head in at the sound. "An absolute pillar of the Church," he repeated. It was a joke they could not share with his pastoral staff. Almost every week, it seemed, one of the resident priests or sisters would hold someone up to Cardinal O'Donnell as "an absolute pillar of the Church."

"Well, I'll give her credit for all her good works, but—"

Sister Agnes' turn now. "Coffee, Your Eminence?"

"Just when I'm finally lighting a fire under this glow? No, thank you, Sister Agnes."

"Well, we're having pepper steak for dinner, prepared just the way you love it, Your Eminence. I'll have you called when dinner is ready."

"Oh, I've no doubt you will, Sister."

"Senator."

"Sister."

Brendan rolled his eyes after Sister Agnes exited gracefully with a deep-staged bow. "But?" he prompted Christine.

"But, oh, it's this thing with Morgan. Really, Bren, even if I let all the other stuff go, how can I ignore that? Is Ramon glossing over the affair to make his argument? Not much of a Jesuit. What if the president and his nominee are the parents of a misbegotten child? Father of his own nominee's son. How can—" *What, again?*

"Just one little thing, Your Eminence. I'm so sorry to interrupt, but there's just this one little, tiny matter—"

Brendan put his glass down so hard the table rattled. "What now?" His voice no longer had even a hint of patience, real or affected.

"Bishop Walker wants to know if you'll be at the St. Vincent's dinner next Friday night. He says—"

"For God's sake, tell him yes. I told him that two days ago. He oughta start taking notes if he can't remember anything. Now Father Clarence, please do me the kindness of getting lost."

"Of course, Your Eminence. I'm so sorry. I meant no harm. Please forgive me, Your Eminence. Senator." The giant bear of a man, whose manner so belied his size, backed out of the room with a look of utter consternation on his face. Christine reached up and stroked Brendan's cheek.

"It's all right."

"No, it isn't," he pouted. "How can it be?"

Silence enveloped the couple, bringing them into each other's intimate presence. *You look so desperately sad,* his eyes said to hers. *As do you,* her gaze answered. Finally, she stirred and leaned her head back against his shoulder again. "How can we say God made a mistake?" Brendan asked softly, stroking her cheek and addressing the unspoken questions that hung between them. "Decisions we made in our youth, for whatever reasons—"

"I have to make the decision now."

"It was made years ago," he said under his breath. His throat felt dry.

She sat up and turned to face him. "Not that," she said thickly. "Tomorrow. The judge. I have to make a decision on how to vote. Knowing full well that, good qualities notwithstanding, she claims to be a practicing Catholic, she did have sexual relations out of wedlock. And with more than one man! She may even have had an illegitimate child baptized under the wrong father's name. How can I condone all of that?"

"Well, maybe she's the lucky one." Brendan's voice had gotten hard. His jaw was set. "After all, if you're right, at least they've got a legacy all these years later. What have we got? Forty years of celibacy and unfulfilled longing? Forty years of torture, of not being able to touch you, or not even having the memory." He shrunk back against the couch and turned his face away, his face showing the familiar pain. Christine touched his hand to bring him back into the room. She used her thumb to wipe the teardrop that had spilled out of the corner of his eye, and then rubbed it gently over his lips. He forced his face into a wan smile.

"Sometimes I regret being Catholic," he said softly, taking her two hands and kissing them. "We lacked courage then, Chrissy. We tried to follow a predestined path and for all the wonder and joy it's brought us in so many ways, we've paid for it a million times over. I can't tell you how to vote. You have to make that choice on your own. No more dictates from on high. Not from me, anyway. Not from anyone. Just listen to your heart. You'll know what to do. Forget everything I said. I can't help you. Sometimes, I don't think I can help anyone. I'm just . . . I don't know . . . just a damned pillar of the Church."

Christine smiled, but not before she heard, "Shall I clear away the martinis, Your Eminence?"

Brendan released Christine's hands. The senator smiled faintly at the blond, unfamiliar, young priest and reached up to smooth her hair once more. The cardinal stared straight ahead. "Yes, Father, thank you. We're finished now."

"In that case, Your Eminence," he said with a soft lisp, "Sister Agnes asked me to inform you that dinner is served."

Brendan stood, and held out his hand to help Christine rise. "Coming, Father," he said with ultimate resignation.

THIRTY-SIX

Friday, June 2

The Senate Chamber is both smaller and more sedately decorated than the House Chamber. It has light-yellow walls and carpeting of red, white, and yellow regal figures on a deep blue background. Vice-presidential busts reside in niches along the rear aisles of the galleries, bearing silent witness to the historic proceedings carried on in this somber room.

Beginning with the opening gavel at 10:00, TV cameramen positioned their equipment centrally and on either side of the chamber. They would bring to an expectant nation the Senate's final debate on Judge Gloria Hernandez's confirmation vote. The afternoon's closing statements from both sides had been brief and usually, but not always, partisan.

"We have a unique opportunity to complete the ground-breaking nomination of the first Latina to the Supreme Court by confirming Judge Gloria Hernandez to the high court today," said Rex St. Clair.

"We must not, we cannot confirm this woman to the Supreme Court. Her ties to the president are too personal, too scandalous. This is one step short of nepotism," weighed in Sinead Sullivan, the Democrat from Oregon.

"Gloria Hernandez—a justice for the twenty-first century. Superbly qualified in every respect. Passionate but dispassionate. Grounded in tradition, but open to change. I call for the Senate to put aside its factional divisions and do the only just thing: Confirm her today," stated Republican Rhode Island senator, John Fitzpatrick.

"Senator Fitzpatrick is correct—this matter must go beyond party lines. That is why I say history will record a confirmation of this nominee as one of the greatest travesties to emerge from this hallowed chamber," shouted Quentin Ravenswood, the Republican from Illinois.

"In every respect, by every criterion—background, knowledge, experience, her keen attention to detail and the spirit of the law—Judge Hernandez is an outstanding nominee. She should be confirmed by us today," said Senator Norah Poole Stafford of New Jersey.

"I have not been persuaded that Judge Hernandez will ever hear or understand the voices of the poor, the undereducated, the legally underrepresented or misrepresented. She should not be confirmed, and I cannot vote for her," conceded Kawai Higashi, the Hawaiian Democrat.

Early that evening after nearly all of the senators had spoken, Vice-President Kyle Lambert entered through a rear door of the chamber at 5:15. He quietly climbed to the top level of the rostrum where Yale Jacobs had been officiating.

Cornell Duckworth was saying, "Ladies and gentlemen of the Senate, my honorable and esteemed colleagues. I implore you today, Friday, the second of June: Let us not allow this to become another day of infamy. Oh, Lord, oh, Lord, give us the courage, the vision, the strength to defeat this woman, this unchaste, immoral creature nominated, not by a leader of high integrity, but by her own bedmate, the possible father of her bast . . . uh, illeg . . . misbegot son! This whole proceeding is the basest, the sickest of jokes. This president is a disgrace to his office. And I say we must reject his totally unacceptable nominee."

"The senator from Alabama has once more displayed his profound ignorance, blatant prejudice, and total lack of class. Judge Hernandez is his polar opposite, and that, ladies and gentlemen, is what scares him to death. Even after enduring the bombardment of his constant, irrelevant abuse, she stands as a beacon of integrity, knowledge, and fairness. She most certainly deserves confirmation. Senator Duckworth, on the other hand, should be immediately recalled from office by the decent and honorable citizens of the great state of Alabama before he gives the rest of us southerners a bad name," asserted North Carolina Republican, Daisy Carlisle.

Kyle leaned over to shake hands with Yale Jacobs. "Ninety-eight here," Yale whispered. "Two democrats missing: Fairchild and Knight. If they don't show, we've got her in with you here to break it."

"Any hope on the dissidents?"

Yale moved his head slightly. "Forrest's been pushing hard, but Albrecht's dug in his heels. Montague's miffed at the president for some reason, I don't know what. Ravenswood planted his flag with the democrats a little earlier. The other six social conservatives probably won't budge either."

"I sincerely regret that Judge Hernandez does not meet my high standards for an associate justice on the United States Supreme Court, and I will respectfully vote against her confirmation this evening," Cotton Blalock, the Arkansas Democrat, restating his previous objections.

"I support Judge Gloria Hernandez one hundred percent. It is my hope that this distinguished jurist from the great state of California will be the Court's strongest voice against bigotry of any kind," Grant Hallstead, the California Democrat, stated emphatically.

"I thought Ravenswood was under pressure from some big Chicago foundation money to vote for Hernandez," Kyle muttered.

Yale turned his head slightly and scratched behind one ear. "It's worth a try. I'll pass it on to Bruce."

Illinois Democrat Stanley Popowski questioned, "How can the Senate confirm to the highest court in the nation a nominee who has so generously financially supported the political ambitions of the president nominating her? If this isn't a classic example of political payback, I don't know what is."

"My thorough analysis of the pros and cons of this nominee leads me to only one conclusion: Judge Hernandez must not win confirmation tonight," pronounced Senator Derek Scott, Democrat from Vermont.

Lorenzo Madrid, the New Mexico Republican, articulated, "The Senate, tonight, has the historic opportunity to confirm the first Hispanic nominee to the United States Supreme Court. It would be an outrage, considering that we have patiently waited for over two hundred years, to deny this confirmation. The time is at hand, the candidate is beyond qualified, the excuses are questionable at best. Judge Hernandez must be confirmed. To not would be to insult the Hispanic population of the entire country."

Kyle glanced up to the central gallery where Estrella, Lorenzo's wife, dabbed a tear from her eye. His white-haired mother stared ahead stoically—the countenance of a pueblo matron.

"I heard direct testimony from Judge Hernandez, for nearly five days, during the Senate Judiciary Committee's hearings. I and other colleagues asked her repeatedly about a number of matters, most notably her strong ties to the president, to the Catholic Church, and to certain high-ranking officials and clergy within the church," declared Carl Albrecht, the influential, Pennsylvania Republican. "We never got a straight answer. Her evasiveness bothers me tremendously. What else is she not forthcoming about? I'm sorry, I cannot vote for her tonight."

Nebraska Republican Paul Worthington retaliated, "The matters Senator Albrecht refers to were all of the most extremely personal nature. Her friends and family members haven't had any influence on her judgments in the past, and for the life of me, I can't see what they have to do with Judge Hernandez's outstanding qualifications and proven achievements. I consider it an honor to support her tonight."

Senate Minority Leader, Blanche St. Antoine was allotted the second-to-last voice in the debate. From behind the speaking stand of her front-row seat, she began: "Fellow senators and millions of Americans watching this vote tonight. I've got to tell you something straight out of my heart. Ya'all see, it'd be awfully tempting for me to endorse this woman of unquestioned ability, and with all her experience and all, but for her close relationship with this president." Senator St. Antoine's deep inhalation elevated her impressive bosom. She narrowed her eyes as she looked rightward and stared directly at Forrest Garrison and Bruce Landes. "The admitted monetary ties between them have opened Judge Hernandez to serious question, as we all got to know more about her and him and all else that went on between them. Ya'all have heard enough about it till you're sick to death of it, so I won't go on about it and all, raising, you know, all the unsavory stuff."

Kyle slid into the presiding officer's chair at the highest level of the rostrum while the Louisiana power broker clasped her speaking stand on either side, and threw herself into her speech.

"Look, I'll be honest: if that were the only problem here, I'd probably support her. But that is not the issue here tonight. No, my friends, the issue tonight is not a question of abilities or money or even partisanship. It all boils down to impropriety, a matter of this president abusing his position of power. My friends, this isn't the president appointing an ambassador to some third-rate place or trying to put an old pal into some obscure cabinet position. This guy is putting up one of his closest and oldest friends, one of his former lovers," she inhaled deeply, "onto the highest court in the land. I don't need to remind the Senate, but, I want to remind you Americans from coast to coast: If confirmed, she's got a lifetime job."

Blanche slammed her fist down on her speaking stand. "Ladies and gentlemen and fellow Americans, I demand our Supreme Court Justices be of the highest personal integrity—and so must you! Judge Hernandez clearly does not stand this test. My friends and fellow Americans, we must not, we cannot confirm her nomination in this honorable chamber tonight."

Blanche paused to acknowledge the outbreak of thunderous applause from democrats and Hernandez opponents in the galleries before taking her seat. She leaned closely across a hunky, male aide to converse with the Minority Whip, Franklin Harmon of Kentucky.

From his lofty position, Kyle Lambert, looked for all the world like the tanned, athletic Texan he was. He gazed down on the legislative clerk who would call the roll, and the assorted aides who sat on the podium and at a long table in front. The nearly full contingent of senators sat at their mahogany desks—separated by the central aisle—forty-seven Democrats to his right, fifty-one Republicans to his left. The rear and side galleries were packed with reporters and VIP spectators. He nodded to Forrest who, as the majority leader, was afforded the right to give the last speech of the debate.

A passing of notes ensued, among whispers, sighs, and an occasional, nervous laugh. An aide darted in with a message for Majority Whip Bruce Landes, also seated in the first row, who read it, and bent to write a response.

Forrest rose to address the chair from his own speaking stand and waited patiently as Lambert gaveled for quiet, fully aware that Blanche had intentionally dropped into her fundamentalist preacher pattern to arouse the opposition for the showdown vote. She'd thrown down the gauntlet.

"Mr. President and members of the Senate," the majority leader began, "we are gathered now to advise and consent on Judge Gloria Hernandez's nomination to serve on the Supreme Court. We have heard eloquent and passionate statements in support of and in opposition to her confirmation in this time-honored room today. High levels of controversy over Supreme Court nominees are hardly new in our history, and I think the controversies regarding Judge Hernandez have now been fully examined and debated."

West Virginia's Senator Knight, a craggy-faced man with thinning brown hair, was admitted to the chamber. He walked quietly to his desk on the democratic side of the aisle.

"Mr. President and distinguished colleagues," Forrest continued, "in the final moments allotted to me by the time constraints we all agreed to earlier, I'd like to get past all the contention and posturing, and refocus on the nominee's superb qualifications for serving on the Court."

"Senator Knight just came in," an aide whispered to Franklin. "Tell Blanche." Harmon nodded and spoke quietly to the youth between him and Blanche, who, in turn, said something to his boss. She grinned, leaned forward, and gave Franklin a victory sign.

"The American Bar Association's Standing Committee on the Federal Judiciary," Forrest thundered on, "interviewed more than six-hundred persons regarding Judge Hernandez—including former Supreme Court Justices, federal and state judges from all over the nation, professors from elite law schools, and dozens of practicing attorneys."

Senator Bluecorn opened the note she had just been handed. "Lily, Morgan signed the Native-American H & E Bill thirty minutes ago. Those amendments of yours all got through. Thought you'd like to know. Forrest." *Why, that son of a bitch is trying to buy my vote*, she reflected, a grin crossing her wrinkled face.

". . . Distinguished herself academically in the prestigious Stanford Law School, graduating number one in her class before moving on to land a position in one of the most respected law firms on the West Coast . . ."

One of the senate pages handed Senator Bowden a piece of paper. He unfolded it and read: "Josh, the

president wanted you to be the first to know that the OU
med school's $5 million maternal-health grant is in the bag.
He spoke to the committee chairman himself just this
morning. Looking forward to stumping with you this fall—
Kyle." The junior senator from Oklahoma combed his
fingers through his hair with a stifled whoop, then looked
up and flashed an "OK" to his golfing buddy.

"For nearly twenty years," Forrest was reminding the
chamber, "Judge Hernandez has served with distinction on
the federal bench, first as a member and chief justice of the
Los Angeles Federal District Court, then, and currently on
the Ninth Circuit Court. She has twice passed the scrutiny
of the U.S. Senate. Twice, mind you, without a single
dissenting vote."

A page with red hair and braces blushed when he
delivered a message to Senator Horvath, and she winked at
him. Then the Wisconsin lawmaker unfolded the paper
quietly. "Babe—Morgan just signed it. Milwaukee's on the
top of the list for inner-city, small-biz opportunity bucks.
The Horvath American Motorcycle Museum in Sheboygan
rider that Grant and I put in stuck. I checked the Weather
Channel—no rain tomorrow. Don't have any leather jeans—
can I wear my Calvins? Yale." Senator Babe Horvath choked
a laugh, then shot a look of apology to Forrest, who gave
no indication he'd noticed either activity.

"Giving her their highest endorsement possible of 'Well
Qualified' by unanimous vote," Forrest was wrapping up.
He extended both arms, "I urge my distinguished
colleagues—on both sides of the aisle—to confirm Judge
Gloria Hernandez's nomination." Forrest stole a glance at
his watch: 5:59. "I request my colleagues remain in their
seats during the roll call, in accordance with senate rules."
He hesitated a few more seconds to demonstrate the full
gravity of the occasion. "Mr. President," he intoned
formally, "I ask for the yeas and nays."

Kyle called for and received a second from the minority
leader, then stood to officially address the assemblage.
"Ladies and gentlemen, before we begin the vote, I remind

the galleries that expressions of approval or disapproval are prohibited, and will be met with expulsion from the chamber. A vote has been motioned and seconded as to the Senate's consent to the nomination of Gloria Hernandez, as an Associate Justice of the United States Supreme Court. The clerk will now call the roll."

In keeping with the formality established over two-hundred years ago, the Legislative Clerk rose from his chair, faced the entire chamber of familiar faces, and began calling their names. The senators rose in turn to respond.

"Mr. Albrecht."

"No."

"Mr. Ashworth."

"Yea."

"Mrs. Bluecorn."

"Yea."

Blanche St. Antoine leaned forward and shot a dirty look across the aisle at her republican counterpart. Forrest answered with lifted eyebrows and a little wave. The clerk continued without pause.

"Mr. Blalock."

"No."

"Mr. Bowden."

"Yes."

Kyle gaveled to suppress the buzz that had erupted on both sides of the aisle. Josh Bowden rested his chin on the bridge of his hands, his elbows on the table, his face defiantly vacant. The clerk cleared his throat.

"Mrs. Caldwell."

"Yea."

"Mrs. Carlisle."

"Yea."

"Mr. Cheever."

"Yea."

Kyle ran his finger down the column of a list of senators' names with their projected votes, as calculated by Andy Grunwald, Forrest Garrison, and Dan Mendelson. So far, so good.

"Mr. Danson."

"No."

"Mr. Duckworth."

"Absolutely, positively, unequivocally no!"

"Mr. . . ."

The clerk stopped. Cornell Duckworth had pounded on his desk in rhythm to his response, which unleashed a ripple of mutterings throughout the chamber. Blanche covered her eyes with both hands. Forrest rolled his. Daisy Carlisle sat laughing quietly to herself. Kyle gaveled once, and the room fell quiet. He nodded to the clerk.

"Mr. Edwards."

"No."

"Ms. Fairchild."

Blanche looked around. Christine had not appeared on the Senate floor. She shrugged when her assistant leaned over and whispered something. The clerk paused only long enough to register the absence, then droned on.

"Mr. Fitzpatrick."

"Yea."

"We've got it even if Chris doesn't show," Blanche whispered to her handsome aide.

"Senator St. Antoine thinks we've won," the aide whispered to Franklin Harmon. The veteran pol, who had witnessed too many past "victories" that surprisingly swept into the hands of defeat, stared straight ahead without answering.

"Mr. Garrison."

"Absolutely, positively, unequivocally yea!"

The titter of chuckles quickly died away as Kyle reached for his gavel.

"Mr. Gurney."

"No."

"Mr. Hallstead."

"Yea."

"Mr. Harmon."

"No."

"Mr. Higashi."

The Hawaiian senator laced his fingers and pursed his lips. His "No" was barely audible.

"Mr. Higashi votes 'No,'" the clerk repeated. Kawai nodded.

"Mrs. Horvath."

"Yes."

"What?"

Kyle pointed out a spectator to the security officer standing behind him. In the back of the gallery, a solidly-built officer plucked on the offender's sleeve and quickly escorted him from the room, ignoring his stutterings of apology and waving hands of protests. Babe Horvath grabbed the handlebars of an invisible bike and winked at Yale Jacobs. He winked back, all the while hoping his face did not reflect the stabbing pain he now felt in his abdomen.

"Mrs. Ivy."

"No."

"Mr. Jacobs."

"Yes."

Bruce Landes handed a folded paper to his aide with whispered instructions. The aide delivered it to Lance Montague, who skimmed it over, and gave it back without comment. The aide returned the note to his boss. "Shit," Bruce said under his breath.

"Mr. Janowski."

"Yea."

"Mr. Kent."

"No."

"Mr. Knight."

"No."

Forrest leaned forward to catch Bruce's attention. Bruce closed his eyes and moved his head slightly from side to side. Forrest puffed out his cheeks in exasperation, making a small popping noise as he let the air out.

"Mr. Landes."

"Yea."

"Mr. Lattimer."

"No."

"Mr. Madrid."

"Yea."

"Mr. Marchbanks."

"Yea."

"Mr. Martindale."

"Yes."

"Mr. Montague."

"No."

Bruce winced. The Reverend Gideon Heartfelt, observing from the gallery, leaned back in his chair with a satisfied smirk. Forrest handed a note to Bruce through his aide. Bruce looked at it, added another line of his own, and sent it to Quentin Ravenswood.

"Mr. Murray."

"No."

"Gwen, I lost count," Forrest mouthed to the intriguing brunette taking notes beside him. "Where are we?"

"Up by four, Sir."

"Mr. Nicholson."

"No."

"Ms. Osborne."

"No."

"Mr. Popowski."

"No."

"Mr. Quince."

"No."

"Mr. Ravel."

"Yea."

"Mr. Ravenswood."

"No."

Quentin raised his arm, pointedly crumpled the note he'd just received, and let it fall to the floor.

"I got it," Bruce muttered under his breath.

You can kiss my tax-shelter vote good-by, buster, Forrest thought.

"Mr. Roberts."

"Yes."

"We've got it, Adonis," Blanche whispered to the young man next to her. He kept his eyes on his tally sheet. "Yeah, Venus, she's history."

"Mr. Scott of Iowa."

"Yea."

"Mr. Scott of Vermont."

The clerk cocked his head. "Mr. Scott of Vermont votes 'No'?"

Derek Scott glanced up from *Bird Watcher's Digest* with an annoyed expression. "That's what I said," he mumbled.

"Mrs. St. Antoine."

"No."

"Mr. St. Clair."

"Yea!" He waved his clasped hands over his head.

"Mrs. Stafford."

"Yea." She wagged a finger at her demonstrative colleague, shaking her head with a bemused look on her face.

"Mrs. Sullivan."

"No."

Well, that's it. Behind projections, Forrest thought. He barely listened to the rest of the vote. It was all over. He loosened his tie, slumped in his seat, and leaned his head back, his eyes closed in defeat. *I've lost another big one,* he concluded, while the clerk recited the assenting and dissenting votes. *Jon counted on me again, and I let him down. Again. Maybe it's time to hang it up. What am I beating my head against the wall for? It's over for me. I should have known that, when Ellen died. Tyler knew, God forgive him. And me. I let my family go. I've let my party down. I should have stopped him that night. God, I need a drink.*

The clerk had stopped calling names. "The vote stands fifty nays to forty-nine . . ." His voice trailed off. Senators, aides, and spectators all turned in their seats to watch Christine Fairchild enter the chamber and walk quietly to the well of the senate floor. Every eye followed her measured gait.

Forrest stifled a groan. *Swell. Just what I need. Another no vote. Thank you, Lord, my failure is now complete.*

"Senator Fairchild," the clerk was saying. "The matter before the Senate is the confirmation vote of Judge Hernandez. What say you, yea or nay?"

Christine paused long enough to make Blanche straighten in her seat. Carl Albrecht tilted his head and clenched his fists. At length, the Maryland senator swallowed hard. "Mr. President," she enunciated deliberately. "After weighing all the pros and cons of this decision, and giving it my utmost careful and soul-searching consideration, I vote . . ." She stared, unseeing, straight ahead. She closed her eyes and let her shoulders lift with a deep inhalation. "I vote . . ." She exhaled, "Yea."

Forrest's head pitched forward, his mouth dropped in amazement. Blanche leaped out of her chair, shaking her hands in distracted disbelief. Cornell Duckworth started banging on his desk, calling on God and the devil, assorted netherworld sinners, and evil spirits to witness this travesty. In the gallery, the Reverend Gideon Heartfelt's face turned gray. He looked quickly around, then made his way down the unruly row of cheering and yelling spectators to the nearest exit. Over the din, Kyle Lambert jumped to his feet and stretched his voice to its full power. "The count being tied," he shouted, "it is my great pleasure to cast a 'Yea' vote for the candidate. The nomination of Gloria Hernandez of California to be Associate Justice of the U.S. Supreme Court is hereby confirmed!"

Through the hazy blur of tears welling up in his eyes, Forrest could barely see Kyle descend the rostrum's stairs and head his way. Suddenly the majority leader was enveloped by a sea of well-wishers, supporters, and fellow republicans—cuffing his shoulders, slapping him on the back.

"Forrest! Great job!"

"Five stars, Senator!"

"Congratulations, old man. You did it!"

"Look this way, Senator!" Flash! Flash! Flash!

On his feet, with regained composure, the white-haired, bespectacled senate icon beamed under the accolades of his peers and staff. He reached in every direction for the hands of colleagues who had stormed into the well from both sides of the aisle. Finally, Kyle pushed through the mob, reached out to make contact, and barely touched his fingers. "Not bad for a couple of useless underdogs, eh?" he shouted at Forrest, trying to be heard over the crowd.

"I guess maybe they'll keep us around for a few more days," Forrest grinned back.

Daisy Carlisle spun him around to plant a kiss smack on his lips. "We did it, darlin'! Brilliant strategy. You came through again!"

With the crush of people split between Forrest, Kyle, and Daisy on the republican side of the room and Blanche, Franklin, and Sinead in the democratic camp, the back of the chamber soon cleared enough for Christine to make her way up the aisle and out into the corridor. There, she found pandemonium had erupted almost as furiously as inside the hall. Reporters pushed and shoved in their haste to extract quotes from frowning democrats, jovial republicans, and either delighted or furious representatives of concerned, public-interest groups. Politicians and journalists jostled against still photographers and TV commentators who tried to establish a position from which to send their live broadcasts.

Christine kept her head down, to avoid eye contact, and threaded her way past thrust-out microphones and the clamoring of broadcasters.

Norah, who had just finished making a jubilant statement to an ABC reporter, trailed after Christine, hoping to catch up and thank her.

In the less-crowded Small Senate Rotunda, Norah pulled back and watched in quiet astonishment as Christine turned her visage up to a tall, handsome, well-dressed, gray-haired man. He took her face in his hands and kissed her fully on the lips. "It's *our* legacy," she said, smiling. The two stood together a moment. Then, hand-in-hand, with their heads bent toward each other in quiet conversation, they proceeded into the massive Capitol Rotunda. Soon they blended into the crowd of government officials, security guards, and media personnel who had assembled for the roll-call vote.

"Mr. President. Mr. President!"

Jonathan Morgan's secretary gestured repeatedly, trying to catch her boss' attention through the cheers, laughter, and mass congratulations that resounded throughout the Oval Office. When she finally caught his eye, the president squeezed his way through the celebrants to where she stood waiting at the outer door.

"Katherine! Did you get a glass of champagne? It's a celebration, for heaven's sake. Let go a little. We just won a big one."

"Sir," she tugged at his sleeve.

Still unable to wipe the grin off his face, he nevertheless bent his head toward her.

"It's the notice you were waiting for, Sir."

"What? I can barely hear you. The notary from Wake Forest?"

"Waiting for! The notice you've been waiting for, Sir!"

"Oh, a notice you say. What about it?"

She waved the white envelope. "The notice you've been waiting for, Sir. From the lab. The test Mr. Carothers arranged."

John still looked puzzled or possibly annoyed.

Calling on all her courage, the president's personal secretary put her mouth directly next to the leader of the free world's ear. "The results from the lab, Sir. You wanted to see these as soon as they came in? The DNA results from the paternity test you said you wanted."

EPILOGUE

Saturday, December 23

The grandly elegant Venetian Room of the Fairmont Hotel, atop San Francisco's Nob Hill, was adorned with banked red and white poinsettias, fresh green wreaths and swags, holly, mistletoe, and silver-flocked angels. On either side of the stage, multicolored lights gleamed on two eighteen-foot Douglas firs. A small chamber ensemble played seasonal music for the over four hundred guests.

Isamu Narita, in a three-button tuxedo with banded-collar shirt and diamond studs, and Eduardo Hernandez, suavely attired in traditional black tie, waited expectantly for the musicians to conclude a rousing performance of "Deck the Halls." Then, shortly before 7:00, Isamu and Eduardo strode to center stage. Isamu tapped the mike grid with his finger, sending a sharp thumping through the room.

"Is this on? Oh, I guess so. If everyone would take their seats, please?" Isamu started again, once the guests had settled themselves in front of the prearranged place cards, "It is my wonderful, complete pleasure to welcome you all to Eduardo's and my first annual Christmas party. We're delighted you could all come, and hope to see you this time every year, from now on!"

He glowed in the polite applause. "I'd like to continue the festivities with a toast to my new second family, and especially to my new second mom, Supreme Court Associate Justice Gloria Hernandez. Mom, may you live a long and happy life, and enjoy many years on the high court."

"His second mom?" Anne hissed from behind her hand. Gloria closed her eyes slightly and rose to return Isamu's shy smile. She lifted her glass to him and took a small sip of champagne.

"Thank you, Isamu. It's good to be home for the holidays. And it's nice to know my son now has someone else he can turn to instead of waking me at 4:30 in the morning." Anne buried her chortles in Jon's shoulder. The rest of the guests chuckled openly. Eduardo stuck his tongue out playfully at his mother, who wrinkled her nose in response. "I'd also like to return the compliment, if I may," she continued. "It gives me great joy to toast you, and your mother and father here at our table. It is indeed an honor to welcome all of you into our family circle."

Glasses clinked around the room. Gloria bowed to Isamu's parents and sat down. "Does this make you his mother-in-law?" Michael asked.

"Shut up," Jon said under his breath.

Gloria turned her head to him deliberately and smiled. "Michael, dear. Don't start."

"You're all looking just great tonight." With a dazzling smile, Eduardo had stepped confidently to the mike. "All the lovely ladies and all the beautiful men."

Cheers, whoops, laughter, and applause erupted from a half dozen tables occupied by expertly coifed and perfectly tailored young to middle-aged men.

Oh, dear God, Gloria prayed, *please make him play this straight tonight.*

Caught up with the *bonhomie* of their friends, Isamu flashed a thumbs up and Eduardo thrust a two-fingered "v" their direction with his free hand, before he raised his glass for quiet. "I'd like to propose a toast."

Anne leaned toward Gloria. "What's he drinking?"

"Supposedly, non-alcoholic wine."

The two women exchanged looks. "Theoretically."

"To the President of the United States," Eduardo was saying. "Congratulations on your landslide re-election. May you have a spectacular second term, Sir, with the help of Republican majorities in both houses of Congress."

The guests stood to raise their glasses in honor of the commander in chief, who remained seated and nodded slightly in recognition of their toast. After everyone settled in again, he rose to loud applause.

"Say something nice, Dad," his son warned.

"I can't reach him, Glory, will you hit him for me?" Anne asked sweetly, from behind her goblet.

"Michael, dear, don't start," Gloria repeated, this time with a look of warning. The president's son, who had begun drinking a few hours earlier, raised his glass in mock apology. The not-quite-beautiful, dark-brown-haired young woman sitting next to him whispered something in his ear. He set his glass down, lifted her hand, and kissed it.

"Ladies and gentlemen," the president began, "I now have, for the first time, the extreme pleasure of toasting my entire extended family." He turned to face his wife. "Anne Sinclair Morgan, my love, my companion, my tower of strength. If not for you, I'd be a crotchety, old attorney trying to figure out which socks match, and getting lost on the back streets of Los Angeles. Instead, I'm now a crotchety, old president whose socks always match, with a driver to keep me from getting lost on the back streets of Washington." He raised his glass. "To my *raison d'être.*"

He touched glasses with Anne's, who laughed with him and took a sip. She looked radiant. In fact, after two trips to Italy in the last six months, she seemed ever radiant. *The weather there must be good for her,* Jon thought. He paused for effect, and then turned toward Gloria. "Gloria Diaz Hernandez, one of my oldest and dearest friends. We've shared many things together through the years: triumphs, defeats, births, deaths. Lots of pizza. I value your friendship, your support, your love of my family. To the best of *compadres.*"

Gloria lifted her glass to him, clinked against Anne's goblet on one side, Michael's on the other, and drank. Jon let a waiter give him a refill before continuing. "Now, to the good stuff," he joked. "First to my son, Michael, and his fiancée, Congresswoman—Republican, of course—Kimberly Lawrence. Kim, take him, with my blessings. Take him without my blessings. Just take him."

Even Michael joined in with the laughter and louder whoops this time. "And finally," the president said, turning to the stage where Eduardo and Isamu were standing, "to the boy who has always been like a second son to me, and now, it turns out, actually is. To Eduardo and his . . ."

"Lover," Michael said with a lascivious leer.

"Significant other," Anne corrected in a whisper. She shot a deadly look at her son, while shaking her head slightly toward Gloria.

"Companion," Gloria muttered, cuffing Michael lightly on the back of his head.

". . . companion, Isamu Narita," Jon finished, the break barely noticeable. "Kim, Isamu—Anne and I are delighted to welcome you and your families into our family group, and wish you both long and satisfying relationships with Michael and Eduardo. Oh, and one more thing," he added. "If for some reason things don't work out between you, just remember: we're not taking either one of them back."

He sat down to the sounds of good-natured laughter, waiters splashing refills into wine goblets, and animated talk, which suffused around the table and throughout the rest of the room. Above the clatter, the chamber quartet struck up an all-string version of "God Rest Ye Merry Gentlemen."

HOW THEY VOTED

Senate: **51** Republicans, **49** Democrats

Confirmation of Gloria Diaz Hernandez to be
an Associate Justice of the U.S. Supreme Court

Senators	Yes	No
Abbott, Donald (D-Ky.)		X
Albrecht, Carl (R-Pa.)		X
Anderson, Glenn (R-Mont.)	X	
Ashworth, Ken (R-Wyo.)	X	
Barrett, Dean (R-Alaska)	X	
Blalock, Cotton (D-Ark.)		X
Bluecorn, Lily (D-Ariz.)	X	
Bowden, Joshua (R-Okla.)	X	
Caldwell, Bryn (R-Fla.)	X	
Carlisle, Daisy (R-N.C.)	X	
Cheever III, Louis (R-Conn.)	X	
Collins, Bryce (D- Wash.)	X	
Danson, Chip (D-Nev.)		X
Dickinson, Caleb (D-Mass.)		X
Donaldson, Dave (R-Ind.)	X	
Duckworth, Cornell (D-Ala.)		X
Edwards, William (D-Minn.)		X

	Yes	No
Senators		
Fairchild, Christine (D-Md.)	X	
Fitzpatrick, John (R-R.I.)	X	
Fowler, Gabe (R-Utah)		X
Garrison, Forrest (R-Ariz.)	X	
Goldring, Jeff (D-Wis.)		X
Gordon, Darrell (R-Colo.)	X	
Greene, Ryan (D-Va.)		X
Gurney, Floyd (D-Miss.)		X
Hallstead, Grant (D-Calif.)	X	
Harmon, Franklin (D-Ky.)		X
Hayes, Gerry (R-Kan.)	X	
Higashi, Kawai (D-Hawaii)		X
Horvath, Dottie (D-Wis.)	X	
Humphrey, Giles (D-La.)		X
Irwin, Lemuel (D-Fla.)	X	
Ivy, Frances (D-N.H.)		X
Jacobs, Yale (R-N.Y.)	X	
Jacoulet, Guy (R-Maine)		X
Janowski, Peter (R-N.J.)	X	
Kent, Milo (D-N.D.)		X
Knight, Byron (D-W.Va.)		X
Kok, Laine (R-Mich.)	X	

Senators	Yes	No
Kurasawa, Yasuo (D-Hawaii)		X
Landes, Bruce (R-Ohio)	X	
Lattimer, Hank (D-S.D.)		X
Leaf, Kirk (D-W.Va.)		X
Madrid, Lorenzo (R-N.M.)	X	
Marchbanks, Russell (R-Mont.)	X	
Martindale, Phil (R-Ida.)	X	
Mayfield, Ward (R-Del.)	X	
Mellon, Christopher (R-Pa.)	X	
Montague, Lance (R-Va.)		X
Murray, Fred (D-Tenn.)		X
Newell, Justin (R-Ind.)		X
Newman, Maxwell (D-S.C.)		X
Nicholson, Albert (D-Mo.)		X
Osborne, Nancy (D-Mich.)		X
Parkening, Charlie (R-Iowa)	X	
Payne, Oliver (R-Maine)	X	
Petty, Stephen ((D-Ga.)		X
Phillips, Quinn (D-S.D.)		X
Plum, Leroy (R-Miss.)	X	
Popowski, Stanley (D-Ill.)		X
Quarles, Patrick (R-Vt.)	X	

	Yes	No
Senators		
Quince, Elliott (D-Del.)		X
Radford, Richard (R-Utah)	X	
Ravel, Jacques (R-Ore.)	X	
Ravenswood, Quentin (R-Ill.)		X
Riley, Will (R-Kan.)	X	
Roberts, Luke (R-Texas)	X	
Ross, Harry (D-Colo.)		X
Ryan, Ben (R-Md.)	X	
St. Antoine, Blanche (D-La.)		X
St. Clair, Rex (R-Calif.)	X	
Scott, Raymond (R-Iowa)	X	
Scott, Derek (D-Vt.)		X
Shapiro, Dov (D-Conn.)		X
Sharp, David (R-Alaska)	X	
Sherman, Stuart (R-Mo.)	X	
Sibley, Rolf (R-S.C.)		X
Smith, Andrew (R-Ark.)	X	
Stafford, Norah (R-N.J.)	X	
Stewart, Lamar (R-Ga.)	X	
Stimson, Ernest (R-Minn.)	X	
Sullivan, Sinead (D-Ore.)		X
Taggart, Ethan (D-N.H.)		X

Senators	Yes	No
Tessaro, Vince (D-N.Y.)		X
Townsend, Campbell (R-Tenn.)	X	
Travis, Gregg (R-Nev.)	X	
Tucker, Dana (D-Neb.)		X
Underwood, Thomas (D-N.M.)	X	
Urban, Ralph (D-N.D.)		X
Valenti, Joseph (D-Ohio)		X
Vanderpool, Taylor (D-R.I.)		X
Vaughan, Henry (D-Texas)	X	
Wallace, Barry (D-N.C.)		X
Warren, Hal (R-Okla.)		X
Whetstone, Leslie (D-Ala.)		X
White, Steve (R-Ida.)	X	
Wiley, Sam (R-Wyo.)		X
Wong, Miles (D-Wash.)		X
Worthington, Paul (R-Neb.)	X	
Young, Wesley (D-Mass.)		X

Acknowledgments

I am grateful to many people for their advice and encouragement during the writing of this novel. Claudia Suzanne, mentor and creative writer, offered innumerable suggestions on both the organization and the content of the manuscript. Shirl Thomas' thoughtful, meticulous copy-editing of the work was vital to the story's clarity, continuity and focus. Professor Delavan Dickson's stimulating courses at the University of San Diego in constitutional law and judicial behavior helped to establish the novel's setting. The suggestions of Attorney Lawrence Zerner of Los Angeles for manuscript improvement were most helpful.

I supplemented my research with articles from the *Los Angeles Times*, the *Wall Street Journal*, the *New York Times*, the *Washington Post*, the *Washington Times*, *USA Today*, *Washingtonian*, *Newsweek* and *Time*.

I acknowledge additional background sources: *Supreme Court Politics*, Susan L. Bloch and Thomas G. Krattenmaker, editors; Louis Fisher's *American Constitutional Law*; *The Oxford Companion to the Supreme Court of the United States*, Kermit L. Hall, editor in chief; David J. Garrow's *Liberty and Sexuality*; *Lesbians, Gay Men and the Law* edited by William B. Rubenstein; *Judicious Choices* by Mark Silverstein; *Courts, Judges & Politics*, Walter F. Murphy and C. Herman Pritchett, editors and *The Brethren* by Bob Woodward and Scott Armstrong.

An excellent, detailed article by David M. O'Brien, appearing in *Yearbook 1989* of the Supreme Court Historical Society, examined the nomination and confirmation of Supreme Court Justice John Paul Stevens. This is a scholarly resource on the selection and approval of a nominee to the U.S. Supreme Court. *Argentina*, edited by Deirdre Ball, from *Insight Guides* is also acknowledged.

I am indebted to staff members of the U.S. Senate Judiciary Committee and of the National Archives for sending me publicly available information about recent, high-court, confirmation hearings and their U.S. Senate, roll-call votes.

I also thank numerous public affairs' officials in the United States Senate, the FBI, the Secret Service and the Washington, D.C. Police Department for providing me with important procedural information. Captain Joel H. Bryden of the San Diego Police Department read portions of the manuscript and offered significant recommendations.

I recognize Carol Mitchell, Jennifer Faden, Catherine Fagan and their associates at Pentland Press, Inc. for their dedication, expertise and guidance in the completion of this novel.

To others whose help I've neglected or forgotten to acknowledge, please accept my apologies.

Finally and most importantly, thanks to my wife, Karen, for her forbearance and support during the production of this work.